# CAROLINE S. KIRKLAND

# Western Clearings

*The American Short Story Series*

VOLUME 68

GARRETT PRESS

512-00443-9

Library of Congress Catalog Card No. 69-11909

*This volume was reprinted from the 1845 edition
published by Wiley & Putnam*
*First Garrett Press Edition published 1969*

*The American Short Story Series*
Volume 68
© 1969

Manufactured in the United States of America

GARRETT PRESS, INC.
*Publishers*
250 West 54th Street, New York, N.Y. 10019

# CONTENTS.

# PREFACE.

To write a book is no great matter—as is very evident from the multitudes of books which are written; to write a preface is quite a different thing. It is the very tyranny of fashion that requires something to be said when there is nothing to say. But if one tells one's publisher so, he only says, "Nothing can come of nothing; try again!" and so one is thrust bodily before the public, like the little boy who clings to his mother's apron, and tries to get behind her chair, while all the family cry out at once, "Johnny, make a bow!" and when Johnny makes his bow after much suffering, the company do not even look at him! In this last particular there is a decided affinity between our case and the little boy's, for the public in whose behalf prefaces are insisted upon, very seldom takes the trouble to glance at them after they are written.

Some cynical people may ask why books must be made at all, since to let them alone is the most easy and obvious way of avoiding the difficulties which beset preface-writing. It would require a whole new book fully to answer such an unreasonable question, so numerous are the inevitable causes of book-making. The first reason that might be given is, that when one is born to write, it is *impossible* to refrain; and if this should not be satisfactory, more than the orthodox thirty-nine might be added, each one unanswerable—so we spare

Goodman Dull the specification. For ourselves in this particular case, we might urge that these are *Western* stories—stories illustrative of a land that was once an El Dorado—stories intended to give more minute and life-like representations of a peculiar people, than can well be given in a grave, straightforward history. To those who left Eastern and civilized homes to try the new Western world, at a period when every one was mad

With visions prompted by intense desire

after golden harvests, no apology for an attempt to convey first impressions of so new a state of things will be needed. A traveller may go to England without finding much that he feels prompted to record for the amusement of friends at home. Almost every body has been there before him ; and while the language and manners are essentially the same as his own, the peculiarities that may strike him have been already reported so often and so well, that even the best sketches seem almost like mere repetitions or *rechauffées* of the observations of others. But the wild West has had few visitors and fewer describers. Its history may be homely, but it is original. It is like nothing else in the wide world, and so various that successive travellers may continue to give their views of it for years to come, without fear of exhausting its peculiarities. Language, ideas, manners, customs—are all new ; yes ! even language ; for to the instructed person from one of our great Eastern cities, the talk of the true back-woodsman is scarce intelligible. His indescribable *twang* is, to be sure, no further from good English than the *patois* of many of the English counties. But at the West this curious talker is your neighbour and equal, while in the elder country he would never come in your way unless you sought him purposely to hear his jargon. And for

ideas, the settler has some of the strangest that ever were har-
boured in human brain, mixed with so much real shrewdness,
practical wisdom, and ready wit, that one cannot but wonder
how nature and a warping or blinding education can be so at
variance.

As to the ordinary manners of the back-woodsman, not a
word can be said in their favour. They are barbarous
enough. Yet he is a gentle creature in sickness; and when
death comes to the family of a friend or neighbour, his whole
soul is melted, and his manners could not be amended by
false Chesterfield himself. A delicacy not always found
among the elegant, will then temper his every look and movement to the very tone of the time. And for substantial kindness at such seasons—but I have tried to say what I thought
of that, elsewhere.

The customs of the West are such as might naturally
be expected to grow up among a most heterogeneous population, contriving to live under the pressure of extreme
difficulties, and living not in the present but in the future. This is the condition of shifts and turns—" expedients and inventions multiform;" encroachments, substitutes,
borrowings; public spirit and individual selfishness; a feeling
of common interest, conflicting strangely with an entire read-
iness to flit with the first offer of " a trade;" neighbourly
kindness struggling against the necessity of looking out sharply for number one. That this combination,—or rather the
combination of which the particulars enumerated are but a
symbol,—should afford amusing materials for one's sketch-
book, is a matter of course. How to refrain, in cases where
to tell would be to infringe upon neighbourly comity, is the
only difficulty. And indeed, to tell at all, in however general
terms, is considered as doing this; since what may be said of

one settlement applies to so many others, that all one's care
does not suffice to avoid the appearance of particularity. It is
a well-known fact that certain sketches of Western life have
been appropriated by more than a dozen communities, each
declaring them personal; while their sole personality lay in
the attempt to adhere closely to the *general*, to the entire
exclusion of the particular.

The papers included in the present collection were all written at the West, and I may say with Goldsmith, "they certainly were new when they were written." Further claims
to originality most of them have not. Yet there is reason to
believe, after all the efforts made to instruct and delight the
people of these United States of Alleghania by Magazine and
Annual stories, very many of them still remain beyond the
pale; and might never acquire this part of their equipment
for the journey of life, if it were not for occasional reprihts
like those of the present series.

Besides these echoes of the past, we entreat the reader to
believe that there is much of new, and (of course) good, to be
found in the following pages. We entreat him to *believe*
this, at least; and that kindly faith will help to give a
grace to what might else have but slender pretensions to his
favour.

# WESTERN CLEARINGS.

## THE LAND-FEVER.

THE wild new country, with all its coarseness and all its disadvantages of various kinds, has yet a fascination for the settler, in consequence of a certain free, hearty tone, which has long since disappeared, if indeed it ever existed, in parts of the country where civilization has made greater progress. The really fastidious, and those who only pretend to be such, may hold this as poor compensation for the many things lacking of another kind; but those to whose apprehension sympathy and sincerity have a pre-eminent and independent charm, prefer the kindly warmth of the untaught, to the icy chill of the half-taught; and would rather be welcomed by the woodsman to his log-cabin, with its rough hearth, than make one of a crowd who feed the ostentation of a *millionaire*, or gaze with sated eyes upon costly feasts which it would be a mockery to dignify with the name of hospitality. The infrequency of inns in a newly settled country leads naturally to the practice of keeping "open house" for strangers; and it is rare indeed that the settler, however poor his accommodations, hesitates to offer the best he has to the tired wayfarer. Where payment is accepted, it is usually very inconsiderable; and it is seldom accepted at all, unless the guest is manifestly better off than his entertainer. But whether a compensation be taken or refused, the heartiness of manner with which every thing that the house affords is offered, cannot but be acceptable to the visitor. Even the ever rampant pride, which comes up so disagreeably at the West, where the outward appearance of the stranger betokens any advantage of condition, slumbers when that stranger claims hospitality. His horse is cared for with more solicitude than the host ever bestows on his own; the table is covered with the best provisions the house affords, set forth in the holiday dishes; the bed is endued with the brightest patchwork quilt—the pride of the housewife's heart; and if there be any fat fowls—any white honey—any good tea—about the premises, the guest will be sure to have it, even though it may have been reserved for "Independence" or "Thanksgiving."

This habit was however reversed, or at least suspended, during the speculating times. The country was then inundated with people who came to buy land,—not to clear and plough, but as men buy a lottery-ticket or dig for gold—in the hope of unreasonable and unearned profits. These people were considered as public enemies. No personal violence was offered them, as might have been the case at the Southwest; but every obstacle, in the shape of extravagant charges, erroneous information, and rude refusal, was thrown in their way. Few were discouraged by this, however; for they came in the spirit of the knights of romance when they had to enter enchanted castles—strong in faith of the boundless treasures which were to reward their perseverance.

To mislead an unpractised land-hunter was a matter of no great difficulty; for few things are more intricate and puzzling, at first, than the system which has been devised to facilitate the identifying of particular spots. Section-corners and quarter-stakes, eighties, and forties, and fractions, are plain enough when one is habituated to them, and they *seem* plain enough to the new man,—on paper. But when he finds himself in the woods, with his maps and his copious memoranda, he is completely at sea, with no guide but the compass. A friend who afterwards became quite a proficient in the mysteries of land-finding tells me that he twice lost himself completely in the woods. "The first time," he says, "my mishap was owing to the wandering habits of a wild Indian pony which I had chosen on account of his power of ceaseless travel. He had been accustomed to pick up his living where he could find it, and he took advantage of my jogging pace, just at dusk, when I did not feel *too* certain of my whereabout, to quit the scarce-defined road, in search of something tempting which he espied at a distance. My resource in this case was to abandon my horse, and fix my eyes on the North Star, which I knew would bring me to a certain State road, in due time. The other occasion was in broad day-light, but when there was only an occasional gleam of sunshine, so that I had no steady guide as to direction. The ground was so thickly strown with leaves that my horse's hoofs left no permanent track, and I found myself in a complete maze. The trees were all alike to my bewildered eyes (I had left my compass at the last lodging-place,) ; and all I knew was that I was south of the road which I had quitted for the sake of saving some miles' distance· After many efforts at marking trees—very ineffectual without an axe—I bethought me of a newspaper, which I tore into pieces and affixed to bushes and low limbs as I went, and so obtained a straight line ; by which means, after some hours' rather anxious wandering, I was finally extricated."

To pass a night in the woods is a small affair for a hunting party ; but it is something quite different for a solitary individual, unprovided with axe or gun, and, of course, unable to make him-self comfortable in any way. To sleep in a tree might do, if trees were not occasionally haunted by wild cats ; or a lair in the heaped leaves of autumn, if there were not a chance of warming into activity a nest of rattlesnakes. These are no doubt partly useless fears, but to the stranger they are very real ; and they tend not a little to the increase of his difficulties by discomposing his nerves when cool reflection would be his best friend.

Mistakes in "locating" land were often very serious, even where there had been no intention to deceive—the purchaser find-ing only swamp or hopeless gravel, when he had purchased fine farming land and maple timber. Every mile square is marked by blazed trees, and the corners especially distinguished by stakes whose place is pointed out by trees called Witness-trees, and so accurate and so minute is the whole system that it seems almost incredible that so many errors should have arisen. The back-woodsman made no mistakes, for to him a stump, or a stone, or a prostrate tree, has individuality ; and he will never confound it with any other. One accustomed to wandering in the woods will know even the points of the compass, in a strange place, without sun or star to guide him. But the fact of the unwillingness of

the actual settler to guide the speculator faithfully, became so
well known, that purchasers often preferred relying on their own
sagacity, backed by what seemed unmistakable rules, to trusting
such disaffected guides. Innumerable stories are current in the
woods of the perplexities of city gentlemen ;—and the following,
if not strictly true, will serve to illustrate somewhat the state
of things in those wild times when sober prudence was forgotten,
and delusion ruled the hour. I shall call it, for want of better
title,

## A REMINISCENCE OF THE LAND-FEVER.

THE years 1835 and 1836 will long be remembered by the
Western settler—and perhaps by some few people at the East,
too—as the period when the madness of speculation in lands had
reached a point to which no historian of the time will ever be
able to do justice. A faithful picture of those wild days would
subject the most veracious chronicler to the charge of exaggera-
tion ; and our great-grand-children can hope to obtain an adequate
idea of the infatuation which led away their forefathers, only by
the study of such detached facts as may be noted down by those
in whose minds the feeling recollection of the delusion is still
fresh. Perhaps when our literary existence shall have become
sufficiently confirmed to call for the collection of Ana, something
more may be gleaned from the correspondence in which were
embodied the exultings of the successful, and the lamentations of
the disappointed.

"Seeing is believing," certainly, in most cases ; but in the days
of the land-fever, we, who were in the midst of the infected district, scarcely found it so. The whirl, the fervour, the flutter, the
rapidity of step, the sparkling of eyes, the beating of hearts, the
striking of hands, the utter *abandon* of the hour, were incredible,
inconceivable. The " man of one idea" was every where : no
man had two. He who had no money, begged, borrowed, or stole
it ; he who had, thought he made a generous sacrifice, if he lent
it at cent per cent. The tradesman forsook his shop ; the farmer
his plough ; the merchant his counter ; the lawyer his office ;
nay, the minister his desk, to join the general chase. Even the

schoolmaster, in his longing to be "abroad" with the rest, laid down his birch, or in the flurry of his hopes, plied it with diminished unction.

> "Tramp! tramp! along the land they rode,
> Splash! splash! along the sea!"

The man with one leg, or he that had none, could at least get on board a steamer, and make for Chicago or Milwaukie; the strong, the able, but above all, the "enterprising," set out with his pocket-map and his pocket-compass, to thread the dim woods, and see with his own eyes. Who would waste time in planting, in building, in hammering iron, in making shoes, when the path to wealth lay wide and flowery before him?

A ditcher was hired by the job to do a certain piece of work in his line. "Well, John, did you make any thing?"

"Pretty well; I cleared about two dollars a day: but I should have made more by *standing round ;*"* i. e., watching the land-market for bargains.

This favourite occupation of all classes was followed by its legitimate consequences. Farmers were as fond of "standing round" as any body; and when harvest time came, it was discovered that many had quite forgotten that the best land requires sowing; and grain, and of course other articles of general necessity, rose to an unprecedented price. The hordes of travellers flying through the country in all directions were often cited as the cause of the distressing scarcity; but the true source must be sought in the diversion, or rather suspension, of the industry of the entire population. Be this as it may, of the wry faces made at the hard fare, the travellers contributed no inconsiderable portion; for they were generally city gentlemen, or at least gentlemen who had lived long enough in the city to have learned to prefer oysters to salt pork. This checked not their ardour, however; for the golden glare before their eyes had power to neutralize the hue of all present objects. On they pressed, with headlong zeal: the silent and pathless forest, the deep miry marsh, the gloom of night, and the fires of noon, beheld alike the march of

* Verbatim.

the speculator. Such searching of trees for town lines! Such
ransacking of the woods for section corners, ranges, and base
lines! Such anxious care in identifying spots possessing particular advantages! And then, alas! after all, such precious
blunders!

These blunders called into action another class of operators,
who became popularly known as "land-lookers." These met
you at every turn, ready to furnish "water-power," "pine lots,"
"choice farming tracts," or any thing else, at a moment's notice.
Bar-rooms and street-corners swarmed with these prowling gentry.
It was impossible to mention any part of the country which they
had not personally surveyed. They would tell you, with the
gravity of astrologers, what sort of timber predominated on any
given tract, drawing sage deductions as to the capabilities of the
soil. Did you incline to city property? Lo! a splendid chart,
setting forth the advantages of some unequalled site, and your
confidential friend, the land-looker, able to tell you more than all
about it, or to accompany you to the happy spot; though that he
would not advise; "bad roads," "nothing fit to eat," etc.; and
all this from a purely disinterested solicitude for your welfare.

These amiable individuals were, strange to tell, no favourites
with the actual settlers. If they disliked the gentleman speculator, they hated with a perfect hatred him who aided by his local
knowledge the immense purchases of non-residents. These
short-sighted and prejudiced persons forgot the honour and distinction which must result from their insignificant farms being
surrounded by the possessions of the magnates of the land.
They saw only the solitude which would probably be entailed on
them for years; and it was counted actual treason in a settler to
give any facilities to the land-looker, of whatever grade. " Let
the land-shark do his own hunting," was their frequent reply to
applications of this kind; and some thought them quite right.
Yet this state of feeling among the Hard-handed, was not without
its inconvenient results to city gentlemen, as witness the case of
our friend Mr. Willoughby, a very prim and smart bachelor,
from ———

It was when the whirlwind was at its height, that a gentleman
wearing the air of a bank-director, at the very least—in other

words, that of an uncommonly fat pigeon—drew bridle at the
bars in front of one of the roughest log houses in the county of
————. The horse and his rider were loaded with all those
unnecessary defences, and cumbrous comforts, which the fashion
of the time prescribed in such cases. Blankets, valise, saddle-
bags, and holsters nearly covered the steed; a most voluminous
enwrapment of India-rubber cloth completely enveloped the rider.
The gallant sorrel seemed indeed fit for his burden. He looked
as if he might have swam any stream in Michigan

> " Barded from counter to tail,
> And the rider arm'd complete in mail ;"

yet he seemed a little jaded, and hung his head languidly, while
his master accosted the tall and meagre tenant of the log cabin.

This individual and his dwelling resembled each other in an
unusual degree. The house was, as we have said, of the roughest; its ribs scarcely half filled in with clay; its "looped and
windowed raggedness" rendered more conspicuous by the tattered
cotton sheets which had long done duty as glass, and which now
fluttered in every breeze; its roof of oak shingles, warped into
every possible curve; and its stick chimney, so like its owner's
hat, open at the top, and jammed in at the sides; all shadowed
forth the contour and equipments of the exceedingly easy and
self-satisfied person who leaned on the fence, and snapped his long
cart-whip, while he gave such answers as suited him to the gentleman in the India-rubbers, taking especial care not to invite him
to alight.

"Can you tell me, my friend,————" civilly began Mr. Willoughby.

"Oh! *friend !*" interrupted the settler; "who told you I was
your friend? Friends is scuss in these parts."

"You have at least no reason to be otherwise," replied the
traveller, who was blessed with a very patient temper, especially
where there was no use in getting angry.

"I don't know that," was the reply. "What fetch'd you into
these woods?"

"If I should say 'my horse,' the answer would perhaps be as
civil as the question."

"Jist as you like," said the other, turning on his heel, and walking off.

"I wished merely to ask you," resumed Mr. Willoughby, talking after the nonchalant son of the forest, "whether this is Mr. Pepper's land."

"How do you know it an't mine?"

"I'm not likely to know, at present, it seems," said the traveller, whose patience was getting a little frayed. And taking out his memorandum-book, he ran over his minutes: "South half of north-west quarter of section fourteen——Your name is Leander Pepper, is it not?"

"Where did you get so much news? You a'n't the sheriff, be ye?"

"Pop!" screamed a white-headed urchin from the house, "Mam says supper's ready."

"So ain't I," replied the papa; "I've got all my chores to do yet." And he busied himself at a log pig-stye on the opposite side of the road, half as large as the dwelling-house. Here he was soon surrounded by a squealing multitude, with whom he seemed to hold a regular conversation.

Mr. Willoughby looked at the westering sun, which was not far above the dense wall of trees that shut in the small clearing; then at the heavy clouds which advanced from the north, threatening a stormy night; then at his watch, and then at his note-book; and after all, at his predicament—on the whole, an unpleasant prospect. But at this moment a female face showed itself at the door. Our traveller's memory reverted at once to the testimony of Ledyard and Mungo Park; and he had also some floating and indistinct poetical recollections of woman's being useful when a man was in difficulties, though hard to please at other times. The result of these reminiscences, which occupied a precious second, was, that Mr. Willoughby dismounted, fastened his horse to the fence, and advanced with a brave and determined air, to throw himself upon female kindness and sympathy.

He naturally looked at the lady, as he approached the door, but she did not return the compliment. She looked at the pigs, and talked to the children, and Mr. Willoughby had time to ob-

serve that she was the very duplicate of her husband ; as tall, as
bony, as ragged, and twice as cross-looking.

"Malviny Jane !" she exclaimed, in no dulcet treble, " be
done a-paddlin' in that 'ere water !  If I come there, I'll——"

"You'd better look at Sophrony, I guess !" was the reply.

"Why, what's she a-doin' ?"

"Well, I guess if you look, you'll see !" responded Miss Mal-
vina, coolly, as she passed into the house, leaving at every step
a full impression of her foot in the same black mud that covered
her sister from head to foot.

The latter was saluted with a hearty cuff, as she emerged from
the puddle ; and it was just at the propitious moment when her
shrill howl aroused the echoes, that Mr. Willoughby, having
reached the threshold, was obliged to set about making the agreeable to the mamma.  And he called up for the occasion all his
politeness.

" I believe I must become an intruder on your hospitality for
the night, madam," he began.  The dame still looked at the
pigs.  Mr. Willoughby tried again, in less courtly phrase.

"Will it be convenient for you to lodge me to-night, ma'am ?
I have been disappointed in my search for a hunting-party, whom
I had engaged to meet, and the night threatens a storm."

" I don't know nothin' about it ; you must ask the old man,"
said the lady, now for the first time taking a survey of the new
comer ; " with *my* will, we'll lodge nobody."

This was not very encouraging, but it was a poor night for the
woods ; so our traveller persevered, and making so bold a push
for the door that the lady was obliged to retreat a little, he entered, and said he would await her husband's coming.

And in truth he could scarcely blame the cool reception he had
experienced, when he beheld the state of affairs within those muddy precincts.  The room was large, but it swarmed with human
beings.  The huge open fire-place, with its hearth of rough stone,
occupied nearly the whole of one end of the apartment ; and near
it stood a long cradle, containing a pair of twins, who cried—a
sort of hopeless cry, as if they knew it would do no good, yet
could not help it.  The schoolmaster, (it was his week,) sat reading a tattered novel, and rocking the cradle occasionally, when

the children cried *too* loud. An old grey-headed Indian was curiously crouched over a large tub, shelling corn on the edge of a
hoe ; but he ceased his noisy employment when he saw the stranger, for no Indian will ever willingly be seen at work, though
he may be sometimes compelled by the fear of starvation or the
longing for whiskey, to degrade himself by labour. Near the
only window was placed the work-bench and entire paraphernalia
of the shoemaker, who in these regions travels from house to
house, shoeing the family and mending the harness as he goes,
with various interludes of songs and jokes, ever new and acceptable. This one, who was a little, bald, twinkling-eyed fellow,
made the smoky rafters ring with the burden of that favourite
ditty of the west :

> " All kinds of game to hunt, my boys, also the buck and doe,
>   All down by the banks of the river O-hi-o ;"

and children of all sizes, clattering in all keys, completed the
picture and the concert.

The supper-table, which maintained its place in the midst of
this living and restless mass, might remind one of the square
stone lying bedded in the bustling leaves of the acanthus ; but
the associations would be any but those of Corinthian elegance.
The only object which at that moment diversified its dingy surface was an iron hoop, into which the mistress of the feast proceeded to turn a quantity of smoking hot potatoes, adding afterward a bowl of salt, and another of pork fat, by courtesy denominated gravy : plates and knives dropped in afterward, at the discretion of the company.

Another call of " Pop ! pop !" brought in the host from the pig-
stye ; the heavy rain which had now began to fall, having no
doubt, expedited the performance of the chores. Mr. Willoughby,
who had established himself resolutely, took advantage of a very
cloudy assent from the proprietor, to lead his horse to a shed, and
to deposit in a corner his cumbrous outer gear ; while the company used in turn the iron skillet which served as a wash-basin,
dipping the water from a large trough outside, overflowing with
the abundant drippings of the eaves. Those who had no pocket-
handkerchiefs, contented themselves with a nondescript article

which seemed to stand for the family towel ; and when this ceremony was concluded, all seriously addressed themselves to the de-
molition of the potatoes. The grown people were accommodated
with chairs and chests; the children prosecuted a series of flying
raids upon the good cheer, snatching a potato now and then as
they could find an opening under the raised arm of one of the
family, and then retreating to the chimney corner, tossing the hot
prize from hand to hand, and blowing it stoutly the while. The
old Indian had disappeared.

To our citizen, though he felt inconveniently hungry, this
primitive meal seemed a little meagre ; and he ventured to ask if
he could not be accommodated with some tea.

" An't my victuals good enough for you ?"

" Oh !—the potatoes are excellent, but I'm very fond of tea."

" So be I, but I can't have every thing I want—can you ?"

This produced a laugh from the shoemaker, who seemed to
think his patron very witty, while the schoolmaster, not knowing
but the stranger might happen to be one of his examiners next
year, produced only a faint giggle, and then reducing his countenance instantly to an awful gravity, helped himself to his seventh potato.

The rain which now poured violently, not only outside but
through many a crevice in the roof, naturally kept Mr. Willoughby cool ; and finding that dry potatoes gave him the hiccups, he
withdrew from the table, and seating himself on the shoemaker's
bench, took a survey of his quarters.

Two double-beds and the long cradle, seemed all the sleeping
apparatus ; but there was a ladder which doubtless led to a lodging above. The sides of the room were hung with abundance
of decent clothing, and the dresser was well stored with the usual
articles, among which a tea-pot and canister shone conspicuous ;
so that the appearance of inhospitality could not arise from poverty, and Mr. Willoughby concluded to set it down to the account
of rustic ignorance.

The eating ceased not until the hoop was empty, and then the
company rose and stretched themselves, and began to guess it
was about time to go to bed. Mr. Willoughby inquired what
was to be done with his horse.

"Well! I s'pose he can stay where he is."

"But what can he have to eat ?"

"I reckon you won't get nothing for him, without you turn him out on the mash."

"He would get off, to a certainty !"

"Tie his legs."

The unfortunate traveller argued in vain. Hay was "scuss," and potatoes were "scusser ;" and in short the "mash" was the only resource, and these natural meadows afford but poor picking after the first of October. But to the "mash" was the good steed despatched, ingloriously hampered, with the privilege of munching wild grass in the rain, after his day's journey.

Then came the question of lodging for his master. The lady, who had by this time drawn out a trundle-bed, and packed it full of children, said there was no bed for him, unless he could sleep "up chamber" with the boys.

Mr. Willoughby declared that he should make out very well with a blanket by the fire.

"Well ! just as you like," said his host; "but Solomon sleeps there, and if you like to sleep by Solomon, it is more than *I* should."

This was the name of the old Indian, and Mr. Willoughby once more cast woful glances toward the ladder.

But now the schoolmaster, who seemed rather disposed to be civil, declared that he could sleep very well in the long cradle, and would relinquish his place beside the shoemaker to the guest, who was obliged to content himself with this arrangement, which was such as was most usual in those times.

The storm continued through the night, and many a crash in the woods attested its power. The sound of a storm in the dense forest is almost precisely similar to that of a heavy surge breaking on a rocky beach; and when our traveller slept, it was only to dream of wreck and disaster at sea, and to wake in horror and affright. The wild rain drove in at every crevice, and wet the poor children in the loft so thoroughly, that they crawled shivering down the ladder, and stretched themselves on the hearth, regardless of Solomon, who had returned after the others were in bed.

But morning came at last; and our friend, who had no desire farther to test the vaunted hospitality of a western settler, was not among the latest astir. The storm had partially subsided; and although the clouds still lowered angrily, and his saddle had enjoyed the benefit of a leak in the roof during the night, Mr. Willoughby resolved to push on as far as the next clearing, at least, hoping for something for breakfast besides potatoes and salt. It took him a weary while to find his horse, and when he had saddled him, and strapped on his various accoutrements, he entered the house, and inquired what he was to pay for his entertainment—laying somewhat of a stress on the last word.

His host, nothing daunted, replied that he guessed he would let him off for a dollar.

Mr. Willoughby took out his purse, and as he placed a silver dollar in the leathern palm outspread to receive it, happening to look toward the hearth, and perceiving the preparations for a very substantial breakfast, the long pent-up vexation burst forth.

"I really must say, Mr. Pepper——" he began: his tone was certainly that of an angry man, but it only made his host laugh.

"If this is your boasted western hospitality, I can tell you——"

"You'd better tell me what the dickens you are peppering me up this fashion for! My name isn't Pepper, no more than yours is! May be that *is* your name; you seem pretty warm."

"Your name not Pepper! Pray what is it, then?"

"Ah! there's the thing now! You land-hunters ought to know sich things without asking."

"Land-hunter! I'm no land-hunter!"

"Well! you're a land-shark, then—swallowin' up poor men's farms. The less I see of such cattle, the better I'm pleased."

"Confound you!" said Mr. Willoughby, who waxed warm, "I tell you I've nothing to do with land. I wouldn't take your whole state for a gift."

"What did you tell my woman you was a land-hunter for, then?"

And now the whole matter became clear in a moment; and it was found that Mr. Willoughby's equipment, with the mention of a "hunting party," had completely misled both host and hostess.

And to do them justice, never were regret and vexation more heartily expressed.

"You needn't judge our new-country folks by me," said Mr. Handy, for such proved to be his name; "any man in these parts would as soon bite off his own nose, as to snub a civil traveller that wanted a supper and a night's lodging. But somehow or other, your lots o' fixin', and your askin' after that 'ere Pepper—one of the worst land-sharks we've ever had here—made me mad; and I know I treated you worse than an Indian."

"Humph!" said Solomon.

"But," continued the host, "you shall see whether my old woman can't set a good breakfast, when she's a mind to. Come, you shan't stir a step till you've had breakfast; and just take back this plaguey dollar. I wonder it didn't burn my fingers when I took it!"

Mrs. Handy set forth her very best, and a famous breakfast it was, considering the times. And before it was finished, the hunting party made their appearance, having had some difficulty in finding their companion, who had made no very uncommon mistake as to section corners and town-lines.

"I'll tell ye what," said Mr. Handy, confidentially, as the cavalcade with its baggage-ponies, loaded with tents, gun-cases, and hampers of provisions, was getting into order for a march to the prairies, "I'll tell ye what; if you've occasion to stop any where in the Bush, you'd better tell 'em at the first goin' off that you a'n't land-hunters."

But Mr. Willoughby had already had "a caution."

# BALL AT THRAM'S HUDDLE.

THE winter being a time of comparative leisure for the farmer and his family, is generally the chosen period for regular, premeditated amusements, such as dancing, seeing "shows," and going to school ;—this last being considered only fit to fill up spare time of such young people as are old enough to do any thing " useful." A ball on Christmas or New-Year night, or in commemoration of Jackson's victory, or Washington's birth, is always in order ; as those eras happen all to occur in the depth of winter. And the raree-shows which traverse the remoter parts of the country, almost invariably offer their attractions about the same period, their owners knowing very well that the farmer never feels so generous or so jovial as when his crops are all safely housed, and his wheat in the ground for next year's harvest.

These exhibitions are a rich treat, sometimes ; not only to those who gaze upon them in good faith, but to the cooler spectator, employed rather in watching the company than the performers. I remember one, the *matériel* of which was a Lecture on Astronomy, with Orrery and Tellurium, (grand-sounding amusements for the woods !) a model of Perkins' steam gun, and a Magic Lantern. The master of ceremonies (feeling very little ceremony himself,) went about quite coolly, with his hat on and a segar in his mouth, marshalling the company, and ordering the boys to make themselves as small as they could, in order that he might the more easily get round to take up a contribution before the " exercises" began. The fee, being left to the generosity of the spectators, was not very burthensome in collecting ; and the orator declared before he began the lecture, that he had not received enough to pay for the candles—of which, by the bye, there were only four, for an audience of nearly an hundred people. This moved a good woman on one of the back seats so deeply, that she asked him to wait a minute, and then passed a sixpence, along a line of ready hands, to the rostrum, where the pathetic speaker, after first examining it on both sides by the nearest candle, put it in his pocket, and then, with a more contented air, ordered the music to begin. The violin accordingly struck up a lively tune, to which all the male part of the audience kept time with their feet; and the lecture, thus gilded over like a bitter pill, began. But such a lecture! It was read off by rote, the reader evidently knowing no more of his subject than of Hebrew, and having merely garbled from some dull treatise, an incomprehensible jumble of facts and theories that would have puzzled Sir John Herschel in the disentangling. The effect of such "amusement" on such an audience may easily be imagined. Some yawned, some nodded, and some went fairly and audibly to sleep. In vain the four candles were snuffed—in vain the lecturer told his audience that he was "just going to bite off"—they evidently began to wish their sixpences back in their pockets, when the lecturer finished and the violin was heard once more. This crisped the spirits of the company admirably, and the most curious blundering expositions of the Orrery and Tellurium found tolerably willing ears. The showman had wisely put the worst first; and now having done with the stars, he came to the steam gun, which took very well; the alcohol burning properly blue, and the reports being managed with the gentleness of any sucking dove.

But the cream of the night was the Magic Lantern, which had at least the merit of being suited to the apprehension of the auditory; its grotesque figures and frightful goblins possessing, too, the additional advantage of being set off by the operator's wit. The extinguishment of the lights set all the babies crying at once; but the violin, or some panacea discovered by the mammas, quieted them after a while; and we saw "the ghost that scared London for twenty years" roll his eyes horribly, and were told by the operator that that was the way the young men cast sheep's eyes when they went a-sparking. This idea created a laugh of course, which seemed a happy relief to some of the spectators, who had begun to feel very squeamish at the sight of a ghost. The night-mare, and several other engaging physiognomies, were still to come, and after all was over, in spite of desperate jokes, some of the ladies declared audibly as they went out, that they did not expect to sleep a wink all night.  Yet they were doubtless sure not to miss the next exhibition of the same kind.

The only exception to the choice of winter for regular amusements, is the ball on Independence night, or rather day, for we take time by the forelock.  In the sketch which follows, I have endeavoured to give an idea of one of these ; but it must be understood that the description applies to a newly settled part of the country, far from the vicinity of any large town.

———

IT was on the sultriest of all melting afternoons, when the flies were taking an ,unanimous siesta, and the bees, baked beyond honey or humming, swung idly on the honeysuckles, that I observed, with half-shut eye, something like activity among the human butterflies of our most peaceful of villages.  If I could have persuaded myself to turn my head, I might doubtless have ascertained to what favoured point were directed the steps (hasty, considering all things,) of the Miss Liggits, Miss Pinn, and my pretty friend, Fanny Russell ; but the hour was unpropitious to research, and slumber beguiled the book from my fingers, before the thought "Where *can* they be going !" had fairly passed through my mind.  Fancy had but just transported me to the focus of a circle of glass-blowers, the furnace directly in front, and the glowing fluid all round me, when I was recalled to almost equally overcoming realities, by a light tap at the door.  I must have given the usual invitation mechanically, for before I was fairly awake, the pink face of one of my own hand-maidens shone before my drowsy eyes.

"If you don't want me for nothin', I'd like to go down to the store to get some notions for the ball."

"The ball! what! a red-hot ball !" I replied, for the drowsy influence was settling over me again, and I was already on the deck of a frigate, in the midst of a sharply-contested action.

"Massy no, marm! this here Independence ball up to Thram's Huddle," said Jane, with a giggle.

I was now wide awake with astonishment.  "A dance, Jane, in such weather as this !"

" Why law ! yes ; nothin' makes a body so cool as dancin' and drinkin' hot tea."

This was beyond argument. Jane departed, and I amused myself with the flittings of gingham sun-bonnets and white aprons up and down the street, in the scorching sun.

It was waxing toward the tea-hour, when that prettiest of Fannies, Fanny Russell, her natural ringlets of shadowy gold, which a duchess might envy, looking all the richer under the melting influence of the time, came tripping into the little porch.

" If you *would* be so kind as to lend me that large feather fan ; I would take such good care of it ! It's for the ball."

Sweet Fanny ! one must be churlish indeed, to deny thee a far greater boon !

Next came that imp, Ring Jones ; but he goes slyly round to the kitchen-door, with an air of great importance. Presently, enter Jane.

" Ring Jones has brought a kind of a bill, marm, for our Mark ; and Mark ain't to hum, and Ring says he can't go without an answer."

" But I cannot answer Mark's billets, you know, Jane."

" No, marm ; but—this 'ere is something about the *team*, I guess."

And in the mean time Jane had, *sans ceremonie*, broken the wafer, and was spelling out the contents of Mark's note.

" I can't justly make it out ; but I know it's something about the *team ;* and they want an answer right off."

Thus urged, I took the note, which was after this fashion :

" The agreeable Cumpany of Mr. Mark Loring and Lady is requested to G. Nobleses Tavern to Thram's huddle Independence the 4th July."

And here followed the names of some eight or ten managers.

" But, Jane, here's nothing about the team, after all."

" Jist look o' t'other side, marm ; you see they didn't want to put it right in the ticket, like."

Upon this hint, I discerned, in the extreme corner of the paper, a flourish which might be interpreted " over." Over I went accordingly, and there came the gist of the matter.

" Mark we want to hav you be ready with your Team at one

o'clock percisely to escort the ladies if you can't let us know and don't forgit to Put in as many Seats as you can and All your Buffaloes."*

I ventured to promise that the team, and the seats, and the buffaloes, should be at Mark's disposal at "one percisely," and Ring Jones departed, highly exalted in his own opinion, by the success of his importunity.

It was to be supposed that we had now contributed our quota of aid on this patriotic occasion; but it seemed that more was expected. The evening was far advanced, when the newly-installed proprietor of the half-finished "hotel" at Thram's Huddle, alighted at our door; and, wiping his dripping brow, made known the astounding fact that he had scoured the country for dried apples, without success, and informed us that he had come, as a *dernier resort*, to beg the loan of some; "for," as he sensibly observed, "a ball without no pies, was a thing that was never heerd on, no wheres."

When this matter was settled, he mustered courage to ask, in addition, for the great favour of a gallon of vinegar, for which he declared himself ready to pay any price; "that is, any thing that was reasonable."

I could not refrain from inquiring what indispensable purpose the vinegar was to serve.

"Why, for the lettuce, you see!—and if it's pretty sharp, it 'll make 'em all the spryer."

Mr. Noble departed, in a happy frame of mind, and we heard no more of the ball that night.

The next day, the eldest Miss Liggitt "jist called in," as she happened to be passing, to ask if I was "a-goin' to want that 'ere flowery white bunnet-curting" of mine.

Some time ago I might not have comprehended that this description applied to a blonde-gauze veil, which had seen its best days, and was now scarce presentable. It did not require any great stretch of feminine generosity to lend this; but when it came to "a pair of white lace gloves," I pleaded poverty, and got off.

* It may be necessary to inform the civilized reader, that the use of buffalo robes in July, is to serve the purpose of cushions, and not of wrappers.

Our Jane, who is really quite a pretty girl, though her hair be
of the sandiest, and her face and neck, at this time of the year,
one continuous freckle, had set her heart upon a certain blue
satin ribbon, which she did not like exactly to borrow, but which
she had none the less made up her mind to have, for the grand
occasion.  So she began, like an able tactician, by showing me
one of faded scarlet, on which she requested my opinion.

" Don't you think this'll look about right ?"

" That horrid thing !  No, Jane, pray don't be seen in that !"

" Well ! what kind o' colour *do* you think would look good
with this belt ?" holding up a cincture, blue as the cloudless vault
above us.

" Blue, or white ; certainly not scarlet."

" Ah ! but I ha'n't got neither one nor t'other ;" and she looked
very pensive.

I was hard-hearted, but Jane was not without resource.

" If you'd a-mind to let me have that 'ere long blue one o'
your'n : you don't never wear it, and I'd be willin' to pay you for't.

Who could hold out ?  The azure streamer became Jane's, in
fee simple.

Spruce and warm looked our good Mark, in his tight blue
coat, with its wealth of brass buttons, his stock five fathoms
—I mean inches—deep, and his exceeding square-toed boots,
bought new for this very solemnity.  And a proud and pleased
heart beat in his honest bosom, I doubt not, as he drove to the
place of rendezvous, buffaloes and all, with cerulean Jane at his
side, a full half hour before the appointed time.  They need not
have cautioned Mark to be " percise."  For my part, I longed for
" the receipt of fern-seed to walk invisible," or some of those other
talismans which used in the good old times to help people into
places where they had no business to be ; and in this instance, the
Fates seemed inclined to be propitious, in a degree at least.

The revellers had scarcely passed on the western road in long
and most rapid procession—the dust they raised had certainly not
subsided—when a black cloud, which had risen stealthily while
all were absorbed in the outfit, began to unfold its ominous shroud.
The fringes of this portentous curtain scarcely passed the
zenith, when a low, distant muttering, and a few scattering but

immense drops, gave token of what was coming; and long ere
the gay *cortége* could have reached the Huddle, which is fully six
miles distant, a heavy shower, with thunder and lightning accompaniments, must have made wet drapery of every damsel's
anxiously elaborate ball-dress. Beaver and broad-cloth might
survive such a deluge, but alas for white dresses, long ringlets,
and blonde-gauze " bunnet-curtings !"

The shower was too violent to last, and when it had subsided,
and all was

> " Fresh as if Day again were born,
> Again upon the lap of Morn,"

I fortunately recollected an excellent reason for a long drive,
("man is his own Fate,") which would bring us into the very
sound of the violins of the Huddle. A young woman who had
filled the very important place of "help" in our family, was
lying very ill at her father's; and the low circumstances of her
parents made it desirable that she should be frequently remembered by her friends during her tedious illness. So in a light
open wagon, with a smart pony, *borrowed* for the nonce, *selon les
regles*, we had a charming drive, and moreover, the much-coveted
pleasure of seeing the heads of the assembled company at Mr.
Noble's; some bobbing up and down, some stretched far out of
the window, getting breath for the next exercise, and some, with
bodies to them, promenading the hall below. I tried hard to
distinguish the " belle chêvelure" of my favourite Fanny Russell,
or the straight back and nascent whiskers of our own Mark; but
we passed too rapidly to see all that was to be seen, and in a few
moments found ourselves at the bars which led to the forlorn
dwelling of poor Mary Anne Simms.

The only apartment that Mr. Simms' log-hut could boast,
was arranged with a degree of neatness which made a visitor
forget its lack of almost all the other requisites for comfort; and
one corner was ingeniously turned into a nice little room for the
sick girl, by the aid of a few rough boards eked out by snow-
white curtains. I raised the light screen, and what bright vision
should meet my eyes, but the identical Fanny, for whom I had
looked in vain among the bobbing heads at the Huddle. She was

whispering kindly to Mary Anne, whose pale cheek had acquired
something like a flush, and her eyes a decided moisture, from the
sense of Fanny's cheering kindness.

Fanny explained very modestly: "I was so near Mary Anne,
and I didn't know when I should get time to come again——"

"Didn't you get wet, coming over?"

"Not so *very*: we—we had an umbrella."

I remembered having lent one to Mark.

"But you are losing the ball, Fanny; you'll not get your
share of the dancing."    And at this moment I heard a new step
in the outer part of the room, and a very familiar voice just outside the curtain:

"Come, Miss Russell, isn't it about time to be a-goin'? There's
another shower a-comin' up."

Fanny started, blushed, and took leave.   Common humanity
obliged us to give time for a retreat, before we followed; for we
well knew that our very precise Mr. Loring would not have been
brought face to face with us, just then, for the world.   When we
did emerge, the sky was threatening enough, and as there was
evidently no room for us where we were, we had no resource but
to make a rapid transit to Mr. Noble's.   We gained the noisy
shelter just in time.   Such a shower !—and it proved much more
pertinacious than its predecessor; so that I had the pleasure of
sitting in " Miss Nobleses" kitchen for an hour or more.   We
were most politely urged to join the festivities which were now
shaking the frail tenement almost to dislocation; but even if we
had been ball-goers, we should have been strikingly *de trop*, where
the company was composed exclusively of young folks.   So we
chose the kitchen.

The empress of this torrid region, a tall and somewhat doleful
looking dame, was in all the agonies of preparation; and she
certainly was put to her utmost stretch of invention, to obtain
access to the fire-place, where some of the destined delicacies of
the evening were still in process of qualification, so dense was the
crowd of damp damsels, who were endeavouring in various ways
to repair the cruel ravages of the shower.   One " jist wanted to
dry her shoes ;" another was dodging after a hot iron, " jist to rub
off her hankercher ;" while others were taking turns in pinching

with the great kitchen tongs the long locks which streamed,
Ophelia-like, around their anxious faces. Poor "Miss Nobles"
edged, and glided, and stooped, among her humid guests, with a
patience worthy of all praise ; supplying this one with a pin, that
with a needle-and-thread, and the other with one of her own side-
combs ; though the last mentidned act of courtesy forced her to
tuck behind her ear one of the black tresses which usually lay
coiled upon her temple. In short, the whole affair was a sort of
prelibation of the Tournament, saving that *my* Queen of Beauty
and Love was more fortunate than the Lady Seymour, in that
her *coiffure* is decidedly improved by wet weather, which is more
than could probably be said of her ladyship's.

At length, but after a weary while, all was done that could be
done toward a general beautification ; and those whose array
was utterly beyond remedy, scampered up stairs with the rest,
wisely resolving not to lose the fun, merely because they were
not fit to be seen.

The dancing now became " fast and furious," and the spirit of
the hour so completely aroused that thirst for knowledge which is
slanderously charged upon my sex as a foible, that I hesitated not
to slip up stairs, and take advantage of one of the various knot-holes
in the oak boards which formed one side of the room, in order
that a glimpse of something like the realities of the thing might
aid an imagination which could never boast of being "all com-
pact." It was but a glimpse, to be sure, for three candles can
do but little toward illuminating a long room, with dark brown
and very rough walls ; but there was a tortuous country-dance,
one side quivering and fluttering in all the colours of the rainbow, the other presenting more nearly the similitude of a funeral ;
for our beaux, in addition to the solemn countenances which they
think proper to adopt on all occasions of festivity, have imbibed
the opinion that nothing but broad-cloth is sufficiently dignified
wear for a dance, be the season what it may. And there
were the four Miss Liggets, Miss Mehitable in white, Miss
Polly Ann in green, Miss Lucindy in pink, and Miss Olive all
over black-and-blue, saving the remains of the blonde-gauze
veil, which streamed after her like a meteor, as she *galoped*
" down the middle." My own Jane was playing off her most

*recherchées* graces at the expense of the deputy sheriff, who seemed for once caught, instead of catching ; and to my great surprise, Fanny Russell, evidently in the pouts, under cover of my fan, was enacting the part of wall-flower, while Mark leaned far out of the window, at the risk of taking an abrupt leave of the company.

Peeping is tiresome. I was not sorry when the dance came to an end, as even country-dances must ; and when I had waited to see the ladies arranged in a strip at one end of the room, and the gentlemen in ditto at the other, and old Knapp the fiddler testing the absorbent powers of a large red cotton handkerchief upon a brow as thickly beaded as the fair neck of any one of the nymphs around him, (and some of them had necklaces which would have satisfied a belle among our neighbours, the Pottowatomies,) I ran down stairs again, to prepare for our moonlight flitting.

Mrs. Noble now renewed her entreaties that we would at least stay for supper; and in the pride of her heart, and the energy of her hospitality, she opened her oven-door, and holding a candle that I might not fail to discern all its temptations, pointed out to me two pigs, a large wild turkey, a mammoth rice-pudding, and an endless array of pies of all sizes ; and these she declared were " not a beginning" of what was intended for the " refreshment" of the company. A cup-board was next displayed, where, among custards, cakes, and " saase," or preserves, of different kinds, figured great dishes of lettuce, " all ready, only jist to pour the vinegar and molasses over it," bowls of large pickled cucumbers, and huge pyramids of dough-nuts. But we continued inexorable, and were just taking our leave, when Fanny Russell, her pretty eyes overflowing and her whole aspect evincing the greatest vexation and discomposure, came running down stairs, and begged we would let her go home with us.

" What *can* be the matter, Fanny !"

" Oh, nothing ! nothing at all ! But—I want to go home."

It is never of much use advising young girls, when they have made up their minds to be foolish ; yet I did just call my little favourite aside, and give her a friendly caution not to expose herself to the charge of being rude or touchy. But this brought

only another shower of tears, and a promise that she would tell
me all about it; so we took her in and drove off.

I could not but reflect, as we went saunteringly home, enjoying the splendour of the moonlight, and the delicious balminess
of that " stilly hour," how much all balls are alike.   Here had
been all the solicitude and sacrifice in the preparation of costume ; all the effort and expense in providing the refreshments ; for
the champagne and ices, the oysters and the perigord pies, are no
more to the pampered citizen, than are the humbler cates we have
attempted to enumerate, to the plain and poor back-woodsman ;
then here was the belle of the evening, in as pretty a paroxysm
of insulted dignity, as could have been displayed on the most
classically-chalked floor ; and, to crown all, judging from past experience in these regions, some of the " gentlemen" at least
would, like their more refined prototypes, vindicate their claims
to the title, by going home vociferously drunk.  We certainly are
growing very elegant.

Fanny's explanation was deferred, at her own request, until
the following morning ; and long before she made her promised
visit, Jane, who came home at day-light, and only allowed herself
a change of dress before she entered soberly upon her domestic
duties, had disclosed to me the mighty mystery.  It had been the
opinion of every body, Jane herself included, (a little green-eyed,
I fancy,) that Fanny and Mark had gone off to Squire Porter's
and got married, under cover of the visit to poor Mary Anne.
This idea once started, the beaux and belles, not better bred than
some I have seen elsewhere, had not suffered the joke to drop, but
pushed their raillery so far, that Fanny had fairly given up and
run away, while Mark, however well pleased in his secret soul,
had thought it necessary to be very angry, and to throw out sundry hints of " thrashing" some of the stouter part of the company.  The peace had not actually been broken, however ; and
when I saw and talked with Fanny, the main difficulty seemed to
relate to the future course of conduct to be observed toward
Mark, who, as Fanny declared, with another sprinkling of tears,
had " never thought of saying such a word to her in his life !"

Women are excellent manœuverers generally, but we were
outdone here.  All our dignified plans for acting " as if nothing

had happened," were routed by a counter scheme of Mark himself, who, before the week was out, not only said "such a word,"
but actually persuaded Fanny to think that the best of all ways
to disprove what had been said, was to go to Squire Porter's, and
make it true, which was accordingly accomplished, within the
fortnight.

"And what for no?" Mark Loring, with a very good-looking
face, and a person "as straight as a gun-barrel" (to borrow a
favourite comparison of his own,) has the wherewithal to make
a simple and industrious country maiden very comfortable. He
has long been earning, by the labour of his hands, far better pay
than is afforded to our district schoolmaster; and with the well-
saved surplus has purchased a small farm, which he and his
pretty wife are improving with all their might. No more balls
for my bright-haired neighbour, or her sober spouse! And if I
should tell my honest sentiments, I should say "so much the better!" for in the hastening of the happy marriage of Mark and
Fanny, may be summed up all the good which I have yet observed to result from the ball at Thram's Huddle, or any other in
our vicinity.

# A FOREST FÊTE.

A LESS common and natural accompaniment of our national holiday is a party of pleasure, or some device to pass the day in quiet amusement, instead of the noisy demonstrations which seem to serve as a safety-valve for the exuberance of animal spirits so habitually repressed throughout the United States during the remainder of the year. Gunpowder in unpractised hands is the cause of so much evil, and its natural friend and ally, whiskey, so inimical to peace and good order, that it is an object of no small solicitude to the soberer classes in the new country to devise some mode of celebrating "Independence" that shall not end in bloodshed and mortal quarrels. A Sunday school celebration—one on a large scale, that should bring children and parents, from far and near, to hear addresses, sing songs, and enjoy a rustic feast under a long bower of fresh branches, was tried one year; but the opposition of the powder party was so bitter that very little was gained in the way of peace, although perhaps some broken bones and blistered faces were saved. Even on that occasion, however, I recollect that a son of one of our neighbours, attempting to blow off some scattered grains of coarse powder from near the touch-hole of the one-pounder that was fired all day by the opposition, suddenly found the whole of it—the powder, not the gun—firmly imbedded in his face, just beneath the skin; and although his mother picked out many grains with her needle, and others made their own way out by suppuration, he will still carry to his grave such a curiously tattooed physiognomy as will serve to remind him of the glorious Fourth, let his lot be cast where it may.

Another device for the more refined enjoyment of the day was a pic-nic party, such as is here sketched under the title of a Forest Fête. This sketch is not to be received as *history* any more than many others of a similar tone.   Real occurrences are introduced, but fancy and general recollections furnished the warp into which such scraps of truth are woven—characteristic correctness being the only aim.

If there be any feeling in the American bosom which may be considered a substitute for that "loyalty" of which the renowned Captain Hall so pathetically notices the lamentable lack, it is the enthusiasm which is annually rekindled, even in the most utilitarian and dollar-worshipping souls among us, by the return of "Independence day."   The first sign of the dawning of this virtue is discoverable in the *penchant* of our younglings for Chinese crackers, and indeed gunpowder in any form, always evinced during the last days of June and the opening ones of July; a season in which he whose pockets will hold money, must be either more or less than boy.   And as "the child is father of the man," the passion for showing joy and gratitude through the medium of gunpowder seems to increase and strengthen with every recurrence of our national festival, till as much "villanous saltpetre" is expended on a single celebration as would have sufficed our revolutionary forefathers to win a pitched battle.   The gentler sex, partaking, by sympathy at least, in the excitement of the time, yet exhibit their patriotism by less noisy demonstrations: by immeasurable pink ribbons; by quadruple consumption of sugar candy; by patient endurance of unmerciful spouting; by unwearied running after the "trainers," and shrill and pretty shrieking at the popping; and sometimes, in primitive and unsophisticated regions, by getting up parties of pleasure, with the aid of such beaux as they cán inveigle from amusements better suited to the dignity of the sex, such as drinking, scrub-racing; firing salutes from hollow logs, or blacksmiths' anvils; playing "fox-and-geese" for sixpences; or shooting at a turkey tied to a post, at a shilling the chance.

One particular Independence day not many years sinsyne is memorable in our village annals.   It was probably qwing to the fact that gunpowder was not very abundant, that some of the élite of the settlement proposed a select pic-nic, to be held on the shore of a beautiful, lonely sheet of water, which having nothing else to do, reflects the flitting clouds at no great distance from our

clearing. A famous time it was, and a still more famous one it
would have been, but for an idea which sprang up among certain
of our rural exclusives, that it was ungenteel to appear pleased
with what delighted others. I say "sprang up," because I feel
assured that our fashionables had never even read of the airs of
their thorough-bred prototypes; and from a retrospect of the
whole affair, I am convinced that the human mind has a natural
tendency toward exclusiveism. This effort at superior refinement, with some slight mistakes and disappointments, clouded
somewhat the enjoyment of the occasion; but on the whole, the
affair went off at least as well as such preconcerted pleasures do
elsewhere. Mr. Towson and Mr. Turner, to be sure —— But
let us begin at the beginning.

Nothing could have been more auspicious than our outset.
All the good stars seemed in conjunction for once, and their
kindly influence lent unwonted lustre to the eyes of the ladies
and the boots of the gentlemen. Every body felt confident that
every thing had been thought of; nobody could recollect any
body tnat *was* any body, who had not been included in the "very
select" circle of invitation. Plenty of "teams" had been engaged—for who thinks of ploughing or haying on Independence
day ?—all the whips were provided with red snappers, and cock-
ades and streamers of every hue decorated the tossing heads of
our gallant steeds. Indeed, to do them justice, the horses seemed
as much excited as any body. Provant in any quantity, from
roast-pig, (the peacock of all our feasts,) to custards, lemonade,
and green tea, had been duly packed and cared for. Music had
not been forgotten, for one of the party played the violin *à mer-
ville*, to the extent of two country dances and half a quadrille,
while another beau was allowed to be a "splendid whistler," and
a third, who had cut his ankle with a scythe, and could not
dance, had borrowed the little triangle from the hotel, which we
all agreed to look upon as a tambourine when it should mark the
time for the dancers, and a gong when employed in its more ac-
oustomed office of calling the hungry to supper. So we were
unexceptionably provided for at all points.

The day was such as we often have during the warm months
—the most delicious that can be imagined. From the first

pearly streak of dawn, to the last fainting crimson of a Claude
sunset, no cloud was any where but where it should have been,
to enhance the intensity of a blue that was truly "Heaven's
own"—inimitable, unapproachable by any effort of human art.
A light crisping breeze ruffled the surface of the lake, whose
shaded borders furnished many a swelling sofa of verdant turf for
the loungers, as well as a wide and smooth area for the exertions
of the nimble-footed.  Here we alighted ; here were our shining
steeds tethered among the oak bushes to browse, to their very
great satisfaction ; our flags were planted, and, to omit nothing
appropriate to the occasion, our salute was fired, with the aid of
what a young lady who went into becoming hysterics declared to
be a six-pounder, but which proved on inquiry to be only a horse-
pistol ; our belle refusing to be convinced, however, on the ground
that she had heard a six-pounder go off at Detroit, and certainly
ought to know.   " *Quelle imagination !*"—as a French gentleman of our acquaintance used to exclaim admiringly, when his
children perpetrated the most elaborate and immeasurable fibs—
" quelle imagination !"

When this was over, Mr. Towson, a very tall and slender
young gentleman, who is considered (and I believe not without
reason,) a promising youth, proposed reading the Declaration of
Independence, and had drawn out his pocket-handkerchief for the
purpose, observing very appositely that if it had not been for that
declaration we should never have been keeping Independence on
the shores of Onion Lake, when he was voted down ; every body
talking at once, to make it clear that a sail on the said lake ought
to precede the reading.  Mr. Towson assented with the best grace
he could muster, to a decision that reduced him, for the present
at least, to a place in the ranks, and offering his arm to Miss
Weatherwax, an imaginative young lady, a belle from a rival
village, he attempted with a very gallant air to lead the way to
the larger of the two boats provided for our accommodation.
Now it so happened that this said large boat, having a red handkerchief displayed aloft, had been by common consent styled
" the Commodore ;" and these advantages being considered, it
may readily be inferred that each and every individual who
meant to " tempt the waves " had secretly resolved to secure a

seat in it. But as the unlucky beau urged his fair companion forward, another, who had been deeply engaged with two of our own belles in the discussion of a paper of sweeties, observing a movement toward the beach, was on the alert in an instant, and with a lady on each arm, made first way to the Commodore; all scattering sugar-plums as they went, to serve as a clue to those who might choose to follow in their wake. Not among these was the spirited Mr. Towson. He declared that the other boat would be far pleasanter, and Miss Weatherwax being quite of his opinion, he led her to the best (*i. e.* the driest) seat in it, and procured a large green branch, which he held over her by way of parasol, or rather awning. The company in general now followed, taking seats, since the *ton* was thus divided, in either boat, as choice or convenience dictated. All seemed very well, though this was in fact the beginning of an unfortunate split, which from that moment divided our company into parties; the largest, viz., that which took possession of "the Commodore," claiming of course to be the orthodox, or regular line, while the other was considered only an upstart, or opposition concern. The latter, as usual, monopolized the wit. They amused themselves by calling the exclusives "squatters," "prëemptioners," &c., and reiterated so frequently their self-congratulations upon having obtained seats in the smaller craft, that it might be shrewdly guessed they wished themselves any where else.

The sail was long and hot, especially to the excluded; for the Commodore having made at once for a narrow part of the lake, shaded by overhanging trees, and enjoying the advantage of a breeze from the south, dignity required that the other boat should take an opposite course. It accordingly meandered about under the broiling sun, until the reflection from the water had baked the ladies' faces into a near resemblance to that of the rising harvest moon; these very ladies, with the heroic self-devotion of martyrs, declaring they never had so pleasant a sail in their lives.

Meanwhile, those of us whom advanced years or soberer taste disposed rather to tea and talk than to songs and sailing, were busily engaged in arranging to the best advantage the variety of good things provided for the refreshment of the company. This proved by no means so easy a task as the uninitiated may suppose. Our party, which was originally to have been a small one, had swelled by degrees to something like forty persons, by the usual process of adding, for various good reasons, people who were at first voted out. No agreement having been entered into as to the classification of the articles to be furnished by each, it proved, on unpacking the baskets, that there had been an inconvenient unanimity of taste in the selection. At least one dozen good housewives had thought it like enough every body would forget butter; so that we had enough of a fluid article so called, to have smoothed the lake in case of a tempest. Then we had dozens and dozens of extra knives and forks, and scarce a single spoon; acres of pie with very few plates to eat it from; tea-kettles and tea-pots, but no cups and saucers. The young men with a never-to-be-sufficiently-commended gallantry, had provided good store of lemons, which do not grow in the oak-openings; but alas! though sugar was reasonably abundant, we searched in vain for any thing which would answer to hold our sherbet, and all the baskets turned out afforded but six tumblers.

These and similar matters were still under discussion, and much ingenuity had been evinced in the suggestion of substitutes, when one of the boating parties announced its return by the discharge of the same piece of ordnance which had frightened Miss Weatherwax from her propriety, on our arrival. We now hastened our preparation for the repast, and some of the gentlemen having procured some deliciously cool water from a spring at a little distance, and borrowed a large tin pail and sundry other conveniences from a lady whose log-house showed picturesquely from the depths of the wood, the lemonade was prepared, and all things declared ready. But the other boat, the opposition line, as it was denominated in somewhat pettish fun, still kept its distance. Handkerchiefs were waved; the six-pounder horse-pistol went off with our last charge of powder; but the "spunky" craft still continued veering about, determined neither to see nor hear our signals. It was now proposed that we should proceed without the seceders, but to this desperate measure the more prudent part of the company made strenuous objection. So we waited with grumbling politeness till it suited the left branch of our troop to rejoin us, which gave time to warm the lemonade and cool the tea. We tried to look good-humoured or indifferent; but there were some on whose unpliant brows frowns left their trace, though smiles shone faint below. The late arrival laughed a good deal; quite boisterously, we thought, and boasted what a charming time they had.

"Had *you* any music?" asked Mr. Towson of Mr. Turner, the hero of the Commodore's crew, with an air of friendly interest.

"No," said the respondent, taken by surprise.

"Ah! there now! what a pity! I wish you had been near us, that you might have had the benefit of ours! The ladies sang 'Bonnie Doon,' and every thing; and 'I see them on their winding way;' and —— it went like ile, Sir."

"'Winding way!' you might have seen yourselves on your winding way, if you'd been where we was!" said the rival beau, with an air of deep scorn. "What made you go wheeling about in the sun so?"

"Fishing, Sir—the ladies were a-fishing, Sir!"

"Fishing! Did you catch any thing?"

"No, Sir! we did not catch any thing! We did not wish to catch any thing! We were fishing for amusement, Sir!"

"Oh!—ah! fishing for amusement, eh!"

But here the call to the banquet came just in time to stop the fermentation before it reached the acetous stage, and brows and pocket-kerchiefs were smoothed as we disposed ourselves in every variety of Roman attitude, and some that Rome in all her glory never knew, reclining round the long-drawn array of table-cloths upon whose undulating surface our multitudinous refreshment was deployed. Shawls, cloaks, and buffalo-robes formed our couches—giant oaks our pillared roof. We had tin pails and cups to match, instead of vases of marble and goblets of burning gold. But nobody missed these imaginary advantages. Talk flagged not, as it is apt to do amid scenes of cumbrous splendour, and the merry laugh of the young and happy rang far through the greenwood, unrestrained by the fear of reproof or ridicule. Exclusiveism and all its concomitants were forgotten during tea-time.

When the repast was finished, the sun was far on his downward way, and the esplanade which had been selected as the ballroom was well shaded by a clump of trees on its western border.

Thitherward all whose dancing days were not over, turned with
hasty steps, and Mr. Kittering's violin might be heard in various
squeaks and groans, giving token of the onset.    But we listened
in vain for farther demonstrations.    No " Morning Star"—no
" Mony-Musk"—no " Poule," or " Trenise" delighted the attendant echoes.    Debate, warm and rapid, if not loud and angry,
seemed to leave no chance for sweeter sounds.    The morning's
feud between Towson and Turner had broken out with fresh acri-
mony, when places were to be claimed for the dance.    Hard
things were said, and harder ones looked, on both sides ; and in
conclusion, Mr. Towson again marched magnanimously off the
field, and contented himself with the sober glory of reading the
Declaration to a select audience ; while the Commodore's crew,
victorious as before, through superior coolness, got up a dance,
and had the violin and triangle all to themselves.

The moon rose full and ruddy before we were packed in our
wagons to return.    The tinkling of bells through the wood, the
ceaseless note of the whip-poor-will, the moaning of the evening
wind, the chill of a heavy dew, all fraught with associations of
repose, gradually quieted the livelier members of the party, and
put the duller or the more fatigued fairly asleep.    Some of the
jokers remained untameable for awhile.    The young ladies kept
up a little whispering and a great deal of giggling among themselves, and the word " Commodore" was so frequently audible,
that one might have thought they were talking of the last war.
Mr. Turner drove so closely upon the vehicle in which Mr. Towson occupied the back seat, as to bring his horses' heads unpleasantly near the new hat of that gentleman.

" Hallo ! Turner ! your horses will be biting me next !" said
Mr. Towson, rather querulously.

" Don't be afraid ; they don't like such lean meat."

" I should think by their looks they'd be glad of any thing to
eat !" said Towson.

" Oh ! you mus'n't judge them by yourself," replied Turner,
coolly ; " they get plenty to eat, every day."

Even this sharp shooting subsided after a while, and before we
alighted, unbroken silence had settled upon the entire *cortège*.
But the pic-nic afforded conversation for a month, and every body
agreed in thinking we had had a charming " Independence."

## LOVE vs. ARISTOCRACY.

THE great ones of the earth might learn many a lesson from
the little. What has a certain dignity on a comparatively large
scale, is so simply laughable when it is seen in miniature, (and,
unlike most other things, perhaps, its real features are better distinguished in the small), that it must be wholesome to observe
how what we love appears in those whom we do not admire.
The monkey and the magpie are imitators; and when the one
makes a thousand superfluous bows and grimaces, and the other
hoards what can be of no possible use to him, we may, even in
those, see a far off reflex of certain things prevalent among ourselves. Next in order come little children; and the boy will
put a napkin about his neck for a cravat, and the girl supply her
ideal of a veil by pinning a pocket handkerchief to her bonnet,
while we laugh at the self-deception, and fancy that *we* value
only realities. But what affords us most amusement, is the awkward attempt of the rustic, to copy the airs and graces which have
caught his fancy as he saw them exhibited in town; or, still
more naturally, those which have been displayed on purpose to
dazzle him, during the stay of some "mould of fashion" in the
country. How exquisitely funny are his efforts and their failure!
How the true hugs himself in full belief that the gulf between
himself and the *pseudo* is impassable! Little dreams he that his
own ill-directed longings after the *distingué* in air or in position
seem to some more fortunate individual as far from being accomplished as those of the rustic to himself, while both, perhaps, owe
more to the tailor and milliner than to any more dignified source.

The country imitates the town, most sadly; and it is really
melancholy, to one who loves his kind, to see how obstinately
people will throw away real comforts and advantages in the vain

chase of what does not belong to solitude and freedom. The restraints necessary to city life are there compensated by many
advantages resulting from close contact with others; while in
the country those restraints are simply odious, curtailing the real
advantages of the position, yet entirely incapable of substituting
those which belong to the city.

Real refinement is as possible in the one case as in the other.
Would it were more heartily sought in both!

---

In the palmy days of alchemy, when the nature and powers
of occult and intangible agents were deemed worthy the study of
princes, the art of sealing hermetically was an essential one;
since many a precious elixir would necessarily become unmanageable and useless if allowed to wander in•the common air.
This art seems now to be among the lost, in spite of the anxious
efforts of cunning projectors; and at the present time a subtle
essence, more volatile than the elixir of life—more valuable than
the philosopher's stone—an invisible and imponderable but most
real agent, long bottled up for the enjoyment of a privileged few,
has burst its bounds and become part of our daily atmosphere.
Some mighty sages still contrive to retain within their own keeping important portions of this treasure; but there are regions of
the earth where it is open to all, and, in the opinion of the exclusive, sadly desecrated by having become an object of pursuit to
the vulgar.    Where it is still under a degree of control, the seal
of Hermes is variously represented.    In Russia, the supreme
will of the Autocrat regulates the distribution of the " airy
good :" in other parts of the Continent, ancient prescription has
still the power to keep it within its due reservoirs.    In France,
its uses and advantages have been publicly denied and repudia-
ted; yet it is said that practically every body stands open-mouth-
ed where it is known to be floating in the air, hoping to inhale as
much as possible without the odium of seeming to grasp at what
has been decided to be worthless.    In England we are told that
the precious fluid is still kept with great solicitude in a dingy re-
ceptacle called Almack's, watched ever by certain priestesses,
who are self-consecrated to an attendance more onerous than that

required for maintaining the Vestal fire, and who yet receive neither respect nor gratitude for their pains.  Indeed, the fine spirit has become so much diffused in England that it reminds us of the riddle of Mother Goose—

> A house-full, a hole-full,
> But can't catch a bowl-full.

If such efforts in England amuse us, what shall we say of the agonized pursuit every where observable in our own country ? We have denounced the fascinating gas as poisonous—we have staked our very existence upon excluding it from the land, yet it is the breath of our nostrils—the soul of our being—the one thing needful—for which we are willing to expend mind, body, and estate.  We exclaim against its operations in other lands, but it is the purchaser decrying to others the treasure he would appropriate to himself.  We take much credit to ourselves for having renounced what all the rest of the world were pursuing, but our practice is like that of the toper who had forsworn drink, yet afterward perceiving the contents of a brother sinner's bottle to be spilt, could not forbear falling on his knees to drink the liquor from the frozen hoof-prints in the road ; or that other votary of indulgence, who, having once had the courage to pass a tavern, afterward turned back that he might " treat resolution." We have satisfied our consciences by theory ; we feel no compunction in making our practice just like that of the rest of the world.

This is true of the country generally; but it is nowhere so strikingly evident as in these remote regions which the noise of the great world reaches but at the rebound—as it were in faint echoes ; and these very echoes changed from their original, as Paddy asserts of those of the Lake of Killarney.  It would seem that our *elixir vitæ*—a strange anomaly—becomes stronger by dilution.  Its power of fascination, at least, increases as it recedes from the fountain head.  The Russian noble may refuse to let his daughter smile upon a suitor whose breast is not covered with orders; the German dignitary may insist on sixteen quarterings; the well-born Englishman may sigh to be admitted into a coterie not half as respectable or as elegant as the one to which

he belongs—all this is consistent enough ; but we *must* laugh
when we see the managers of a city ball admit the daughters of
*wholesale* merchants, while they exclude the families of merchants who sell at *retail ;* and still more when we come to the
"new country" and observe that Mrs. Penniman, who takes *in*
sewing, utterly refuses to associate with her neighbour Mrs.
Clapp, because she goes *out* sewing by the day ; and that our
friend Mr. Diggins, being raised a step in the world by the last
election, signs all his letters of friendship, "D. Diggins, Sheriff."

There is Persis Allen, the best and the prettiest girl to be
found within a wide belt of forest, must be quite neglected by the
leaders of the *ton* among us, because she goes out to spin, in order
to help her "unlucky" father.   Not that spinning is in itself considered vulgar—far from it !   Flocks are but newly introduced
among us, and all that relates to them is in high vogue ; but going out ! there is the rub !   Persis might have lounged about at
home, with her hair uncombed and her shoes down at heel, only
"helping" some neighbour occasionally for a short time to earn
a new dress,—without losing caste.   But to engage herself as a
regular drudge, to spin day after day in old Mr. Hicks' great
upper chamber all alone, and never have time or finery to go to a
ball or a training—she must be a poor, mean-spirited creature,
not fit to associate with "genteel" people.

The father of Persis is a blacksmith, and an honest and worthy
man, but he is one of those who are described in the country as
having "such bad luck !"   When he first came into the wilds, he
put a sum of money that constituted his all, in a handkerchief
about his head, and then swam over a deep and rapid river,
because he was too intent on pursuing his journey to await the
return of a boat which had just left the shore.   He saved
his hour, but lost the price of his land ; and so was obliged to
run in debt for a beginning.   During the haying of his first western summer he was too ardent in his endeavours to retrieve his
loss to allow himself a long rest at noon, as the other mowers
did ; and the consequence was an attack of fever which put him
still further back in the world.   Once more at work, and no less
determined than before, he employed his leisure time in assisting
the neighbours in the heavy and dangerous business of "logging ;"

and once more "unlucky," he attempted to stop by his single arm
a log which threatened to roll down a slope, and the next moment
he lay helpless with a dislocated shoulder and a hand so mash-
ed that it was long doubtful whether it would ever regain its
powers.

All through these disasters his faithful help-meet struggled on,
enfeebled by ague, and worn with nursing and watching and
pitying her husband.   Early and late—out of doors and within—
she was at work, endeavouring to preserve a remnant from the
general wreck, aided and cheered by her eldest daughter, who,
like many children so situated, became prematurely thoughtful
and laborious, and seemed never to have known the careless joy-
ousness of childhood.   At length Mrs. Allen took a heavy cold
in searching all the evening for her cow, through grass and bushes
dripping with dew, and she was seized with a rheumatism which
made a cripple of her, just as her husband was able to go to his
forge again. , So our pretty Persis seemed, as I have said, born
the "predestined child of care," but she held the blessed place of
comforter, and that consciousness can throw somewhat of an
angelic radiance over even the face of care.   She looked neither
pale nor sad, though she was seldom smiling ; and from the habit
of constant effort and solicitude at home, she seemed, when away
and among young people, as if she hardly knew what to do with
herself.   But in old Mr. Hicks' spinning-room she was in her
element ; the great unfurnished chamber is cool and shady, and
across its ample floor Persis has paced back and forth, at her light
labour, till she has acquired an elastic grace of motion which
dancing-masters often try in vain to teach.   Indeed, I fancy that
few of my fair readers know the real advantages of a thorough
acquaintance with the spinning-wheel ; the expanded chest, the
well developed bust, the firm, springing step which belong to this
healthiest and most graceful of all in-door employments.   And
let me whisper to some of my pretty, mincing, pit-a-pat friends,
that an easy and elastic step is no trifling point in the estimation
of those who know what real elegance is, independently of stupid
fashions.   Many a young lady can manage the curve of the wrist
prescribed by the French prints, and let her shoulders fall so low
that one can hardly help trembling for the consequences, yet her

walk, after all, needs all the charitable shadow afforded by long dresses. But we must not indulge in impertinent digressions.

Spinning differs from other feminine labours, inasmuch as its profits are dependent on the superior skill or industry of the spinner. Let a poor girl sew ever so steadily, she can earn but little addition to her miserable *per diem ;* but in spinning there is, by ancient custom, a measure to the day's work ; and a good hand may by extra exertion accomplish this twice in a June day. So poor Persis worked incessantly when she could be spared from home, encouraged by the thought that all she could accomplish over and above her " run and a half" was so much clear gain. A gain in home comforts, sweet Persis ! but a terrible loss elsewhere.

The loss of caste was, however, less an evil to the Allens, because their home troubles had hitherto prevented their mingling much with the people about them, and so, they had not yet fully adopted the public sentiment. But they learned to know all about it in time.

There is one white and green house in the village, and that, where paint is still so rare, is by good right the Palazzo Pitti of our bounds. It is shown to the passing traveller as a proof of the civilization of the country, and elicits not a few remarks from the farmers who pass it slowly in their huge wagons. It is worth looking at, too, for even its outer decorations are a masterpiece of taste. The siding is plain white to be sure ; but the frames of doors and windows, the cornices, the " corner-boards" and the piazza railing are all bright green. The sashes are in black— rather prison-like but vastly " genteel"—and the front door is in an elaborate mahogany style, with more " curly-wurlies" than usual. Within doors, a taste no less gorgeous is evident, for the wood-work is all of the brightest blue—probably in imitation of lapis-lazuli.

In this favoured and much-envied dwelling resides a lady who is considered by the public in general, and herself in particular, as the very cream of our aristocracy.

Mrs. Burnet is a fair and plump dame, whose age can only be guessed by considering a grown-up son. Not a wrinkle mars her smooth brow ; not a gray hair mingles with the smooth brown tresses that are laid so demurely on either temple. Her coun-

tenance wears a fixed smile, and her words are measured by the
strictest rule of propriety ; and the tones which convey them to
the ear are of so silvery a softness that one can hardly think the
most yielding of all substances could melt between those correct
lips.   (This paraphrase is the result of much laborious thought.)
But in the full brown eye above them there lurks—what shall we
call it ?—to say the least, a latent power which is felt through all
those silvery tones, and in spite of all that winning softness.   The
initiated are exceedingly careful how they rouse this sleeping
power ; for in those singular tones—to convey which to the reader
would require music-paper and some skill at annotation—things
are sometimes said which other people might say passionately or
sharply, but which Mrs. Burnet knows how to make the more
bitter by sweetness.

This lady's household consisted usually of only two members
beside herself—a serving-maid with a flat white face and a threatening beard—for Mrs. Burnet had an instinctive dislike of youth
and beauty—and a young man toward whom nature had been more
bounteous, but whom fortune had so neglected that he was fain to
"do chores" for his board at Mrs. Burnet's, while he picked a
very scanty education out of the village school.   This poor youth,
Cyprian Amory, was the nephew of the great lady, but only the
gloom of her glory fell on him ; for his mother had made an
imprudent marriage, and her orphan boy was a heavy burthen to
Mrs. Burnet's pride.   She could not quite make an outcast of her
sister's son, but she revenged the mortification which his poverty
occasioned her, by rendering his situation as odious as possible ;
taking care always to represent him as an object of charity,
although his services were such as would have earned ungrudged
bread any where else.   Cyprian was of a mild and quiet temper,
and being unfitted by delicate health for the labour of farming,
he was intent on preparing himself for that poorest of all drudgery,
the teaching of a district school.   So he bore all in a silence
which his aunt ascribed to stupidity, but which a few friends that
he loved, and whose love consoled him, considered the result of a
patience and resignation almost saintly.

Besides Cyprian and the flat-faced serving-maid, Mrs. Burnet's family boasted yet one member more—her only son and heir, of whom more, presently.

Mrs. Burnet's establishment was at no great distance from the humble dwelling of William Allen; indeed the two gardens joined at their farther extremity. And at that corner the wide difference between the two was not so evident, for the fruit-trees hid the splendid white and green mansion, while the roses and lilies which adorned Mr. Allen's garden had evidently never heard of our aristocracy, since they bloomed with a provoking splendour which Mrs. Burnet's did not always exhibit. That lady's general plan was so thrifty, that her grounds were largely devoted to corn and potatoes; and she did not remember to pay much attention to flowers, unless she longed for their decorative powers on some great occasion.

Such an occasion had arrived; for George Burnet had just come home after finishing what he called his " law studies ;" studies which we rather think were comprised in six months' " sharp practice," as clerk to a gentleman who had quitted the shoe-maker's bench for the law, on the supposition that the art of pet-tifogging would prove a stepping-stone to a bench of more dignity. This gentleman's neophyte, Mr. George Burnet, was such a youth as the only son of a doting mother is apt to be—wilful, conceited and very hard to please ; in short, not voted particularly agree-able for any qualities of his own, but much reverenced as the heir-presumptive of the white and green house, and also on account of his aristocratic pretensions—his father having once been elected to the legislature. He was fully sensible of his advantages, and not a little apt to boast of his expectations ; was good-natured when he was pleased, and very kind where he took a fancy—in short, one of those people who intend well, or at least intend no ill, but are never to be depended on for a day.

Mr. George Burnet came home in high spirits, determined to enjoy to the uttermost the interval between the finish of his prepa-ration and the opening of sharp practice on his own account. He was extravagantly fond of dancing, and his mother had always promised him a grand party when he should have got through his studies, on the express condition, however, that he was to return immediately to business, and not stay to hunt and fish and sere-

nade about the neighbourhood.    George found it easy to promise,
and the party was now to come off.

The preparations for this great event had for some time been
foreshadowed in the active brain of Mrs. Burnet ; and George's
" freedom suit" was duly bespoken, and two violins secured,
long before the arrival of the graduate.    But, as the appointed
day drew nigh, who shall tell of the hopes and fears, the consul-
tations and the arguments, which were·expended on and over the
list of favoured guests.    Enough to say that it was almost the
ditto of those familiar to the town-bred getters-up of splendid hospitality, (!) and that the principle of the whole thing was precisely
the same, though set forth and put in practice in homelier guise.
Who will do to invite ?    Who may be left out ?    Who will look
best ?    Whose presence will reflect most honour on the enter-
tainers ?    Whose enmity will be least formidable among those
who ought to be excluded on account of want of *caste*, or want of
*savoir faire ?*    George Burnet and his lady mother found it hard
to agree in their estimate of the guests ; George insisting upon
all the pretty girls, and these, for the most part, portionless belles,
being the last to be selected by Mrs. Burnet.

" Mary Stevens," said George.

" Poh !  She goes out sewing !" said Mrs. Burnet.

" I don't care for that," said the dutiful son, " she has rosy
cheeks, and I'll have her."

" There's Mary Drinkwater, I shall ask, of course," observed
Mrs. Burnet.

" Squint-eyed !" said George.

" No matter for that," was the reply, " she's got a farm of her
own.   I hope you'll be very civil to her."

" Mother," said George Burnet, " I wouldn't marry Polly
Drinkwater if there wasn't another girl in the world !"

" I haven't asked you to marry her ; though, for that matter,
it is just as easy to love a rich girl as a poor one," said Mrs.
Burnet.   " But, George, it is high time for you to have done with
nonsense, and behave like a man.   Mary Drinkwater is, after
all—"

" Hush ! mother," said George, politely laying his hand on his

mamma's mouth; " no use talking—let's go on with the party.
There's Jane Lawton is a nice girl."

" But her mother's a fright," said Mrs. Burnet.

" Leave her out, then," said George.

" No, no ; if you ask Jane, we must have the old folks."

" Lump 'em, then," said George ; " and who has Phebe Penniman got tacked to her ?"

" Nobody, thank fortune !" said his mother ; " her old lame
grandmother can't go out ; but Phebe 'll come in a shilling
calico."

" I don't care what she comes in," said the youth, " if she only
brings those pretty bright eyes of hers with her ; and Phebe's a
good hearty girl, too ; she can dance all night. But who was
that splendid looking girl that was with her this morning ? By
George ! I never saw such a step !"

" That was Persis Allen," said Mrs. Burnet ; " a new family
that moved in after you went away. But I will *not* have her, so
that's settled ! She's as proud as a peacock, for all she goes out
to spin by the day at old Hicks's. I won't have her, though I
long for some of those lilies to dress the supper-table with. I
can't get the lilies without asking her, but I'd rather go without."

" But she's a screamer of a girl," persisted Master George ;
" I'd rather have her than all the rest."

" But you won't have her, though," said Mrs. Burnet ; and
George, seeing her so determined, let the matter drop, a sure sign
that he was determined, too.

But all his strategy was vain. No surprise, no coaxing, no
pouting, had the least effect upon Mrs. Burnet. The Allen family had pertinaciously omitted all that courting which, we regret
to say, follows wealth and power even to the wilds ; and they had,
moreover, found occasion, more than once, to resent certain im-
pertinences which Mrs. Burnet was in the habit of offering to her
poorer neighbours. So the lady was inexorable ; and, strong in
her smooth bitterness, she carried her point. Persis was left out.

But, on the eve of the great day, when the preparations were
in great forwardness, those dazzling lilies were again mentioned ;
and George, who was never much hampered by the restraints of
good breeding, declared he would get the lilies without inviting the

damsel, and, on this glorious thought intent, he climbed the intervening fence, by moonlight, and made directly for the spot rendered lovely by the choicest flowers of our poor Persis. This was the neighbourhood of a little arbour, over the rustic framework of which a luxuriant wild-grape had been trained, to shade a soft bank covered with abundant mosses. The overpowering perfume of the lilies, called forth in double measure by the dew, guided our adventurer directly to their place, even before they became visible in the moonlight; and he was about to rifle the bed, when his eye was caught by as white an object in the arbour. George's conscience whispered that it was a " sperrit;" but, after the first moment's start, he could not resist venturing a little nearer; and there was Persis Allen, fast asleep on her mossy couch, her fair forehead upward toward the sky, a book still open on her lap, and a lily fallen at her feet, fit emblem of her own purity and beauty.

Mr. George Burnet stood entranced. He had seen no such personification of beauty and romance in the whole course of his law-studies. He ventured nearer,—nearer still—until he could distinguish the lightest curl waved by the evening breeze, and even the satin smoothness of the skin beneath. But while he still gazed, the sleeping beauty stirred—opened her eyes—uttered a slight exclamation, as if not quite sure that what she saw was real—and our gallant youth darted off, as much frightened as if the opening of those eyes had threatened literal instead of only figurative death. The young girl did not scream, although she ought, in propriety, to have done so. She had no presentiment that she was to be made a heroine of; and, in truth, men of all sorts are too plenty, and too unceremonious, at the West, to excite much alarm. So, concluding that the intruder had been only some neighbouring marauder in search of her father's fine raspberries, she picked up her bonnet, and walked quietly into the house.

Meanwhile, our scared swain had reached his own maternal mansion; and, coming empty-handed, was closely questioned, and not a little laughed at when he recounted the failure of his adventure.

" But, hold on a little till I tell ye !" interposed Master George: " If she hadn't been there I'd have got 'em easy enough ; but the

sight of such a white thing, you know, right in the moonlight,
made my heart beat so that I could hardly see. But, by George!
what a girl! Mother! I must and will have that girl at my
party, and so there's an end of it."

"How can you be so vulgar, George?" replied his mother.

"Vulgar or not," persisted he, "if she don't come, I don't!
I'll go and spend the evening with her, instead of those dowdies."

"George," said Mrs. Burnet, "you always were an obstinate
boy, but I was in hopes you had more sense now."

"So I have," said the dutiful youth, "and that's the reason I
want my own way. Come, mother, get your bonnet and shawl,
and let's go over and invite that pretty—what's her name? and
then we'll ask her for the flowers."

And George at length carried his point, and dragged his mother over to William Allen's.

"Persis, dear," said Mrs. Burnet, in her most seducing and
mellifluent tones, as soon as the requisite salutations were over,
"will you come and spend the evening to-morrow? We shall
have a number of young people—"

"And fiddles," interposed George, in way of parenthesis.

Persis murmured something in reply, but Mrs. Burnet proceeded without waiting for an answer.

"And, if you *can't* come, you will at least give me a few of
your beautiful flowers to dress my supper-table. I must have
some of those lilies. You have so many that I am sure you can
spare me some."

"Oh yes, certainly," Persis said; "you shall have the lilies
in welcome."

"But you'll come," said George, whose eyes had devoured the
beautiful face with no measured stare all this time; "you'll
come, won't you?"

"I—I don't know—I'll ask mother," said Persis.

"Well! I'll send for the flowers in the morning," said Mrs.
Burnet, hurrying away quite unceremoniously.

George was very reluctant to be dragged off without a promise
from Persis, but he was obliged to be content with the advantage
he had gained. He felt that the tone of his mother's invitation
had not béen what it should be, but he hoped his own urgency

had supplied all deficiencies.   An invitation to the Palazzo was not likely to be contemned by any of the village damsels.   We must confess, it occasioned no little flutter in the innocent heart of Persis; but she was, as we have said, prematurely sober and self-restrained, and sought good advice before she ventured to decide on a point so important.   She did not even think " What shall I wear ?" perhaps the scantiness of her wardrobe saved her the trouble.   She only said to her parents, " Had I better go ?"

They were naturally disposed to think Persis might safely follow her own inclination in the matter; and the young girl had as naturally been inclined to what all young people love.   But the next morning, when Persis went as usual to her spinning, she mentioned the whole affair to old Mr. Hicks and his good sister ; the visit of the evening before, the hasty tone of the mother as contrasted with the urgency of the son; and also, for we must own that Persis, like many a simple country damsel, had a quick perception of the ludicrous—the odd way Mrs. Burnet had of coupling her request for the lilies so closely with the invitation for the evening.

" Just like her !" said Aunt Hetty, " she's the coldest-heartedest crittur that ever spoke."

" She is a proud, unfeeling woman," said old Mr. Hicks, " and, if you'll take my advice, my dear, you'll keep clear of the Burnets altogether.   George is always crazy after some pretty face or another, and it's no credit to a young girl like you to have his acquaintance.   If he or his mother should meet you in the street, at B——, they wouldn't know you at all.   Don't go, Persis."

At this advice from the plain-spoken old man, Persis blushed deeply, and the vision of the grand party, which had begun to loom large in her imagination, faded away almost entirely.   She had so much respect for farmer Hicks, who was known as the oldest settler and universally looked up to by the neighbours, that she resolved at once to follow his advice, and decline the tempting invitation.   Besides, in a cooler view, an instinctive self-respect whispered that Mrs. Burnet's manner was any thing but what it should have been, and that the only urgency had been on the part of the young man.   So she told her good old friend that she would not go to Mrs. Burnet's.

The lilies went, however, and formed the crowning decoration of the feast, dividing the public eye with the splendid " pediment" of maccaroons which had been brought with great care and solicitude from B——. The entire gentility of the neighbouring village was collected. There was the lawyer's lady, and the clergyman's lady, and the storekeeper's lady, all drest as primly as possible, and looking as solemn as the occasion required. Then, there was Mrs. Millbank, the tailor's lady, a very " genteel" woman, and she wore an elegant black bombazine, with pink satin bows on the shoulders, and a flounce half a yard deep. Mrs. Perine, the harness-maker's lady, was in plain white, but she wore a scarf of rainbow hues, and a most superb and towering head-dress of black feathers and pale blue roses. Miss Adriance, the school-ma'am, was invited, because she was " genteel" and wore spectacles, though her calling was scarcely the thing for a select party ; and she honoured the occasion by appearing in a green merino, and a mob-cap, full trimmed with yellow ribbons. But it would require the accuracy of a court-circular to describe the costume of every star that twinkled in Mrs. Burnet's parlour on that distinguished evening. We can but observe that the eyes were brighter than the candles, and the conversation much less blue than the cerulean mantelpiece. The very beaux were inspired, and, instead of sneaking into corners, or getting behind the door, they came boldly forward, talked and laughed among themselves, and looked sideways at the girls, with most unwonted assurance.

George, arrayed in the " freedom suit"—solemn black, of course, as became his profession—made the agreeable to his male guests after the most approved style—shaking hands heartily, and asking them to " take something to drink." But the festivities had reached no great height, when the youthful heir, scanning closely the tittering circle, missed the bright mistress of the lilies, and, finding or making an opportunity to speak to his mamma, asked if " the Allen girl" had not come.

" No, my dear," said the honey-voiced Mrs. Burnet, " I dare say she couldn't get her frock washed in time, or she would have been here."

As the lady turned away, with a gentle titter at her own wit, her young hopeful vanished by the nearest door.

"Where's your girl ?" said he a few moments after, addressing Mr. Allen.

"Gone to bed," was the cool reply.

"Why! isn't she coming to our 'us ?"

"Not this night, I think," replied her father, very composedly for, be it known, that the ceremonies of acceptance and apology are not in vogue among us—every body exercising his democratic privilege of going or staying away, without rendering account to any one.

"Why! that beats all !" exclaimed Mr. George, in considerable vexation. "Why didn't she come ?"

"Well—I believe she didn't want to," said Mr. Allen.

"I don't believe that," muttered George, and, going out of the door, he looked up at the only upper window.

"Halloo! Persis—I say, Persis !"

No answer.

"Persis Allen; what's the matter with you ?"

Dead silence; and poor George, casting a wrathful look at the papa quietly smoking his pipe in the kitchen, went his way back to the party, resolving to pay the most provoking attention to Miss Drinkwater, by way of revenging himself on Fate and Persis Allen.

The party went off in the usual style—that is to say, dull and stiff at first, chattering and warm secondly, and then, after due attention to the vivers, coming to an uproarious finale. Mr. George, early excited by drinking with his "dear five hundred friends," more or less, became quite stupid before the company departed; and, when the last shawl had left the entry-table, and the second supply of tallow candles began to burn low in the sockets, Mrs. Burnet was obliged to call in the strong arm of Huldy from the kitchen to get Mr. George up to bed.

The next day, it became too evident that the freedom-party had cost Mr. George Burnet a violent fever. He awoke out of a long sleep with an agonizing pain in his head, and a pulse going at railroad speed. Before evening medical aid had been summoned, heads and vials shaken, and a cot put into George's room for Mrs.

Burnet, and a smoked ham put into the pot for the "watchers."
(Watchers are always expected to be very hungry.)  In short, it
was a serious case, and excited much interest with the two Ga-
lens of the neighbourhood.

"Midnight!—and not a nose—" from one end of the village to
the other—"snored"—for the screams and ravings of the unfortunate youth freighted the weary echoes.

"Persis!  Persis Allen!  why don't she come?" rung in the
night air, so distinctly that the owner of the appellation lay trembling in her little attic, with the vague dread of distress and im-
pending disaster.  All night long did the heart-rending tones of
the sufferer keep her awake, and it was scarcely daylight when
a messenger from Mrs. Burnet knocked loudly at her father's
door, to entreat Persis to come but for a moment to George's bedside, hoping that the sight of her might have some effect in soothing his irritation.  She went, though trembling and almost fainting with fright and agitation, never doubting, in her simplicity,
whether it was proper for her to comply with so unusual a request.
There is a sort of sacred reverence for the sick in those regions,
where there is scarce any reverence for any thing else.

The moment George's delirious brain became aware of the
presence of the pale beauty, he would have sprung from his bed
but for strong arms that held him down.  It was indeed surprising that her image should have taken so firm a hold on his memory and imagination ; but it soon became evident that nothing but
her presence would soothe his more than "midsummer madness."
So there the poor girl was obliged to sit, her cold hand clasped between his burning palms, and his wild eyes fixed upon her face,
hour after hour, listening to his raving vows that she and she only
should be his wife, spite of his mother and—a less smooth-looking
personage.

We are not to suppose that Persis was unmoved by the sound
of all these passionate words.  Words have a power of their own,
as we have all doubtless experienced, and besides, George Burnet
was rather a handsome young man, and the certain heir of a still
handsomer property.  So that we shall not pretend that his pro-
testations, though made in all the wildness of delirium, fell upon
deaf ears or a stony heart.  On the other side of the bed stood

Cyprian Amory, unwearied in his attention to the sick man, but watching with a painful anxiety the changes in the pale face of Persis, and frequently suggesting something which might tend to quiet George and relieve her unpleasant situation. At length George's ravings grew fainter, his grasp gradually slackened, his eyes closed, and he fell asleep, murmuring blessings on the fair being who had so kindly soothed his wretchedness. Persis was removed, half fainting, and it was not until some hours' rest that she was able to return home, so completely had her nerves been overwrought by this distressing scene. Yet Mrs. Burnet dismissed her without the slightest acknowledgment of the sacrifice she had made to humanity; evidently rejoiced to get rid of so dangerous a friend.

But there was further trouble in store for the politic mamma. George's delirium subsided, it is true, but his memory proved wonderfully tenacious of the subject of his ravings. As he gained strength his natural willfulness showed itself, and a determination to make good all he had said to Persis was but too apparent. The violence of his disease was not of long duration, but it had so shattered him that his convalescence was slow; and, during the weeks of his scarce perceptible amendment, his talk was continually of his fair neighbour. His mother would not stay in the room to listen to what so deeply offended her; but Cyprian was always there, and into his unwilling ear did George pour all his plans for the future.

"We shan't live here, Cyp," he would say; "she's too splendid a creature for the woods, and beside, mother would worry her life out. Isn't she a sweet creature, Cyp? Stay—what do you go away for? You shall be my clerk, Cyp, you write so much better than I do—you shall study law with me—take care of my business whenever I'm away. I shall be sent to Congress by and bye, and, while I'm gone to Washington, you'll be head man at home. Only help me to persuade my mother. Won't *she* make a figure at Washington? Such a step! and how she carries her head !" and he would run on by the hour after this fashion, holding Cyprian fast till his new found strength would be entirely exhausted, and he would fall asleep only to wake and renew the strain.

Matters could not long go on thus.  It never entered the head
of either mother or son that Persis Allen would have to be asked
more than once ; and Mrs. Burnet only waited her son's more
complete recovery to put an end to his fine dreams.  When the
time came for the execution of this her fixed purpose, there was a
scene indeed.  George cried and swore alternately, while his
mother, calm as usual, with her lips compressed to a thready thinness, and that unearthly light in her eye which malicious eyes
*will* perversely emit when their owner most desires to seem an-
gelically virtuous, she expressed her unalterable determination to
disinherit him if he persisted in marrying a girl who earned her
living by spinning.

This was a tremendous engine, and wielded with the coolness
so peculiar to Mrs. Burnet, it bore with terrible force upon poor
George, who had been brought up to expect a fortune which was
entirely in his mother's power.  But opposition only contributed
to keep alive a determination which would otherwise most probably have shared the fate of many others which George had made
and broken.  He did not venture to defy his mother openly, for,
in his eyes as well as hers, the possession of property was all that
made any essential difference between one man and another.  But
there had been nothing in his education which forbade his pursuing covertly what he had not courage to defend ; and Persis was
doomed to be waylaid on all occasions by her impetuous admirer,
till she was almost ready to marry him to get rid of him.

George had now entirely recovered, and his mother insisted on
his returning to his business according to promise.  Cyprian took
charge of the village school, and the white and green house presented a silent and very haughty-looking exterior—Mrs. Burnet
having subsided into her usual aristocratic grandeur, and not
even knowing the poor spinning-girl when she met her.  Cyprian
Amory, it is true, though he belonged to the great house, was
troubled with no such shortness of memory—indeed, it would
have been fortunate for him if he had, poor fellow ! for why
should he remember Persis ?  They often encountered at sunset,
when each was returning from the day's task ; and it was perhaps
from an idea that Persis' own youth had not passed without its
trials and struggles, that Cyprian was led at times to be rather

confidential on the subject of his condition and its difficulties.   It
was thus that the fair spinning-girl learned that the only chance
to which Cyprian looked for an escape from the horrors of a dis-
trict-school, was George's consenting to receive him as a clerk, a
destiny not in itself to be coveted, yet far preferable to its alter
native.   Such was the pity and sympathy excited in the gen.
breast of Persis, that she almost wished sometimes that she had
accepted George, since she might then have been of so much service to poor Cyprian !

But the time came when Cyprian no longer met Persis, as he
sauntered along the road, after shutting up the school-house.
She was bound, day and night almost, to the death-bed of her
kind old friend, farmer Hicks, whose sister, quite infirm, and almost imbecile, depended on Persis as on a daughter.   Inured as
she was to care and to personal sacrifice, the aid of Persis about
the sick-bed was invaluable, and the old man, with his dying
breath, blessed her, and recommended his sister to her kindness.

After he was gone, and his will came to be opened, it was
found that he had left Persis his entire property, with the sole
burthen of a comfortable support for the aged sister, "feeling,"
the will said, "that she could not be in better hands.'

Here was an overturn of affairs ! and, at first, it seemed likely
to be the overturn of poor Persis' wits, too ; not that she was ela-
ted, but perplexed and embarrassed in the extreme by the surprise, and by the sudden weight of responsibility.   She was to
live in her own house, that the old lady might not be subject to
the pain of a removal ; and, as Persis' younger sister was now
able to supply in part her place at home, this was soon arranged ;
but other matters presented more formidable difficulties.

We must not pretend that our village maiden had been indifferent to the addresses of a young gentleman who was considered
by the entire democracy about her to be so much "above" her.
She had a kind and noble heart, but, after all, she was human.
and subject to the influence of *caste,* as well as the rest of us.
George Burnet, a young "lawyer," the beau of the country, and
heir of the splendid white and green house and the fine farm appended to it, would have been irresistible, perhaps, but for a something—an unexplained, troublesome something, which presented

itself before Persis' mental vision whenever she had time to think of the matter.   There was drawn, by some magical or invisible power, on the retina of her mind's eye, a pretty rural scene—a log-house, plain and small, shaded with trees and surrounded with gay flowers.   In the upper chamber of this humble abode was a neatly dressed damsel plying the great wheel, and in the little garden which her window commanded, was a tall, slender young man, busily tending some well-kept rows of vegetables, and occasionally casting a glance upward at the window.   The damsel at the wheel was Persis herself, the youth in the garden, her friend, Cyprian Amory.

This pretty picture had often presented itself to Persis, while she was still a simple spinning-girl, and it stood very much in the way of George Burnet's interest.   And yet, if Persis could only marry George, how much might she brighten the lot of her friend, Cyprian.   George would take Cyprian into his office, and, once on the way, Cyprian might, nay, must, rise to a condition in life so much better suited to a mind like his.   A farmer's life would never do for that delicate frame, and a school in the country is only another name for starvation, and not reputable starvation either.   It was such considerations as these that had caused Persis sometimes to listen to George Burnet, and try to make up her mind to like him, though she had told him no a thousand times.

It was only a few days after the funeral of old Mr. Hicks, that the old aunty and her young guardian were still seated at the tea-table, when they were surprised by a visit from Mrs. Burnet. That agreeable lady was decked in her sweetest smiles, and paid her compliments of condolence in the choicest phrase, crowning all by hoping that as Miss Allen must be quite at leisure she should have the pleasure of seeing her often—very often.   She was so fond of the society of young people ! and now they were to be such near neighbours, she hoped Persis would be "sociable."

This visit was followed at no great distance by another, with the avowed object of pleading George's cause, the match being now warmly desired by the devoted mother.   She had understood, she said, that there had been an attachment, (she did not say a mutual one, though her manner implied it,) but Miss Allen must be aware that nothing could be more imprudent than engagements hastily made, and without proper provision for the future. *Now* there could be no possible objection; and she hoped her dear Persis would not object to an early day, since poor George would find it impossible to engage in business until his mind was at rest.

All this was delivered so volubly that Persis had no opportunity for a word, but even while Mrs. Burnet was speaking, her mind had been unconsciously applying all these prudential observations in another direction. It was a brilliant thought, truly, and it was marvelous that it had not suggested itself before—that she was an heiress, and could do as she liked. She had money enough for two, and Cyprian could hire workmen, and oversee the farm as old Mr. Hicks had done. All this was concluded in a moment; and, as a finish to the cogitation, grown worldly wise by suffering, she considered that if any thing should yet be lacking, she could still ply the wheel as before, and so make all right.

And, when Mrs. Burnet had exhausted all her eloquence, and paused for a reply, she got only a plain and somewhat absent negative.

Who shall give the faintest idea of her rage? Who paint the gleam of that eye, or the sharp thinness of the compressed lips? Bitter sweet was she at parting, but Persis was so occupied with her new idea that she felt no embarrassment at having offended the great lady.

But how to put her plan in Cyprian's head? We can account for what follows only in one way—the intensity of the thought which dwelt on him for so long a time must have drawn him to her side; for he no sooner understood that Mrs. Burnet had been to see Persis than he found himself irresistibly impelled toward the old farm-house.

And there, in the parlour, by the great western window, sat Persis; her head leaning on her hand, her eyes fixed on vacancy, and her thoughts so absorbing that she did not perceive Cyprian's entrance until he stood before her. A start—a fluttering blush, and the magnetic influence was evident to both. Cyprian was not yet so much of a schoolmaster that he could talk nothing but grammar; and though you might have found it difficult to parse what he said to Persis on that occasion, the meaning was, on the

whole, remarkably clear to her mind.   She felt satisfactorily convinced that Cyprian had long loved her, though pride and poverty would forever have sealed his lips, but for the rumour that
she had decidedly refused a rich lover.

And what did poor George Burnet do ?   He talked undutifully
to his amiable mamma, and swore he would go and be a Patriot.
Mrs. Burnet took both these things quietly, and George, after all,
had to marry Polly Drinkwater.

# HARVEST MUSINGS.

WHO can help falling into a reverie at the decline of a sultry summer day? Who can pass unnoticed the delicious changes in the light and in the air; the orange tints darkening into purple, and the hot breath of Day freshened by the soft-falling dew? The whip-poor-wills " striving one with the other which could in most dainty variety recount their wrong-caused sorrow,"* fill the woods with their plaints; the harvest-moon rises in the blue depths of ether, globular to the sight, not merely round; and of a deep golden orange colour, like—like—Jerry Dingle says it is like "the yelk of an egg that's been froze, and then dropt into a great tub o' bluin'-water." Not so very unlike, good Jerry, as mine own observation witnesseth at this moment; and so, in the barrenness of our own sun-burnt and wilted fancy, we will let thy homely comparison stand for want of a better.

How still is this evening atmosphere! The breeze is not yet strong enough to wave the curtain; it only stirs it, as with an expectant thrill! Would it might come! with force sufficient to drive away some of these musquitoes, whose attacks are enough to put to flight all romantic thoughts except those of boarding-school girls and midshipmen. The night-hawks are very busy; they have scented our broods of young turkeys; and there are owls enough hooting and flying about, to " scare" any body that was not " born in the woods." The cows come lowing home, bringing with them a circumambient cloud of musquitoes, to "spell" those which have exhausted their energies upon us. One lone and lorn individual of the horned people stays mourning in the forest; probably calling with fruitless iteration upon her tender offspring,

* Sir Philip Sydney's " Arcadia."

doomed to the knife at this season of "boarding hands." The katydids are high in their eternal disputation; and somewhere within hearing, though out of sight, is Jerry Dingle, with a rifle, getting his cradle ready for to-morrow.

Oh, mystery of mysteries were once these dark sayings to my uninitiated ear! Why should a "rifle" be needed for reaping, since though grain shoots, nobody every heard of its being shot? And the "cradle?" Wheat waves, but why should it be rocked? Wild music called me once to the gate, and there stood Jerry with a whetstone sharpening a scythe, which had several slender rods arranged parallel with its curved blade, and now the riddle was read. But I have never learned to this day why a whetstone should be called a "rifle," while there is so different an implement of the same name so much in use among us. The "cradle" seems more intelligible, because the pretty slender curved bars which help to lay the grain in regular rows as fast as it is cut, do bear some little resemblance to the form of rockers.

The operation of cradling is worth a journey to see. The sickle may be more classical, but it cannot compare in beauty with the swaying, regular motion of the cradle, which cuts at once a space as wide as strong arms, aided by a long blade, can describe; and at the same time lays the golden treasure in beautiful lines, like well-ordered hosts in array of battle. There is no movement more graceful and harmonious than that of a row of cradlers; none on which one can gaze by the hour with more pleasure. It suggests the idea of soft music—*siciliano* or *gracioso*.

The subject of the weather, always so valuable a resource in the way of conversation, is never more prominent than during the harvest time. Saving and excepting new year's day, when the beaux are apt to be, as Mr. C. said, "hard up for talk," and some few bitter days in February, when tingling fingers and crimson noses remind one inevitably of the state of the atmosphere, there is indeed no period when the weather is so universally the theme for young and old, rich and poor. In town this subjection to the skyey influences wears one aspect, in the country another. There is no part of the year when the difference between city and country views and habits is more striking.

Those who have brought city habits with them to this green and
growing world, and who naturally look back very frequently with
feelings of affectionate reminiscence to the roasting brick houses
and the broiling flag pavements which helped to ripen their earlier
summers, are particularly alive to the change in their location
and circumstances when this time comes round. How the citizen
labours to be cool! How pathetically he descants on each particular stage of sweltering! How do magazines and dailies teem
with articles which only to read bring the drops to one's forehead! What listless hours! what groans, what fans, what lemonade, what ice-cream, are associated in civic minds with the
idea of the dog-days! What racing to springs and watering-
places, what crowding in ferry-boats and rail-road cars, attest the
anxiety of the urbane world for a breath of cool air! Recreation has become a serious business; amusement a solemn duty;
for who can work in such weather? At Saratoga or the Falls,
at Rockaway or Nahant, strenuous Idleness has but one aim—the
killing of the sultry hours; and nobody will deny, that after all,
the hours sometimes die hard.

We too labour to be cool, but it is after another sort. The
citizen who finds it difficult to sustain life at this season, even
with the aid of baths and ices, may be curious to know how the
wretched being whom necessity forces to labour under the sun of
August, endures the burden of existence; how often he seeks the
cooling shade; what drinks moisten his parched throat; by what
means he contrives to fan his burning brow. Fear nothing, oh!
sympathizing reader! Save thy sensibilities for a more urgent
call. This is a world of compensations. The labourer has
neither shade, nor *punkah*, nor lemonade, nor even ginger-beer.
He may get a drink of buttermilk occasionally; but the sparkling, ice-cold spring supplies his best beverage; and in place of
all thy luxuries he lives from sunrise till sunset in a perpetual
vapour-bath, of Nature's own providing; more refreshing by far
than even the famed solace of the Turk; and he does his own
shampooing so well that every power of his frame is kept incessantly in the very best condition. He would die on thy sofa.

Yes! in the country all is activity and bustle, at the very time
when the seekers of pleasure are at their wit's end for pastime.

It is the era not only *from* which, but *toward* which all reckon for
weeks.  "I can't undertake it afore harvest."  "Well, I'll see
about it after harvest."  "Wait till we know how the harvest turns
out."  Does wife or daughter long for a new dress?  "I'd rather give you two after harvest."  Is a jaunt in question?  The
grain must be secured before it is talked of.  Is a man "under the
harrows," that is, hard pressed by his creditors?  He begs only
for a delay till after harvest.  Not that all things turn out always according to the expectations of these sanguine calculators.
But with the husbandman this time is the boundary of his immediate hope—his mental sensible horizon—the natural limit of his
view.  Hope, it is true, is in this as in other cases, often delusive
enough; but the return of the season affords many a peg on
which to hang bright promises that cheer from afar the weary
way of the farmer.

When it comes, as we have said, all is activity and bustle.  All
energies are concentrated upon it, and every thing gives way to
it.  Politics for a time let go their hold upon the rustic partisan.
He cares not for vetoes, nor even for tariffs; bad legislation
stays not the ripening of corn; (fortunately for us all.)  When
the beneficent Sun has done his work, and wheat nods its brown
head and sways languidly in the faint breath of the morning;
when corn flings its silken banners abroad, and the earth seems
every where burdened with Heaven's bounty; at this glorious
season the farmer, with his heart and his arm nerved by hope,
goes forth to put the finishing stroke to the year's labours.  No
fear of the sun's fervours deters or disheartens him.  He fears
only the delicious cooling shower which would drive his "hands"
to the barn, and perhaps detain his grain on the ground long
enough materially to injure its quality.

To be early in the field is the farmer's maxim.  He waits only
for light enough to work by, before calling up his men, who are
apt to be up before he calls them, so contagious is the enthusiasm
of the hour.  No one likes to be a laggard in harvest.  And then
the early morning air is so fresh and so inspiriting; the brighten-
ing hues of the pearly East so irresistibly glorious, the rising of
the sun so majestic, that even the dull soul feels, and the dull eye
gazes, with an admiration not unmixed with awe.  Two hours'

labour before the six o'clock breakfast lays bare a wide space in the field, for very numerous are the strong arms brought up to the work. This season is the test of the husbandman's capabilities, whether as master or man. The unthrifty is behindhand in his preparations. He has depended upon *luck* for his assistants, and put off looking for or engaging them until the last moment. Luck, as usual, takes care of those who take care of themselves, and so neighbour Feckless is obliged to take up with the leavings. When it is time to begin, scythes want sharpening and rifles are worn out or lost, and perhaps a ride of ten miles is necessary to repair the deficiency. Before harvest is half over, the stock of provisions proves scanty, and half a day must be spent in borrowing of the neighbours. With all these and many more drawbacks, the work goes on but slowly, and the crop is perhaps not properly secured in season. Wheat will become so dead ripe that much is lost in the gathering, or perhaps successive rains, when it ought to be under cover, will rust and ruin it entirely. Neighbour Feckless has of course no barn; (in the new country better farmers cannot always afford one ;) and being obliged to put up his grain in a hurry, it is perhaps not sufficiently dried, or not well stacked ; in which case every grain will sprout and grow in such a way that the entire mass becomes one body of shoots, so that it must be torn apart, and is only fit to feed the cattle with. "Bad luck!" sighs our poor friend.

Far otherwise runs the experience of the thriving farmer. All is ready betimes, and due allowance made for lee-way and "peradventures." He is not obliged to overwork himself or his people. He goes forward in his own business in order to insure its success. It is proverbial in the country that "Come, boys!" is always better than "Go, boys!" Neighbour Thrifty knows this so well that if he be not in the freshness of his strength, so that he can take the lead in mowing or reaping, he will yet engage in some part of the day's labours, which will keep him in the midst of his men, so that the influence of his eye and of his voice may be felt, without his incurring the odious suspicion of being a mere overseer or task-master. And what a various congregation is that which does his bidding ! Not mere day-labourers—for the country furnishes comparatively few of these—but all men of all

kinds. Do you want your wagon-wheel mended? The wheel-
wright, if he have no fields of his own, is busy in those of his
neighbour. The carpenter will not drive a nail for love or money, for he too is "bespoke." You are unlucky if your nag
need shoeing at this critical period, for the son of Vulcan will
not have time to light a fire in his own smithy, perhaps for a
fortnight. Peep into the village school-house; you will find
none there but minors, in a very literal sense; wee things who
would be only in the way at home. All boys who are old enough
to rake or run on errands are sure to be in the field, and the girls
are helping at home to boil and bake. The interests of learning
have for the time the go-by. This is so well understood that in
most places the master abdicates for the season in favour of the
female sovereign, again to resume the sceptre when Winter
grasps his.

Stranger than all, even law-suits are suspended, for the justice
is in the field; witnesses are swinging the cradle; all possible
jurymen are scattered miles apart, mowing the broad savannahs;
and the contending parties themselves are too much engrossed,
each with his own business, to wish matters pushed to extremities
at such a crisis. Even the young lover almost forgets the flaxen
ringlets of his sweetheart in the bustle of a field-day, and if he
meet the damsel at evening will be apt to entertain her with an
account of his achievements with the cradle or the sickle. Idleness is banished so completely that even the incurably lazy bustle
about as if they too wished to do something. It is amusing to
see one of this class at this juncture. In the general rush of business and consequent scarcity of strong arms, he knows that
even his aid is of consequence. Feeling this to be emphatically
his day, he is disposed to make the most of it. He accordingly
assumes a swaggering air; don't know whether he'll come or
not: but, on the whole, guesses he'll help! He braces up for
the occasion, lays by his rifle and his fishing-tackle, and like a
spinning-top whirls round bravely for a while, but if not now and
then lashed into speed by some new motive, soon subsides into
his natural state of repose. We have known a worthy of this
tone promise to "help" four different farmers, and after all, take

down his rifle and "guess he'd better go and try if he couldn't
see a deer!"

The good woman within doors is far from being idle all this
time.   Hers is the pleasant though rather arduous task of keeping
the harvesters in heart for the labours of the day, and for this
purpose she summons all her skill and forethought, and sets forth
all her good cheer.   Pies and cake and all manner of rustic
dainties grace her bounteous board; for her reputation is at stake,
since she is supposed at this time to do her very best.   To set a
poor table at harvest is death to any housewifely reputation.   Good
humour too is very desirable, where work is to be done; and to
this we all know good cheer is apt to contribute; and no mistress likes to see her table surrounded by sour faces, even if
the work should go on as well as ever.   The providing for a
dozen or two of harvest-hands is not a matter of any especial research; since although, as we have hinted, some delicacies are
always included, yet the main body of the meal, three times a
day, is formed of pork and hot bread.   Where these are abundant, (and no Western farmer need lack either,) the adjuncts are
matter of small moment.   Pork and hot bread three times a day!
No wonder they can work twelve hours out of the twenty-four.
To labour any less on such diet would be suicide.

One of the pretty sights of these days is the passing of the
huge loads of grain and hay as they are brought home to their
several owners.   There are generally three or four men and
boys on the top of each load, chattering merrily, urging on the
cattle, and evincing in their tones and gestures a glad sense of
bustle and importance which is quite infectious.   One cannot
help watching them as they toss and stack their graceful burdens,
and sympathizing in their merry laughter, and almost envying
them their light-hearted jocularity.   By and by the wagon passes
again, a mere frame, with a man or boy at every stake, holding
on for life, and laughing and talking louder than ever, since the
speed is tenfold and the jolting in proportion.   The gradual com-
pletion of a stack and the final pointing out and thatching which
is to secure all within from the weather, is an operation in which
we often find amusement by the hour.

The harvest-moon is a phenomenon which can hardly be passed

over, in thinking of this season. As if to cheer and aid the husbandman on whose apparently humble labours the comfort, the
very existence of the proudest is absolutely dependant, the moon
shows her glowing face at nearly the same hour for a whole
week, lengthening out the day with some hours of refreshing
coolness. The surpassing beauty of her mild light can be fully
appreciated only after a day of heat and dust and exertion. In
the country, in the true wild forest, and after the labours of the
harvest field, it has an ineffable charm. We will not call the
harvest-moon a miracle, for astronomers explain her constancy;
but we will say that a phenomenon so admirably adapted to the
consolation and refreshment of the weary tiller of the soil, seems
to refer us directly to the divine benignity, which disdains not to
watch over the comforts as well as the necessities of all.

Would I might add to this sketch of the labours of the harvest,
that we do honour to its close by some innocent festivities like
those which used to be known under the name of harvest-home.
But alas! our holydays are only political; election days, when it
is our business to vote, and "Independence," when it is our business to rejoice. We have no days consecrated to innocent hilarity; no days of the feast of in-gathering, over which harmless
Sport may preside, gladdening at once the heart of young and
old, and strengthening the links of human sympathy. But
this is a work-a-day world, and we are a working people.
Granted; yet we should work no whit the less for an occasional
interval of gayety. But there's "Thanksgiving"—true; and
good as far as it goes. It is a family gathering; a set season for
the meeting of near friends, and renewing of all thoughts of affectionate interest. In this new world we have scarcely begun
to pay respect to this occasion: the custom is regarded partly as
sectional, partly as inappropriate; for our family-friends, where
are they? With our joy there would mingle a touch of sadness.
We could not rejoice in thinking of the absent.

Are we wiser than our forefathers?—those of the olden time,
when it was supposed there was a time for merry-making, among
other good things in this world? Were the feast of harvest and
the feast of in-gathering, which were ordained to the Jews by the
highest authority, purely ceremonial? Imperative obligation is

allowed to attach to the command, "Six days shalt thou labour,
and on the seventh thou shalt rest." Is no weight whatever to be
given to that which immediately follows: " Thou shalt keep the
feast of harvest, the first-fruits of thy labours  .  .  .  and the
feast of in-gathering, which is in the end of the year ?" A plain
reader may reasonably be puzzled by the very great stress we
lay upon the one, and the absolute neglect with which we treat
the other.   It is true we know but little of the especial form of
these festivals, but we know that rejoicing made a part of them,
and that the joy was heightened by feasting and music.   Not only
were these permitted, but commanded ; only the revelry which attended them, when manners became corrupt, was condemned.
Has the nature of man so changed that all this has now become
unsuitable ?   Does he really eschew pleasures, or have his
pleasures assumed a darker character ?

# THE BEE-TREE.

AMONG the various settlers of the wide West, there is no class which exhibits more striking peculiarities than that which, in spite of hard work, honesty, and sobriety, still continues hopelessly poor. None find more difficulty in the solution of the enigma presented by this state of things, than the sufferers themselves; and it is with some bitterness of spirit that they come at last to the conclusion, that the difference between their own condition and that of their prosperous neighbours, is entirely owing to their own " bad luck ;" while the prosperous neighbours look musingly at the ragged children and squalid wife, and regret that the head of the house " ha'n't no faculty." Perhaps neither view is quite correct.

In the very last place one would have selected for a dwelling, —in the centre of a wide expanse of low, marshy land,—on a swelling knoll, which looks like an island,—stands the forlorn dwelling of my good friend, Silas Ashburn, one of the most conspicuous victims of the " bad luck" alluded to. Silas was among the earliest settlers of our part of the country, and had half a county to choose from when he " located" in the swamp, —half a county of as beautiful dale and upland as can be found in the vicinity of the great lakes. But he says there is " the very first-rate of pasturing" for his cows, (and well there may be, on forty acres of wet grass !) and as for the agues which have nearly made skeletons of himself and his family, his opinion is that it would not have made a bit of difference if he had settled on the highest land in Michigan, since " every body knows if you've got to have the ague, why you've got to, and all the high land and dry land, and *Queen Ann*\* in the world wouldn't make no odds."

\* Quinine.

Silas does not get rich, nor even comfortably well off, although he works, as he says, " like a tiger." This he thinks is because " rich folks ain't willing poor folks should live," and because he, in particular, always has such bad luck. Why shouldn't he make money ? Why should he not have a farm as well stocked, a house as well supplied, and a family as well clothed and cared for in all respects, as his old neighbour John Dean, who came with him from " York State ?" Dean has never speculated, nor hunted, nor fished, nor found honey, nor sent his family to pick berries for sale. All these has Silas done, and more. His family have worked hard ; they have worn their old clothes till they well nigh dropped off; many a day, nay, month, has passed, seeing potatoes almost their sole sustenance ; and all this time Dean's family had plenty of every thing they wanted, and Dean just jogged on, as easy as could be ; hardly ever stirring from home, except on 'lection days ; wasting a great deal of time, too, (so Silas thinks,) " helping the women folks." " But some people get all the luck."

These and similar reflections seem to be scarcely ever absent from the mind of Silas Ashburn, producing any but favourable results upon his character and temper. He cannot be brought to believe that Dean has made more money by splitting rails in the winter than his more enterprising neighbour by hunting deer, skilful and successful as he is. He will not notice that Dean often buys his venison for half the money he has earned while Silas was hunting it. He has never observed, that while his own sallow helpmate goes barefoot and bonnetless to the brush-heap to fill her ragged apron with miserable fuel, the cold wind careering through her scanty covering, Mrs. Dean sits by a good fire, amply provided by her careful husband, patching for the twentieth time his great overcoat ; and that by the time his Betsey has kindled her poor blaze, and sits cowering over it, shaking with ague, Mrs. Dean, with well-swept hearth, is busied in preparing her husband's comfortable supper.

These things Silas does not and will not see ; and he ever resents fiercely any hint, however kindly and cautiously given, that the steady exercise of his own ability for labour, and a *little* more thrift on the part of his wife, would soon set all things right.

When he spends a whole night " 'coon-hunting," and is obliged to
sleep half the next day, and feels good for nothing the day after,
it is impossible to convince him that the " varmint" had better
been left to cumber the ground, and the two or three dollars
that the expedition cost him been bestowed in the purchase of a
blanket.

" A blanket !" he would exclaim angrily ; " don't be puttin'
sich uppish notions into my folks' heads ! Let 'em make com-
fortables out o' their old gowns, and if that don't do, let 'em
sleep in their day-clothes, as I do ! Nobody needn't suffer with a
great fire to sleep by."

The children of this house are just what one would expect
from such training. Labouring beyond their strength at such
times as it suits their father to work, they have nevertheless
abundant opportunity for idleness ; and as the mother scarcely
attempts to control them, they usually lounge listlessly by the
fireside, or bask in the sunshine, when Ashburn is absent ; and
as a natural consequence of this irregular mode of life, the whole
family are frequently prostrate with agues, suffering every variety
of wretchedness, while there is perhaps no other case of disease
in the neighbourhood. Then comes the two-fold evil of a long
period of inactivity, and a proportionately long doctor's bill ; and
as Silas is strictly honest, and means to wrong no man of his due,
the scanty comforts of the convalescents are cut down to almost
nothing, and their recovery sadly delayed, that the heavy expenses of illness may be provided for. This is some of poor Ashburn's " bad luck."

One of the greatest temptations to our friend Silas, and to most
of his class, is a bee-hunt. Neither deer, nor 'coons, nor prairie-
hens, nor even bears, prove half as powerful enemies to any thing
like regular business, as do these little thrifty vagrants of the
forest. The slightest hint of a bee-tree will entice Silas Ashburn
and his sons from the most profitable job of the season, even
though the defection is sure to result in entire loss of the offered
advantage ; and if the hunt prove successful, the luscious spoil is
generally too tempting to allow of any care for the future, so long
as the " sweet'nin" can be persuaded to last. " It costs nothing,"
will poor Mrs. Ashburn observe, " let 'em enjoy it. It isn't often

we have such good luck." As to the cost, close computation might lead to a different conclusion; but the Ashburns are no calculators.

It was on one of the lovely mornings of our ever lovely autumn, so early that the sun had scarcely touched the tops of the still verdant forest, that Silas Ashburn and his eldest son sallied forth for a day's chopping on the newly-purchased land of a rich settler, who had been but a few months among us. The tall form of the father, lean and gaunt as the very image of Famine, derived little grace from the rags which streamed from the elbows of his almost sleeveless coat, or flapped round the tops of his heavy boots, as he strode across the long causeway that formed the communication from his house to the dry land. Poor Joe's costume showed, if possible, a still greater need of the aid of that useful implement, the needle. His mother is one who thinks little of the ancient proverb which commends the stitch in time ; and the clothing under her care sometimes falls in pieces, seam by seam, for want of the occasional aid is rendered more especially necessary by the slightness of the original sewing; so that the brisk breeze of the morning gave the poor boy no faint resemblance to a tall young aspen,

"With all its leaves fast fluttering, all at once."

The little conversation which passed between the father and son was such as necessarily makes up much of the talk of the poor,—turning on the difficulties and disappointments of life, and the expedients by which there may seem some slight hope of eluding these disagreeables.

" If we hadn't had sich bad luck this summer," said Mr. Ashburn, " losing that heifer, and the pony, and them three hogs,—all in that plaguy spring-hole, too,—I thought to have bought that timbered forty of Dean. It would have squared out my farm jist about right."

" The pony didn't die in the spring-hole, father," said Joe.

" No, he did not, but he got his death there, for all. He never stopped shiverin' from the time he fell in. You thought he had the agur, but I know'd well enough what ailded him ; but I wasn't a goin' to let Dean know, because he'd ha' thought himself so

blam'd cunning, after all he'd said to me about that spring-hole.
If the agur could kill, Joe, we'd all ha' been dead long ago."

Joe sighed,—a sigh of assent.   They walked on musingly.

"This is going to be a good job of Keene's," continued Mr.
Ashburn, turning to a brighter theme, as they crossed the road
and struck into the "timbered land," on their way to the scene
of the day's operations.   "He has bought three eighties, all lying close together, and he'll want as much as one forty cleared
right off; and I've a good notion to take the fencin' of it as well
as the choppin'.   He's got plenty of money, and they say he
don't shave quite so close as some.   But I tell you, Joe, if I do
take the job, you must turn to like a catamount, for I ain't a-go-
ing to make a nigger o' myself, and let my children do nothing
but eat."

"Well, father," responded Joe, whose pale face gave token of
any thing but high living, "I'll do what I can; but you know I
never work two days at choppin' but what I have the agur like
sixty,—and a feller can't work when he's got the agur."

"Not while the fit's on, to be sure," said the father; "but I've
worked many an afternoon after my fit was over, when my head
felt as big as a half-bushel, and my hands would ha' sizzed if I'd
put 'em in water.   Poor folks has got to work——but, Joe! if
there isn't bees, by golley!   I wonder if any body's been a
baitin' for 'em ?   Stop! hush! watch which way they go!"

And with breathless interest—forgetful of all troubles, past,
present, and future—they paused to observe the capricious
wheelings and flittings of the little cluster, as they tried every
flower on which the sun shone, or returned again and again to
such as suited best their discriminating taste.   At length, after a
weary while, one suddenly rose into the air with a loud whizz,
and after balancing a moment on a level with the tree-tops, darted off, like a well-sent arrow, toward the east, followed instantly
by the whole busy company, till not a loiterer remained.

"Well! if this isn't luck!" exclaimed Ashburn, exultingly;
"they make right for Keene's land!   We'll have 'em! go ahead,
Joe, and keep your eye on 'em!"

Joe obeyed so well in both points, that he not only outran his
father, but very soon turned a summerset over a gnarled root or

*grub* which lay in his path. This *faux pas* nearly demolished one side of his face, and what remained of his jacket sleeve, while his father, not quite so heedless, escaped falling, but tore his boot almost off with what he called " a contwisted stub of the toe."

But these were trifling inconveniences, and only taught·them to use a little more caution in their eagerness. They followed on, unweariedly ; crossed several fences, and threaded much of Mr. Keene's tract of forest-land, scanning with practised eye every decayed tree, whether standing or prostrate, until at length, in the side of a gigantic but leafless oak, they espied, some forty feet from the ground, the " sweet home" of the immense swarm whose scouts had betrayed their hiding-place.

" The Indians have been here ;" said Ashburn ; " you see they've felled this saplin' agin the bee-tree, so as they could climb up to the hole ; but the red devils have been disturbed afore they had time to dig it out. If they'd had axes to cut down the big tree, they wouldn't have left a smitchin o' honey, they're such tarnal thieves !"

Mr. Ashburn's ideas of morality were much shocked at the thought of the dishonesty of the Indians, who, as is well known, have no rights of any kind ; but considering himself as first finder, the lawful proprietor of this much-coveted treasure, gained too without the trouble of a protracted search, or the usual amount of baiting, and burning of honeycombs, he lost no time in taking possession after the established mode.

To cut his initials with his axe on the trunk of the bee-tree, and to make *blazes* on several of the trees he had passed, to serve as way-marks to the fortunate spot, detained him but few minutes ; and with many a cautious noting of the surrounding localities, and many a charge to Joe " not to say nothing to nobody," Silas turned his steps homeward, musing on the important fact that he had had good luck for once, and planning important business quite foreign to the day's chopping.

Now it so happened that Mr. Keene, who is a restless old gentleman, and, moreover, quite green in the dignity of a land-holder, thought proper to turn his horse's head, for this particular morning ride, directly towards these same "three eighties," on which

he had engaged Ashburn and his son to commence the important
work of clearing. Mr. Keene is low of stature, rather globular
in contour, and exceedingly parrot-nosed ; wearing, moreover, a
face red enough to lead one to suppose he had made his money
as a dealer in claret; but, in truth, one of the kindest of men, in
spite of a little quickness of temper. He is profoundly versed in
the art and mystery of store-keeping, and as profoundly ignorant
of all that must sooner or later be learned by every resident land-
owner of the western country.

Thus much being premised, we shall hardly wonder that our
good old friend felt exceedingly aggrieved at meeting Silas Ashburn and the " lang-legged chiel" Joe, (who has grown longer
with every shake of ague,) on the way *from* his tract, instead of
*to* it.

" What in the world's the matter now !" began Mr. Keene, rather testily.  " Are you never going to begin that work ?"

" I don't know but I shall ;" was the cool reply of Ashburn ; " I
can't begin it to-day, though."

" And why not, pray, when I've been so long waiting ?"

" Because, I've got something else that must be done first.
You don't think your work is all the work there is in the world,
do you ?"

Mr. Keene was almost too angry to reply, but he made an
effort to say, " When am I to expect you, then ?"

" Why, I guess we'll come on in a day or two, and then I'll
bring both the boys."

So saying, and not dreaming of having been guilty of an
incivility, Mr. Ashburn passed on, intent only on his bee-tree.

Mr. Keene could not help looking after the ragged pair for a
moment, and he muttered angrily as he turned away, " Aye !
pride and beggary go together in this confounded new country !
You feel very independent, no doubt, but I'll try if I can't find
somebody that wants money."

And Mr. Keene's pony, as if sympathizing with his master's
vexation, started off at a sharp, passionate trot, which he has
learned, no doubt, under the habitual influence of the spicy temper of his rider.

To find labourers who wanted money, or who would own that

they wanted it, was at that time no easy task. Our poorer neighbours have been so little accustomed to value household comforts,
that the opportunity to obtain them presents but feeble incitement
to that continuous industry which is usually expected of one
who works in the employ of another. However, it happened
in this case that Mr. Keene's star was in the ascendant, and the
woods resounded, ere long, under the sturdy strokes of several
choppers.

The Ashburns, in tne mean time, set themselves busily at work
to make due preparations for the expedition which they had
planned for the following night. They felt, as does every one
who finds a bee-tree in this region, that the prize was their own
—that nobody else had the slightest claim to its rich stores; yet
the gathering in of the spoils was to be performed, according to
the invariable custom where the country is much settled, in the
silence of night, and with every precaution of secrecy. This
seems inconsistent, yet such is the fact.

The remainder of the "lucky" day and the whole of the suc-
ceeding one, passed in scooping troughs for the reception of the
honey,—tedious work at best, but unusually so in this instance,
because several of the family were prostrate with the ague.
Ashburn's anxiety lest some of his customary bad luck should
intervene between discovery and possession, made him more
impatient and harsh than usual; and the interior of that comfort-
less cabin would have presented to a chance visiter, who knew
not of the golden hopes which cheered its inmates, an aspect of
unmitigated wretchedness. Mrs. Ashburn sat almost in the fire,
with a tattered hood on her head and the relics of a bed-quilt
wrapped about her person; while the emaciated limbs of the baby
on her lap,—two years old, yet unweaned,—seemed almost to
reach the floor, so preternaturally were they lengthened by the
stretches of a four months' ague. Two of the boys lay in the
trundle-bed, which was drawn as near to the fire as possible; and
every spare article of clothing that the house afforded was thrown
over them, in the vain attempt to warm their shivering frames.
"Stop your whimperin', can't ye!" said Ashburn, as he hewed
away with hatchet and jack-knife; "you'll be hot enough before

long." And when the fever came his words were more than
verified.

Two nights had passed before the preparations were completed.
Ashburn and such of his boys as could work, had laboured inde-
fatigably at the troughs, and Mrs. Ashburn had thrown away the
milk, and the few other stores which cumbered her small supply of household utensils, to free as many as possible for the
grand occasion. This third day had been "well day" to most of
the invalids, and after the moon had risen to light them through
the dense wood, the family set off, in high spirits, on their long,
dewy walk. They had passed the causeway, and were turning
from the highway into the skirts of the forest, when they were
accosted by a stranger, a young man in a hunter's dress, evidently
a traveller, and one who knew nothing of the place or its inhabitants, as Mr. Ashburn ascertained, to his entire satisfaction, by
the usual number of queries. The stranger, a handsome youth
of one or two and twenty, had that frank, joyous air which takes
so well with us Wolverines; and after he had fully satisfied our
bee-hunter's curiosity, he seemed disposed to ask some questions
in his turn. One of the first of these related to the moving cause
of the procession and their voluminous display of *containers*.

"Why, we're goin' straight to a bee-tree that I lit upon two or
three days ago, and if you've a mind to, you may go 'long, and
welcome. It's a real peeler, I tell ye! There's a hundred and
fifty weight of honey in it, if there's a pound."

The young traveller waited no second invitation. His light
knapsack was but small incumbrance, and he took upon himself
the weight of several troughs, that seemed too heavy for the
weaker members of the expedition. They walked on at a rapid
and steady pace for a good half hour, over paths which were none
of the smoothest, and only here and there lighted by the moon-
beams. The mother and children were but ill fitted for the
exertion, but Aladdin, on his midnight way to the wondrous
vault of treasure, would as soon have thought of complaining of
fatigue.

Who then shall describe the astonishment, the almost breathless
rage of Silas Ashburn,—the bitter disappointment of the rest,—
when they found, instead of the bee-tree, a great gap in the dense

forest, and the bright moon shining on the shattered fragments of
the immense oak that had contained their prize? The poor
children, fainting with toil now that the stimulus was gone, threw
themselves on the ground; and Mrs. Ashburn, seating her wasted
form on a huge branch, burst into tears.

"It's all one!" exclaimed Ashburn, when at length he could
find words; "it's all alike! this is just my luck! It ain't none
of my neighbours, work, though! They know better than to be
so mean! It's the rich! Them that begrudges the poor man the
breath of life!" And he cursed bitterly and with clenched teeth,
whoever had robbed him of his right.

"Don't cry, Betsey," he continued; "let's go home. I'll find
out who has done this, and I'll let 'em know there's law for the
poor man as well as the rich. Come along, young 'uns, and stop
your blubberin', and let them splinters alone!" The poor little
things were trying to gather up some of the fragments to which
the honey still adhered, but their father was too angry to be kind.

"Was the tree on your own land?" now inquired the young
stranger, who had stood by in sympathizing silence during this
scene.

"No! but that don't make any difference. The man that
found it first, and marked it, had a right to it afore the President
of the United States, and that I'll let 'em know, if it costs me my
farm. It's on old Keene's land, and I shouldn't wonder if the
old miser had done it himself,—but I'll let him know what's the
law in Michigan!"

"Mr. Keene a miser!" exclaimed the young stranger, rather
hastily.

"Why, what do you know about him?"

"O! nothing!—that is, nothing very particular—but I have
heard him well spoken of. What I was going to say was, that I
fear you will not find the law able to do any thing for you. If
the tree was on another person's property——"

"Property! that's just so much as you know about it!" replied
Ashburn, angrily. "I tell ye I know the law well enough, and
I know the honey was mine—and old Keene shall know it too, if
he's the man that stole it."

The stranger politely forbore further reply, and the whole

party walked on in sad silence till they reached the village road, when the young stranger left them with a kindly "good night!"

It was soon after an early breakfast on the morning which succeeded poor Ashburn's disappointment, that Mr. Keene, attended by his lovely orphan niece, Clarissa Bensley, was engaged in his little court-yard, tending with paternal care the brilliant array of autumnal flowers which graced its narrow limits. Beds in size and shape nearly resembling patty-pans, were filled to overflowing with dahlias, china-asters and marigolds, while the walks which surrounded them, daily "swept with a woman's neatness," set off to the best advantage these resplendent children of Flora. A vine-hung porch, that opened upon the miniature Paradise, was lined with bird-cages of all sizes, and on a yard-square grass-plot stood the tin cage of a squirrel, almost too fat to be lively.

Mr. Keene was childless, and consoled himself as childless people are apt to do if they are wise, by taking into favour, in addition to his destitute niece, as many troublesome pets as he could procure. His wife, less philosophical, expended her superfluous energies upon a multiplication of household cares which her ingenuity alone could have devised within a domain like a nut-shell. Such rubbing and polishing—such arranging and re-arranging of useless nick-nacks, had never yet been known in these utilitarian regions. And, what seemed amusing enough, Mrs. Keene, whose time passed in laborious nothings, often reproved her lawful lord very sharply for wasting *his* precious hours upon birds and flowers, squirrels and guinea-pigs, to say nothing of the turkeys and the magnificent peacock, which screamed at least half of every night, so that his master was fain to lock him up in an outhouse, for fear the neighbours should kill him in revenge for the murder of their sleep. These forms of solace Mrs. Keene often condemned as "really ridic'lous," yet she cleaned the bird-cages with indefatigable punctuality, and seemed never happier than when polishing with anxious care the bars of the squirrel's tread-mill. But there was one never-dying subject of debate between this worthy couple,—the company and services of the fair Clarissa, who was equally the darling of both, and superlatively useful in every department which claimed the attention of either. How the maiden, light-footed as she was, ever contrived to satisfy both uncle and aunt, seemed really mysterious. It was, " Mr. Keene, don't keep Clary wasting her time there when I've *so much* to do !"—or, on the other hand, " My dear ! do send Clary out to help *me* a little ! I'm sure she's been stewing there long enough !" And Clary, though she could not perhaps be in two places at once, certainly accomplished as much as if she could.

On the morning of which we speak, the young lady, having risen very early, and brushed and polished to her aunt's content, was now busily engaged in performing the various behests of her uncle, a service much more to her taste. She was as completely at home among birds and flowers as a poet or a Peri ; and not Ariel himself, (of whom I dare say she had never heard,) accomplished with more grace his gentle spiriting. After all was " perform'd to point,"—when no dahlia remained unsupported,— no cluster of many-hued asters without its neat hoop,—when no intrusive weed could be discerned, even through Mr. Keene's spectacles,—Clarissa took the opportunity to ask if she might take the pony for a ride.

" To see those poor Ashburns, uncle."

" They're a lazy, impudent set, Clary."

" But they are all sick, uncle ; almost every one of the family down with ague. Do let me go and carry them something. I hear they are completely destitute of comforts."

" And so they ought to be, my dear," said Mr. Keene, who could not forget what he considered Ashburn's impertinence.

But his habitual kindness prevailed, and he concluded his remonstrance (after giving voice to some few remarks which would not have gratified the Ashburns particularly,) by saddling the pony himself, arranging Clarissa's riding-dress with all the assiduity of a gallant cavalier, and giving into her hand, with her neat silver-mounted whip, a little basket, well crammed by his wife's kind care with delicacies for the invalids. No wonder that he looked after her with pride as she rode off! There are few prettier girls than the bright-eyed Clarissa.

When the pony reached the log-causeway,—just where the thick copse of witch-hazel skirts Mr. Ashburn's moist domain,—some unexpected occurrence is said to have startled, not the sober pony, but his very sensitive rider ; and it has been asserted that the pony stirred not from the said hazel screen for a longer time than it would take to count a hundred, very deliberately.   What faith is to be attached to this rumour, the historian ventures not to determine.   It may be relied on as a fact, however, that a strong arm led the pony over the slippery corduroy, but no fur-ther ; for Clarissa Bensley cantered alone up the green slope which leads to Mr. Ashburn's door.

" How are you this morning, Mrs. Ashburn ?" asked the young visitant as she entered the wretched den, her little basket on her arm, her sweet face all flushed, and her eyes more than half-suffused with tears,—the effect of the keen morning wind, we suppose.

" Law sakes alive !" was the reply, " I ain't no how.  I'm clear tuckered out with these young 'uns.  They've had the agur already this morning, and they're as cross as bear-cubs."

" Ma !" screamed one, as if in confirmation of the maternal remark, " I want some tea !"

" Tea ! I ha'n't got no tea, and you know that well enough !"

" Well, give me a piece o' sweetcake then, and a pickle."

" The sweetcake was gone long ago, and I ha'n't nothing to make more—so shut your head !"   And as Clarissa whispered to the poor pallid child that she would bring him some if he would be a good boy and not tease his mother, Mrs. Ashburn produced, from a barrel of similar delicacies, a yellow cucumber, some-thing less than a foot long, " pickled " in whiskey and water—and this the child began devouring eagerly.

Miss Bensley now set out upon the table the varied contents of her basket.  " This honey," she said, showing some as limpid as water, " was found a day or two ago in uncle's woods—wild honey —isn't it beautiful ?"

Mrs. Ashburn fixed her eyes on it without speaking, but her husband, who just then came in, did not command himself so far.  " Where did you say you got that honey ?" he asked.

"In our woods," repeated Clarissa; "I never saw such quantities; and a good deal of it as clear and beautiful as this."

"I thought as much!" said Ashburn angrily; "and now, Clary Bensley," he added, "you'll just take that cursed honey back to your uncle, and tell him to keep it, and eat it, and I hope it will choke him! and if I live, I'll make him rue the day he ever touched it."

Miss Bensley gazed on him, lost in astonishment. She could think of nothing but that he must have gone suddenly mad, and this idea made her instinctively hasten her steps toward the pony.

"Well! if you won't take it, I'll send it after ye!" cried Ashburn, who had lashed himself into a rage; and he hurled the little jar, with all the force of his powerful arm, far down the path by which Clarissa was about to depart, while his poor wife tried to restrain him with a piteous "Oh, father! don't! don't!"

Then, recollecting himself a little,—for he is far from being habitually brutal,—he made an awkward apology to the frightened girl.

"I ha'n't nothing agin *you*, Miss Bensley; you've always been kind to me and mine; but that old devil of an uncle of yours, that can't bear to let a poor man live,—I'll larn him who he's got to deal with! Tell him to look out, for he'll have reason!"

He held the pony while Clarissa mounted, as if to atone for his rudeness to herself; but he ceased not to repeat his denunciations against Mr. Keene as long as she was within hearing. As she paced over the logs, Ashburn, his rage much cooled by this ebullition, stood looking after her.

"I swan!" he exclaimed; "if there ain't that very feller that went with us to the bee-tree, leading Clary Bensley's horse over the cross-way!"

Clarissa felt obliged to repeat to her uncle the rude threats which had so much terrified her; and it needed but this to confirm Mr. Keene's suspicious dislike of Ashburn, whom he had already learned to regard as one of the worst specimens of western character that had yet crossed his path. He had often felt the vexations of his new position to be almost intolerable, and was disposed to imagine himself the predestined victim of all the ill-

will and all the impositions of the neighbourhood. It unfortunately happened, about this particular time, that he had been
more than usually visited with disasters which are too common
in a new country to be much regarded by those who know what
they mean. His fences had been thrown down, his corn-field
robbed, and even the lodging-place of the peacock forcibly attempted. But from the moment he discovered that Ashburn had
a grudge against him, he thought neither of unruly oxen, mischievous boys, nor exasperated neighbours, but concluded that the
one unlucky house in the swamp was the ever-welling fountain
of all this bitterness. He had not yet been long enough among
us to discern how much our " bark is waur than our bite."

And, more unfortunate still, from the date of this unlucky
morning call, (I have long considered morning calls particularly
unlucky), the fair Clarissa seemed to have lost all her sprightli-
ness. She shunned her usual haunts, or if she took a walk, or a
short ride, she was sure to return sadder than she went. Her
uncle noted the change immediately, but forbore to question her,
though he pointed out the symptoms to his more obtuse lady, with
a request that she would " find out what Clary wanted." In the
performance of this delicate duty, Mrs. Keene fortunately limited
herself to the subjects of health and new clothes,—so that Clarissa,
though at first a little fluttered, answered very satisfactorily without stretching her conscience.

" Perhaps it's young company, my dear," continued the good
woman ; " to be sure there's not much of that as yet ; but you
never seemed to care for it when we lived at L——. You used
to sit as contented over your work or your book, in the long evenings, with nobody but your uncle and me, and Charles Darwin,
—why can't you now ?"

" So I can, dear aunt," said Clarissa ; and she spoke the truth
so warmly that her aunt was quite satisfied.

It was on a very raw and gusty evening, not long after the
occurrences we have noted, that Mr. Keene, with his handkerchief carefully wrapped round his chin, sallied forth after dark,
on an expedition to the post-office. He was thinking how vexatious it was—how like every thing else in this disorganized, or

rather unorganized new country, that the weekly mail should not
be obliged to arrive at regular hours, and those early enough to
allow of one's getting one's letters before dark. As he proceeded
he became aware of the approach of two persons, and though it
was too dark to distinguish faces, he heard distinctly the dreaded
tones of Silas Ashburn.

"No! I found you were right enough there! I couldn't get
at him that way; but I'll pay him for it yet!"

He lost the reply of the other party in this iniquitous scheme,
in the rushing of the wild wind which hurried him on his course;
but he had heard enough! He made out to reach the office, and
receiving his paper, and hastening desperately homeward, had
scarcely spirits even to read the price-current, (though he did
mechanically glance at that corner of the "Trumpet of Com-
merce,") before he retired to bed in meditative sadness; feeling
quite unable to await the striking of nine on the kitchen clock,
which, in all ordinary circumstances, "toll'd the hour for re-
tiring."

It is really surprising the propensity which young people have
for sitting up late! Here was Clarissa Bensley, who was so busy
all day that one would have thought she might be glad to retire
with the chickens,—here she was, sitting in her aunt's great
rocking-chair by the remains of the kitchen fire, at almost ten
o'clock at night! And such a night too! The very roaring of
the wind was enough to have affrighted a stouter heart than hers,
yet she scarcely seemed even to hear it! And how lonely she
must have been! Mr. and Mrs. Keene had been gone an hour,
and in all the range of bird-cages that lined the room, not a feather was stirring, unless it might have been the green eyebrow of
an old parrot, who was slily watching the fireside with one optic,
while the other pretended to be fast asleep. And what was old
Poll watching? We shall be obliged to tell tales.

There was another chair besides the great rocking-chair,—a
high-backed chair of the olden time; and this second chair was
drawn up quite near the first, and on the back of the tall antiqui-
ty leaned a young gentleman. This must account for Clary's

not being terrified, and for the shrewd old parrot's staring so knowingly.

"I will wait no longer," said the stranger, in a low, but very decided tone ; (and as he speaks, we recognise the voice of the young hunter.) "You are too timid, Clarissa, and you don't do your uncle justice. To be sure he was most unreasonably angry when we parted, and I am ashamed to think that I was angry too. To-morrow I will see him and tell him so ; and I shall tell him too, little trembler, that I have you on my side ; and we shall see if together we cannot persuade him to forget and forgive."

This, and much more that we shall not betray, was said by the tall young gentleman, who, now that his cap was off, showed brow and eyes such as are apt to go a good way in convincing young ladies; while Miss Bensley seemed partly to acquiesce, and partly to cling to her previous fears of her uncle's resentment against his former protégé, which, first excited by some trifling offence, had been rendered serious by the pride of the young man and the pepperiness of the old one.

When the moment came which Clarissa insisted should be the very last of the stranger's stay, some difficulty occurred in unbolting the kitchen door, and Miss Bensley proceeded with her guest through an open passage-way to the front part of the house, when she undid the front door, and dismissed him with a strict charge to tie up the gate just as he found it, lest some unlucky chance should realize Mr. Keene's fears of nocturnal invasion. And we must leave our perplexed heroine standing, in meditative mood, candle in hand, in the very centre of the little parlour, which served both for entrance-hall and *salon*.

We have seen that Mr. Keene's nerves had received a terrible shock on this fated evening, and it is certain that for a man of sober imagination, his dreams were terrific. He saw Ashburn, covered from crown to sole with a buzzing shroud of bees, trampling on his flower-beds, tearing up his honey-suckles root and branch, and letting his canaries and Java sparrows out of their cages ; and, as his eyes recoiled from this horrible scene, they encountered the shambling form of Joe, who, besides aiding and abetting in these enormities, was making awful strides, axe in hand, toward the sanctuary of the pea-fowls.

He awoke with a cry of horror, and found his bed-room full of smoke. Starting up in agonized alarm, he awoke Mrs. Keene, and half-dressed, by the red light which glimmered around them, they rushed together to Clarissa's chamber. It was empty. To find the stairs was the next thought, but at the very top they met the dreaded bee-finder armed with a prodigious club!

"Oh mercy! don't murder us!" shrieked Mrs. Keene, falling on her knees; while her husband, whose capsicum was completely roused, began pummelling Ashburn as high as he could reach, bestowing on him at the same time, in no very choice terms, his candid opinion as to the propriety of setting people's houses on fire, by way of revenge.

"Why, you're both as crazy as loons!" was Mr. Ashburn's polite exclamation, as he held off Mr. Keene at arm's length. "I was comin' up o' purpose to tell you that you needn't be frightened. It's only the ruff o' the shanty there,—the kitchen, as you call it."

"And what have you done with Clarissa?"—"Ay! where's my niece?" cried the distracted pair.

"Where is she? why, down stairs to be sure, takin' care o' the traps they throw'd out o' the shanty. I was out a 'coon-hunting, and see the light, but I was so far off that they'd got it pretty well down before I got here. That 'ere young spark o' Clary's worked like a beaver, I tell ye!"

It must not be supposed that one half of Ashburn's hasty explanation "penetrated the interior" of his hearers' heads. They took in the idea of Clary's safety, but as for the rest, they concluded it only an effort to mystify them as to the real cause of the disaster.

"You need not attempt," solemnly began Mr. Keene, "you need not think to make me believe, that you are not the man that set my house on fire. I know your revengeful temper; I have heard of your threats, and you shall answer for all, sir! before you're a day older!"

Ashburn seemed struck dumb, between his involuntary respect for Mr. Keene's age and character, and the contemptuous anger

with which his accusations filled him. "Well! I swan!" said
he after a pause; "but here comes Clary; *she's* got common
sense; ask her how the fire happened."

"It's all over now, uncle," she exclaimed, almost breathless;
"it has not done so *very* much damage."

"Damage!" said Mrs. Keene, dolefully; "we shall never get
things clean again while the world stands!"

"And where are my birds?" inquired the old gentleman.

"All safe—quite safe; we moved them into the parlour."

"We! who, pray?"

"Oh! the neighbours came, you know, uncle; and—Mr.
Ashburn—"

"Give the devil his due," interposed Ashburn; "you know
very well that the whole concern would have gone if it hadn't
been for that young feller."

"What young fellow? where?"

"Why here," said Silas, pulling forward our young stranger;
"this here chap."

"Young man," began Mr. Keene,—but at the moment, up
came somebody with a light, and while Clarissa retreated behind
Mr. Ashburn, the stranger was recognised by her aunt and uncle
as Charles Darwin.

"Charles! what on earth brought you here?"

"Ask Clary," said Ashburn, with grim jocoseness.

Mr. Keene turned mechanically to obey, but Clarissa had disappeared.

"Well! I guess I can tell you something about it, if nobody
else won't," said Ashburn; "I'm something of a Yankee, and
it's my notion that there was some sparkin' a goin' on in your
kitchen, and that somehow or other the young folks managed to
set it a-fire."

The old folks looked more puzzled than ever. "*Do* speak,
Charles," said Mr. Keene; "what *does* it all mean? Did you
set my house on fire?"

"I'm afraid I must have had some hand in it, sir," said
Charles, whose self-possession seemed quite to have deserted him.

"You!" exclaimed Mr. Keene; "and I've been laying it to
this man!"

"Yes! you know'd I owed you a spite, on account o' that plaguy bee-tree," said Ashburn; "a guilty conscience needs no accuser. But you was much mistaken if you thought I was sich a bloody-minded villain as to burn your gimcrackery for that! If I could have paid you for it, fair and even, I'd ha' done it with all my heart and soul. But I don't set men's houses a-fire when I get mad at 'em."

"But you threatened vengeance," said Mr. Keene.

"So I did, but that was when I expected to get it by law, though; and this here young man knows that, if he'd only speak."

Thus adjured, Charles did speak, and so much to the purpose that it did not take many minutes to convince Mr. Keene that Ashburn's evil-mindedness was bounded by the limits of the law, that precious privilege of the Wolverine. But there was still the mystery of Charles's apparition, and in order to its full unravel-ment, the blushing Clarissa had to be enticed from her hiding-place, and brought to confession. And then it was made clear that she, with all her innocent looks, was the moving cause of the mighty mischief. She it was who encouraged Charles to be-lieve that her uncle's anger would not last for ever; and this had led Charles to venture into the neighbourhood; and it was while consulting together, (on this particular point, of course,) that they managed to set the kitchen curtain on fire, and then—the reader knows the rest.

These things occupied some time in explaining,—but they were at length, by the aid of words and more eloquent blushes, made so clear, that Mr. Keene concluded, not only to new roof the kitchen, but to add a very pretty wing to one side of the house. And at the present time, the steps of Charles Darwin, when he returns from a surveying tour, seek the little gate as naturally as if he had never lived any where else. And the sweet face of Clarissa is always there, ready to welcome him, though she still finds plenty of time to keep in order the complicated affairs of both uncle and aunt.

And how goes life with our friends the Ashburns? Mr. Keene has done his very best to atone for his injurious estimate of Wol-verine honour, by giving constant employment to Ashburn and his sons, and owning himself always the obliged party, without which concession all he could do would avail nothing. And Mrs. Keene and Clarissa have been unwearied in their kind attentions to the family, supplying them with so many comforts that most of them have got rid of the ague, in spite of themselves. The house has assumed so cheerful an appearance that I could scarcely recognise it for the same squalid den it had often made my heart ache to look upon. As I was returning from my last visit there, I encountered Mr. Ashburn, and remarked to him how very comfortable they seemed.

"Yes," he replied; "I've had pretty good luck lately; but I'm a goin' to pull up stakes and move to Wisconsin. I think I can do better, further West."

# IDLE PEOPLE.

THOSE who never work—those who number among their most precious privileges a complete exemption from not only the spur of necessity, but the pressure of duty—must find it hard to believe that there are people in the world whose destiny it seems to be to work all the time.  Yet no—these are the very beings who think God has so ordered the lot of a portion of his children, in contrast to the all-embracing beneficence of his providence in other respects.  These might be called the butterflies of the earth, if the butterfly was not an established emblem of *soul*.  Their self-complacency is much soothed by the conviction that they are of "the porcelain clay of human kind," and they are thankful—or rather, glad—that there *is* a coarser race, to whom hard work and hard fare are well suited.

The fate of these two divisions of mankind is, after all, much more justly balanced than either portion is apt to imagine.  There is a universal necessity for labour, and those who obstinately close their understandings against this fact, whether rich or poor, inevitably join the class of sufferers sooner or later.  There is nothing in which what we call *fate* is more impartial.  The poor are admonished by destitution, and the rich by ill health—the mere idler by ennui, and the scheming sharper by disappointment and disgrace.  Yet this same universal necessity is not more evident than is the undying effort to elude it.  After centuries of warning, the struggle still continues; its energy sustained sometimes by pride, sometimes by a downright love of ease, so blind that it looks no farther than the present moment.  Thus much of the outer and obvious world—a theatre whose actors, from being, or supposing themselves to be, " th' observed of all observers," have fallen into many unnatural views and artificial habits of

life, all tending to the one darling end of drawing a broad line of
distinction between themselves and the "common" and the "vulgar."

In these western wilds, where nature, scarce redeemed from
primeval barbarism, seems to demand, with an especial earnestness, the best aid of her denizens, and where she pays with gold
every drop that falls on her bosom from the brow of labour, there
may be danger sometimes, methinks, danger of falling into an
error of an opposite character.  There is so much work to be
done, and so few people to do it, that the idea of labour is apt to
absorb the entire area of the mind, to the exclusion of some other
ideas not only useful but pleasant withal, and humanizing, and
softening, and calculated to cherish the higher attributes of our
nature.  So far is this carried that idleness is emphatically *the*
vice for which public opinion reserves its severest frown, and in
whose behalf no voice ventures an apologetic word.  If a man
drink, he may reform; even if he should steal, we permit him to
rebuild his character upon repentance; but if he be lazy, we
have neither hope nor charity.

Still, even among us, there are those to whose imagination the
*dolce far niente* is irresistible; and it must be confessed that they
form a class which is not likely to raise the reputation of the
followers of pleasure.  They have one thing in common with
the fashionables of the earth—a determination to eschew every
conceivable form of labour; but, however dignified this trait
may appear when set off by an imposing *hauteur* and an elegant
costume, it makes but a sorry figure in the woods, where the prevailing tone is far different.  Yet these kindred souls are as incorrigible as their betters; and, like them, will often perform as
much labour, and exert as much ingenuity in avoiding work, as
would, if differently directed, suffice to place them in an independent and honourable position.

It must be owned that this land of hard work presents a thousand temptations to idleness.  Not to mention the sacrifice with
which we begin—the giving up of all that gave life a rosy or a
golden tint in the older world—there may be other excuses for a
longing after amusement, in minds of a certain class.  There
is an aspect of severe effort—of closeness—of grinding care in

the general constitution of society; the natural consequence of
the fact that poverty, or at least narrow circumstances at home,
was the impetus that drove nine-tenths of the population westward; and this aspect being in striking opposition to the free,
glowing, and abundant one which characterizes unworn nature
in this scarce-trodden region, suggests and connects with labour a
certain idea of slavery—of confinement; and creates a pro-
portionate desire for all the liberty that so narrow a fate will permit.   He who possesses abundant leisure for amusement, will perhaps be heard to complain that it is hard to find; but he who is
every hour spurred on by necessity to the most toilsome employments, cannot but snatch with delight every available form of
recreation;* and will be apt to devote to the coveted indulgence
hours which must be dearly purchased by the sufferings of the
future.   Let us judge him with a charity which we may hardly
be disposed to exercise towards his prototype in high places.

So unpopular, as we have said, so contrary to the prevailing
spirit, is this desire for amusement, that those among us who are
so unfortunate as to be born with something of a poetical temperament—which delights in quiet musings, long rambles in the
woods, and other forms of idleness—generally disguise to themselves and try to disguise to others the true nature of this propensity, by contriving many new and ingenious ways of earning
money, all agreeing in one point—a determined avoidance of
every thing that is usually called *work*.

In the early spring time, while a thin covering of very fragile
ice still encrusts the marshes, there may be seen around their
borders a tangled fringe of seemingly bare bushes.   On nearer
approach these bushes are found stripped indeed as to their upper
branches, but garnished at the water's edge with berries of the
brightest coral, each shrined separately in a little ring of crystal.
These are the most delicate and highly prized cranberries; mellowed, not wilted, by the severest frosts, and now peeping through
their icy veil, and glowing in the first warm rays of approaching
spring.

These are an irresistible temptation to our fashionable of the
woods.   Armed in boots, not seven-leagued, but thick as the sev-
en-fold shield of Ajax, he plunges into the crackling pool; and

there, as long as a berry is to be found, he stands or wades; snatching, perhaps, a shilling's worth of cranberries, and a six months' rheumatism. No matter; this is not *work*.

You may see him next, if you are an early riser, setting off, at peep of dawn, on a fishing expedition. He winds through the dreary woods, yawning portentously, and stretching as if he were emulous of the height of the hickory trees. Dexterously sway-ing his long rod, he follows the little stream till it is lost in the bosom of the woodland lake; if unsuccessful from the bank, he seeks the frail skiff, which is the common property of laborious idlers like himself, and, pushing off shore, sits dreaming under the sun's wilting beams, until he has secured a supply for the day. Home again—an irregular meal at any time of day—and he goes to bed with the ague; but he murmurs not, for fishing is not *work*.

Here is a strawberry field—well may it claim the name! It is a wide fallow which has been ploughed late in the last autumn, and is now lying in ridges to court the fertilizing sunbeams. It is already clothed, though scantily, with a luxuriant growth of fresh verdure, and among, and through, and over all, glows the rich crimson of the field strawberry—the ruby-crowned queen of all wild fruits. Here—and who can blame him?—will our ex-quisite, with wife and children, if he be the fortunate proprietor of so many fingers, spend the long June day; eating as many berries as possible, and amassing in leafy baskets the rich re-mainder, to be sold to the happy holders of splendid shillings, or to dry in the burning sun for next winter's "tea-saase." Plough-ing would be more profitable, certainly, but not half so pleasant, for ploughing is *work*.

Then come the whortleberries; not the little, stunted, seedy things that grow on dry uplands and sandy commons; but the produce of towering bushes in the plashy meadow; generous, pulpy berries, covered with a fine bloom; the "blae-berry" of Scotland; a delicious fruit, though of humble reputation, and, it must be confessed, somewhat enhanced in value by the scarcity of the more refined productions of the garden. We scorn thee not, oh! bloom-covered neighbour! but gladly buy whole bushels of thy prolific family from the lounging Indian, or the still lazier white man. We must not condemn the gatherers of whortleberries, but it is a melancholy truth that they do not get rich.

Wild plums follow closely in the wake of whortleberries, and these are usually picked when they are so sour and bitter as to be totally uneatable ; because the rush for them is so great, among the class alluded to, that each thinks nobody else will wait for them to ripen ; and whoever succeeds in stripping all the trees in his neighbourhood, even though he can neither use nor sell a particle of his treasure, deems himself the fortunate man. This seems ridiculous, truly ; but is it not exactly the spirit of the miser ? What matters whether the thing be gold or green plums, if they are equally useless ? This blind haste to secure any thing bearing the form of fruit, is only an extreme exemplification of the desire to snatch a precarious subsistence from the lap of Nature, instead of paying the price which she ever demands for a due and full enjoyment of her bounties.

Baiting for wild bees beguiles the busy shunner of work into many a wearisome tramp, many a night-watch, and many a lost day. This is a most fascinating chase, and sometimes excites the very spirit of gambling. The stake seems so small in comparison with the possible prize—and gamblers and honey-seekers think all possible things probable—that some, who are scarcely ever tempted from regular business by any other disguise of idleness, cannot withstand a bee-hunt. A man whose arms and axe are all-sufficient to insure a comfortable livelihood for himself and his family, is chopping, perhaps, in a thick wood, where the voices of the locust, the cricket, the grasshopper, and the wild bee, with their kindred, are the only sounds that reach his ear from sunrise till sunset. He feels lonely and listless ; and as noon draws on, he ceases from his hot toil, and, seating himself on the tree which has just fallen beneath his axe, he takes out his lunch of bread and butter, and, musing as he eats, thinks how hard his life is, and how much better it must be to have bread and butter without working for it. His eye wanders through the thick forest, and follows, with a feeling of envy, the winged inhabitants of the trees and flowers, till at length he notes among the singing throng some half dozen of bees.

The lunch is soon despatched; a honey tree must be near; and the chopper spends the remainder of the daylight in endeavouring to discover it. But the cunning insects scent the human robber, and will not approach their home until nightfall. So our weary wight plods homeward laying plans for their destruction.

The next morning's sun, as he peeps above the horizon, finds the bee-hunter burning honey-comb and old honey near the scene of yesterday's inkling. Stealthily does he watch his line of bait, and cautiously does he wait until the first glutton that finds himself sated with the luscious feast sets off in a " bee-line"—" like arrow darting from the bow"—blind betrayer of his home, like the human inebriate. This is enough. The spoiler asks no more; and the first moonlight night sees the rich hoard transferred to his cottage; where it sometimes serves, almost unaided, as food for the whole family, until the last drop is consumed. One hundred and fifty pounds of honey are sometimes found in a single tree, and it must be owned the temptation is great; but the luxury is generally dearly purchased, if the whole cost and consequences be counted. To be content with what supplies the wants of the body for the present moment, is, after all, the characteristic rather of the brute than of the man; and a family accustomed to this view of life will grow more and more idle and thriftless, until poverty and filth and even beggary lose all their terrors. It is almost proverbial among farmers that bee-hunters are always behindhand.

Wild grapes must be left until after the hard frosts have mellowed their pulp; and the gathering of them is not a work of much cost of time or labour, since the whole vine is taken down at once, and rifled in a few moments; its bounteous clusters being reserved for the ignoble death of a protracted withering, as they hang on strings from the smoky rafters of the log-house.

Hazel-nuts are not very abundant, and they must therefore— so think our wiseacres—be pulled before they are fit for any thing, lest somebody else should have the benefit of them. So we seldom see a full ripe hazel-nut. I have had desperate thoughts of transplanting a hazel-bush or two; but I am assured it would only be buying Punchinello. Its powers are gone when it leaves its proper place.

Hickory-nuts afford a most encouraging resource. They are so plentiful in some seasons that one might almost live on them ; and then the gathering of them is such famous pastime ! An occasional risk of life and limb to be sure, but no *work !*

Hunting the deer, in forests which seem to have been planted to shelter him, and in which he is seldom far to seek, is a sort of middle term—a something *between* play and work—which is not very severely censured even by our utilitarians. Venison is not "meat," to be sure, in our parlance ; for we reserve that term for pork, *par excellence ;* but venison has some solid value, and may be salted and smoked, which seems to place it among the articles of household thrift. But our better farmers, though they may see deer-tracks in every direction round the scene of their daily rail-splitting, seldom hunt, unless in some degree debilitated by sickness, or from some other cause incapacitated for their usual daily course of downright, regular industry. " It is cheaper to buy venison of the Indians," say they ; and now that the Indians are all gone, there are white Indians enough—white skins with Indian tastes and habits under them—to make hunting a business of questionable respectability. Ere long it will be left in the hands of such, with an occasional exception in favour of city gentlemen who wander into the wilds with the hope of rebracing enervated frames by some form of exercise which is not *work.*

# CHANCES AND CHANGES;

## OR, A CLERICAL WOOING.

THIS disquisition upon some of the different phases of that sweet sin—idleness, has no particular reference to the little story that follows, except so far as it was suggested by the subduing influences of the delicious season at which the incidents here related are supposed to have occurred. It must be a dry and impracticable mind, indeed, that is not filled to overflowing with the beauty of our Indian summer; when every winding valley, every softly swelling upland, in the picturesque "openings," is clothed in such colours as no mortal pencil can imitate, blended together with such magical effect, that it is as if the most magnificent of all sunsets had fallen suddenly from heaven to earth, and lay, unchanged, on forest, hill, and river. Not a tree, from the almost black green of tamarack and hemlock, to the pale willow and the flaunting scarlet maple, the crimson-brown oak and the golden beech—not a shrub, however insignificant its name or homely its form — but contributes to the general splendour. Frequent showers, soft and silent as the very mist, cover the leaves with dewy moisture; and upon this glittering veil shines out the tempered autumn sun, calling forth at once glowing hues and nutty odours, which had been lost in a drier and less changeful atmosphere. Low in the bosom of almost every valley lies either a little lake ready to mirror back the wondrous pageant, or a bright winding stream, seldom musical here where scarce a stone of any size is to be found, but always crystal clear, and watched over by bending willows, or parting to give place to tiny islands loaded with evergreens. The sharp crack of the rifle or fowling-piece seems like sacrilege in such scenes; yet the multi-

tude of wild, shy, glancing creatures, that venture forth to enjoy
the balmy air and regale themselves upon the abundance of nature at this season, tempts into the woods so many of those to
whom the idea of game is irresistible, that we must take the
sportsman with his fine dogs, his glittering gun and his gay hunting gear, as part of the picture, if we would have it true to the
life ; and we cannot deny that he makes a picturesque adjunct,
though we hate the " barbarous art" that brings him to these
sweet solitudes.

But not alone on the wild wood and the silent lake does the Indian summer shed its tender light, making beautiful what might
else have seemed rough and common-place.  The harvest has
been nearly all gathered, and the ploughing for next year's crop
has made some progress, as the deep rich brown of some fields
and the plough itself slowly moving in others can tell us.  See
those unerring furrows, those ridges, sometimes curving a little
round some lingering stump, but always parallel, be the area
ever so extensive.  Or look yonder, beyond the line of crimson
and brown shrubs that line the rough fence, at the sower, pacing
the wide field with the measured tread of the soldier, that each
spot may get its due proportion of the golden treasure ; and
keeping exact time with foot and hand, his own thoughts furnish-
ing his only music.  No hireling or giddy youth is entrusted with
this nice operation.  The foundation for next year's riches is laid
by the master himself; but you may perhaps see the harrow
which follows his footsteps attended only by one of the younglings
of the house, whose little hands wield the slender willow wand
which urges on old Dobbin ; and whose shrill piping tones are a
far off imitation of the gruffer shouting of the elder.  The adjoin-
ing field is like a fairy camp, with its ranges of tent-like stacks
of corn, and a young maple left standing here and there as if on
purpose to supply the flaring red banners necessary to the illusion.
"Fallows gray" are not wanting, to temper the general gorgeous-
ness, nor parties of " huskers" to give a human interest to the
picture.  Here and there a cluster of hay-stacks of all sizes,
covered with roofs shaped like those of a Chinese pagoda, give
quite an oriental touch ;' while, close at hand, a long shambling
Yankee teamster, coaxing and scolding his oxen in the most un-

couth of all possible voices, will recall the whereabout, with a shock, as it were; reminding one that the prevailing human tone of the region is any thing but poetical.

One very striking feature in our autumn scenery is one that was undreamed of in the days when people ventured to be poetical upon rural themes. Cowper sings with homely truth—

> Thump after thump resounds the constant *flail*,
> That seems to swing uncertain, and yet falls
> Full on the destin'd ear. Wide flies the chaff,
> The rustling straw sends up a frequent mist
> Of atoms sparkling in the noon-day beam ——

But he would listen in vain for the flail at the West, at least during the autumn. The threshing-machine has superseded all slower modes of extracting the grain from the ear; and though a "machine" has a paltry sound, the operation of this mighty instrument gives rise to scenes of the greatest animation and interest. Half a dozen horses and all the stout arms of the neighbourhood are kept busy by its requisitions. One of the more active youths climbs the tall stack to toss down the sheaves; the next hand cuts the "binder," and passes the sheaf to the "feeder," who throws it into the monster's mouth. Round goes the cylinder, at the rate of several hundred revolutions in a minute, and the sheaf comes from among the iron teeth completely crushed; the grain, straw, and chaff in one mass, but entirely detached from each other—the work of a whole day of old-fashioned threshing being performed in a few minutes. Several persons are busied in raking away the straw from the machine as rapidly as possible; and shouts and laughter and darting movements testify to the excitement of the hour. A day with the machine is considered one of the most laborious of the whole season; yet it is a favourite time, for it requires a gathering, which is always the signal for hilarity in the country.

So tremendous a power does not work without danger; and, accordingly, the excitement of the occupation is heightened by the fear of broken arms, dislocated shoulders, torn hands, and the like—even death itself being no unusual attendant on the threshing-machine. But no one ever hesitates to use it on this account;

since rail-road speed is as much the foible of the backwoodsman
as of his civilized brother.   No inconsiderable portion of the grain
is wasted by this tearing process ; and the straw, considered so
important by the thorough farmer, is rendered nearly useless ;
but the lack of barns in which to store the grain for the slower
process of threshing, and the desire to have a great job finished
at once, reconciles the farmer to all this.   The birds profit by it,
at least.

The "making a business" of marriage, which forms the nu-
cleus of the following story, is by no means peculiar to the new
country, though it is certainly better suited to a half savage tone
of manners, than to society which pretends to civilization.  Strange
to say, marriages contracted without any previous acquaintance
between the parties, are almost confined to a class which, of all
others, is bound to teach the sacredness of the tie.   For such to
treat marriage as a mere business contract, without the least
reference to the undivided and exclusive affection which alone
can make it holy and ennobling, is indeed a marvel ; and I trust
that so coarse a form of utilitarianism may become less and less
popular among us.   If I appear to have done any thing in the
following little sketch calculated to make the practice seem less
revolting, let it be ascribed to the state of society in which the
circumstances are supposed to have occurred.   Among isolated
and uneducated people, we may tolerate what should be held unpardonable where greater advantages and greater pretensions en-
title us to look for a higher degree of refinement.

# CHAPTER I.

Let India boast her groves, nor envy we
The weeping amber and the balmy tree.

THESE western colonies, gatherings as they are from the four corners of the earth, of people whose manners, habits, and ideas are various as their origin, present a thousand little oddities of custom and character, sometimes amusing and sometimes vexatious enough to the looker-on, whose own peculiarities afford in turn their share of marvel and diversion. The Yankee smiles when the Scotsman asks for "a few o' they molasses" for his cake; the Scot stares in his turn when the man of Connecticut calls that cake a "griddle" or a "slap-jack." The Englishman describes gravely a machine which is to be "perpelled by the hair;" and the Maineman who indulges a joke at his expense will talk the next moment of his "ca-ow," which, with an indescribable twang, he will declare to be "the beatermost critter under the canopy." And in actions as well as words—in modes as well as manners—is this variety constantly presenting itself. We may see glimpses of half our United States within the compass of a school-district. We may travel without stirring from the cottage fireside, and, in one sense, (not the poet's,)

"Run the great cycle, and be still at home."

An odd affair which occurred last autumn within our bounds gave rise to these reflections, though perhaps the critical reader may decide that the association is not a very obvious one. A slender thread serves sometimes to string female reveries, and it is doubtless best they should not aim too much at "consecution of discourse," lest they be accused of lecturing. I shall tell my little story "promiscuous like," claiming my feminine privilege.

The occasion was a nutting-party—a regularly planned and numerously attended expedition in search of hickory-nuts; a cold-blooded conspiracy against the domestic comfort of the squirrels, whose despairing sighs probably swelled the soft southern breeze which we enjoyed so thoughtlessly. But this nutting is a wondrous pleasant kind of laborious idleness. Leaving out of view the desirableness of the spoil—forgetting the talk-promoting influence of a dish of well-cracked nuts placed on the little table before the fire at Christmas-tide, or in some bitter evening in February, when the snapping and cracking of the more distant articles of furniture tell of the struggle between the frosty influences without and the glowing warmth within,—the gathering is a toil to be coveted for its own sake. It is a mode of getting at the very essence and heart of a delicious autumn day, when the misty air glows with an indistinct diffusion of sunlight, so softened and so universal that we can scarce point out the spot whence it emanates, and all the tints of earth are blended and neutralized into a perfect harmony with this enchanting atmosphere. Green is almost or quite gone; scarlet has sobered into crimson, and that again into a golden brown. The leaves still hang in isolated clusters upon the oaks, dry, and rustling ever and anon with a melancholy, sighing music; but the hickory trees stretch their long branches and lift their lofty heads, denuded of every thing but their fragrant fruit, which, looked at from below, dwindles to the size of dots on the rich sky.

This is the time, of all others, for long rambles; and when October brings it round, we moralizers upon the thriftless and vagrant habits of certain of our neighbours, are disposed to be at least as idle as the idlest, and think no day better, or at least more delightfully spent, than that on which we repair to a strip of untouched forest land a mile or two from our village, and there waste the short afternoon in such sport as fascinates the truant schoolboy, until the declining sun, and the chilly breeze of approaching night, warn us off, tired trespassers upon nature's blest domain. Is it possible any body ever had the heart to whip a truant boy in such weather, when the forest was accessible?

Oh! the pleasures of the cart ride, even with its unfailing accompaniment of shrieks of pretty terror, as the patient oxen draw us up and down and sidling through hills on whose impracticable roughness no horses could be trusted! Then comes the racing

search after the oldest trees, which are always supposed to promise the largest nuts, and then the scramble when some strong arm
shakes down a rattling shower on the unequal floor formed around
the foot of the tree by means of shawls and cloaks and buffalo-
robes, spread on the ground lest the thick bed of leaves should hide
the falling treasure.   Many is the wild shout of youthful glee
when some older or less accustomed face is unwarily turned upward for a moment to ask another shower, and receives, perchance,
a billeted bullet on the tip of its nose.   And not a little consoling
is required by the infant heroes upon whom the bounties of autumn descend too copiously, administering more and harder
thumps than their green philosophy has yet been trained to endure.

These frolics are not without their perils, howevei, and those
more serious than a bruised nose or a thumped shoulder ; and
the especial nut-gathering of which I began to tell, will, I am
sure, be long remembered by all concerned, though perhaps for
very various reasons.

## II.

> Ye list to the songs of the same forest bird,
> Your own merry music together is heard:
> Nor can Echo, sweet sisters! amid the rocks tell
> Your voices apart in her moss-covered cell.

OUR party was a large one, and as merry as it was large.
Three great wagons, drawn by oxen, were our vehicles ; and
into these were crammed as many giggling girls as possible, with
a few older heads by way of ballast.   Three stout farmers went
along, to shout at the teams, and to pilot us safely over hill and
hollow—no sinecure, as I before hinted.   These were to officiate
also as shakers or *pounders ;* for, be it known, whenever the at-
tendants on these occasions are too old or too lazy to climb, they
make their services effectual by upheaving great stones, which
they throw against the tree with main force, producing concus-
sions which might bring down toppling cliffs, let alone hickory-
nuts.   Our friends, Haw and Gee, were of the order of the ele-

phant, and could not be induced to climb; but they were admirable pounders, and we were soon well pelted with nuts, and busily engaged in freeing them from their aromatic wrappers—an operation which we of the West call "shucking."

Among our bright-eyed company were the twin-daughters of a worthy neighbour of ours, generally known among the villagers by the title of Deacon Lightbody, though I believe he has not any other claim to the dignity than that which rests upon a particularly grave face, and a devoted attention to the secular affairs of his church. He always makes the fire in the meeting-house—sees to the sweeping and lighting—asks the minister to dinner—hands up all notices—turns out the dogs that sometimes intrude during service—and does all necessary frowning and head-shaking at the unlucky urchins who laugh when the said dogs howl just outside the door. All this Mr. Lightbody does, not for the lucre of gain, but from pure love of what he calls the " good cause," though I doubt he deceives himself a little as to the catholicity of his regard for religion. Yet he declares he *does* try to have charity for those who do not think as he does in matters of faith, though it is certain that no Christian can object to any of his favourite doctrines, since they are Bible truths and nothing else. We must leave the worthy deacon to reconcile these incongruities, as they have no immediate bearing on our little story, and were introduced solely for the purpose of making our reader acquainted with Mr. Lightbody's turn of mind.

Those twin-daughters of his were " as like as two peas "— sweet peas—or pea blossoms rather. Such cloudless azure eyes —such diaphanous complexions—such dimpling roses and such sunny hair! If one should undertake to describe them, nothing but superlatives would do. Yet their hands had handled the churn-dasher too often to be very satiny in the palm, and their feet, having never been coaxed into shoes of the size and shape of a scissors-sheath, were unfashionably well-proportioned. Charming fairies were they, nevertheless, and wonderfully alike, yet with a difference, perceptible enough to their intimates. Ruth was the demure fairy—Elsie the tricksy sprite. Ruth was born a careful, tidy housewife ; Elsie an incorrigible shatter-brain. Ruth never did wrong, while Elsie had to atone for all sorts of offences against good order and good government twenty times a day. Yet she made up so sweetly, and was withal so kind and loving, that her father, who meant to be considered a stern stickler for family discipline, could seldom find it in his heart to scold her for her faults, except when she laughed in meeting, which always cost her a laborious pacification.

These two lilies of the valley were arrayed in white, as was meet : Ruth's ribands being lilac, and Elsie's pale green, for the convenience of being known apart. As an offset to their wood-nymph costume, we had Miss Cotgrave in a purple silk, with her coal-black locks brought down to her chin, and then wound round her large ears, and a pinch-back brooch by way of *ferronière*. Then there was Ellen Shirley, prepared for a game at her dearly beloved romps, wisely preferring a pink gingham dress to any sort of finery ; and Patty Chandler grasping her great basket and staring silently with round eyes, seemingly full of nothing but anxiety lest she should not manage to secure her share of the spoils. These, with half a dozen or more of little folks, who were any thing but *personnages muets*, made up our "load," and the other vehicles carried crews neither less numerous nor less noisy.

The young ladies talked and laughed moderately, for there were no beaux ; and Miss Cotgrave said she rejoiced that it was so, for she did hate to have a parcel of young men hanging about.

## III.

These arms
Invite the chain, this naked breast the steel.

IT could not have been long after we left the village that two sober-looking individuals, drest in comely and reverend black, greeted the pleased eyes of Deacon Lightbody as he stood at his own door, looking at the meeting-house, (as was his habit,) and noting the curious effect of the level beams of the afternoon sun, which shone through and through the little building, making it glow like a lantern. Light brought warmth to mind, and the

deacon, by a natural transition, began thinking that the very next
week he must bestir himself and get up a " bee " to bank up his
beloved meeting-house.

Are there any of my readers so benighted as not to take the
sense of this home-bred phrase ?   Then I must stop to tell them
that a " bee" is a collection of volunteers who agree to meet at
some specified time to accomplish any object of public or private utility which requires the concurrence of numbers.   And
" banking up " is a service rendered very necessary by the severity of our winters and the slightness of our dwellings, and
consists in piling earth round the foundations, so as to prevent the
frosty winds from intruding below the floor.   All this has nothing
at all to do with our important history, but is merely a private
hint for the enlightenment of the unlearned.

The deacon, then, was devising liberal things for the good of
his dear meeting-house, when the two suits of black, with faces
to correspond, (not to match,) crossed his line of vision and brought
a pleased expression into his solemn countenance.   The gentlemen alighted, and proved to be—one a church-officer from a
neighbouring town, and the other a young clergyman, who being
just come there, and likely to officiate within our bounds occasionally, was an object of the first interest to Mr. Lightbody.

After a short prelude, Mr. Poppleton, the elder gentleman,
began.   " I called, Mr. Lightbody, to introduce this reverend gentleman to your acquaintance."

Mr. Lightbody shook hands, and then shook hands again, and
asked the gentlemen to walk in.

Mr. Poppleton, with a somewhat impatient wave of the hand,
as much as to say he had come on business, and had no time for
ceremony, proceeded in his speech.

" This gentleman, sir, is Mr. Hammond,—the reverend Mr.
Hammond, sir—who is going to be with us for a spell, and perhaps longer—and as he thinks some of settling at the West, he
judges it best, and so do we all—that he should take a wife, and
so keep house, for you know it isn't pleasant for a minister to be
boarding round.   And he has been recommended—"

The young man upon this turned, Deacon Lightbody says, " as
red as a fire-coal," (as well he might,) and stammered out some-

thing about his having heard that Mr. Lightbody had two daughters. " Why, yes, sir—yes,—I have so"—said the deacon—a
snug parsonage appearing at the end of a short vista in his imagination—" I have so—and the neighbours *do* say that they are
pretty likely girls—but walk in—walk in ;" and the guests were
ushered in with reverential alacrity.

In the " keepin-room" they found Mrs. Lightbody, with her
hearth scrupulously swept and her white apron shining with
cleanliness, and her fair hair most primly arranged under a
transparent cap, which was yet not so clear as her complexion.
The ceremony of introduction having been repeated, Mr. Poppleton, with very little circumlocution, gave Mrs. Lightbody to
understand the especial purport of the visit.

The good lady shared her husband's reverence for all that
belonged to the church, but she was a woman and a mother, and
she coloured deeply,—almost painfully, at this abrupt reference
to the disposal of a daughter. But Mr. Poppleton had come on
business, and he knew only one way of doing it ; and Mr. Hammond said but little, having, indeed, but little opportunity. After
some ineffectual attempts, he kept his eyes fixed firmly on the
floor while his mouth-piece set forth his claims and enlarged upon
his plans and prospects.

In Mr. Lightbody's mind, however, all was sunshine. To have
a minister for a son-in-law, was all that his ambition coveted ;
and to do the candidate justice, his countenance and manner,—
setting aside the unmanageable awkwardness of his present position—were much in his favour.

" As far as I'm concerned," said Mr. Lightbody in winding up
the conference, "as far as I'm concerned, I'm perfectly agreeable. I give my consent, and I dare say Miss Lightbody won't
say no—you can take your choice—airy one of 'em—airy one of
'em—that is—if they are agreeable, you know ! I shouldn't put
any force upon 'em, nor over-persuade 'em—but if they're agreeable I am !"

Thus encouraged, the principal and his *double* took leave, in
spite of pressing invitations to stay tea. They were on their
way to some convocation of their order, and were to call as they
returned. But meanwhile, as their way onward lay near the

nutting-ground, Mr. Hammond suggested that it might not be amiss to make some small tarry in that vicinity. Perhaps he thought his choice need not be restricted to the deacon's fair twins —or perhaps—but they came—saw—

## IV.

Alive, I would be loved of one—
I would be wept when I am gone.

In the midst—the very acme—of our frolic, when Ruth was swinging in a grape-vine which had been slung so conveniently by the freakish hand of Nature that it needed very little aid from man,—and Elsie, shrieking like a Banshee, was flying through the dry leaves, pursued by Patty Chandler, whose basket she had mischievously abstracted—this was the time, of all others, when the two sober-looking horsemen rode up the hillside and presented themselves to the view of our abashed damsels, who had forgotten that there were any grave people in the world. A wet blanket! and all our fire was extinguished accordingly. Every body fell to picking up nuts with an air of conscious delinquency.

Mr. Poppleton was acquainted with most of the party, and gave his companion a general introduction; singling out Ruth and Elsie, however, and endeavouring, by sundry not very far-sought questions, to make them shine out for Mr. Hammond's 'encouragement, just as we pat and coax a shy horse when we wish to show his paces to advantage. But the twins were more than shy, and could not be brought to say any thing but yes and no, so that Mr. Poppleton, discouraged by the result of this his first effort at a more diplomatic mode of proceeding, fairly called them aside, leaving Mr. Hammond staring and unprotected among a parcel of giddy girls.

The reverend youth had no long trial, however, for it was but a moment before Mr. Poppleton returned, and with a grave sigh beckoned him away.

It took us a good while to find the fair sisters, and when they did show themselves, Ruth looked primmer than ever, and Elsie had certainly been shedding tears, though her face gave us no small reason to suspect they had been tears of laughter.

"What *did* Mr. Poppleton want ?" was the question of half a dozen pairs of lips.

"Who is that handsome young man ? Is he a minister ?" asked not a few.

The answers to these questions were very vague. Ruth, and even Elsie seemed seized with a fit of the silents, and conjecture was left to float wide and pick up all sorts of things.

"I'll tell you !" said Miss Cotgrave, whose thoughts were a good deal turned towards matrimony, "I'll tell you all about it ! I see it all now ! Old Pop is looking for a wife for that young man. He always takes care of the young ministers, and he's been to Deacon Lightbody's to speak for one of his girls !"

The truth thus blurted out was almost too much for the heroines of Mr. Poppleton's anti-romance. They blushed, they laughed, they made up all sorts of improbable stories, and to escape from the storm of raillery, began seeking for nuts with renewed industry.

"How provoking that we have no one to climb the trees !" said Elsie ; "the nuts hang on the upper boughs after all the shaking !" and at the word, the best climber in the country was at her elbow.

Joe Fenton, a son of the forest, dark-eyed and ruddy-cheeked, and withal slender and elastic as a willow wand, had long been suspected of a bashful liking for Elsie, and yet no one,—not even Miss Cotgrave,—had ever been able to ascertain whether there had actually been any "love-passages" between them or not. The principal ground for any suspicion of partiality on the side of the young lady was an over-scrupulous avoidance of Master Fenton upon every occasion. This, Miss Cotgrave says, is " a sure sign."

Joe had been ploughing in a neighbouring field, (Burns has made ploughing glorious, O gentle reader !) and hearing the merry shouts of the nut-gatherers, could not resist the temptation to come and see if his help was not needed.

"Oh ! climb the tree, Joe !" said the little folks, for the grown damsels were somewhat ceremonious, although Joe was in his every-day clothes, and did not look half the beau he appears on Sundays and high occasions.

Not another word was needed, and it was scarcely a moment before Joe was poised on a bough which it made one dizzy to look up at. Down came the pelting showers on all sides, and we were fain to run away until the rain had ceased from the exhausted condition of the reservoirs. Baskets were filled, and bags were brought from the wagons. Another and another tree did young Fenton climb, and with equal success, until Miss Cotgrave, in pursuing her running changes upon her favourite theme, inflicted a cruel pinch upon Ruth's arm, asking her whether the young parson was in treaty for herself or her sister.

A scream from Ruth at the moment when Fenton was making a perilous transit from one branch to another, caused him to miss his hold, and the next instant he lay on the ground at her feet— dead, as we all supposed. His lips were colourless, and his breathing had ceased entirely.

It were vain to tell of the consternation, the distress which followed. Ruth's grief was terrific. The poor girl, feeling that she had been the cause, though innocently, of this sad accident, hung over him, wringing her hands in helpless anguish, beseeching him to open his eyes and speak to her, and this in tones which could hardly fail to awaken life if a glimmering remained.

We had begun to despair of the success of the simple remedies which were within our reach when a deep-drawn sigh from the sufferer relieved us. As one of the company observed, " The minute he ketch'd his breath, his cheeks begun to look streaked," and the red streaks soon overpowered the white ones. Our efforts were now renewed, and Ruth—the prim, the demure Ruth,—transported beyond herself by the first violent emotion she had ever experienced, was as profuse in her exclamations of hope and joy, as she had before been in those of agonizing self-reproach. It was at this moment that Elsie made her appearance for the first time since the accident. She was pale, but most of us were so, and no one seemed so little inclined to assist in recovering poor Joe's scattered senses.

" La !" said Miss Cotgrave, " if nobody had cared any more

about Joe Fenton than you did, Elsie, he might have been dead
by this time!"

Joe turned his opening eyes full upon Elsie.

" Are you much hurt ?" she inquired, with an indifferent air.
Ruth replied for him, with a most eloquent exposition of the danger, and the terror, and the joy; but Elsie turned away as if she
had not heard the words.

We got our patient into a wagon by the aid of our stout team-
sters; we had him bled when we reached home, and he felt almost well before bed-time,—well bodily, we mean, for Elsie's
coldness had found a very sensitive spot in his heart, and the
poor boy could hardly think of it without shivering.

## V.

What wicked and dissembling glass of mine
Made me compare with Hermia's sphery eyne?

In two days Joe Fenton's lithe limbs were as active as ever,
but the bleeding had done nothing for the blow on his heart. He
had never, we are assured, told his love to Elsie, but he thought
she knew all about it, and now to be treated in this killing sort of
way ! It was plain that he must have deceived himself entirely;
and, lacking courage to encounter Elsie's frigid looks again, he
resolved to make Ruth the confidant of his troubles, and to engage her good offices with her less approachable sister.

As to his shy Doris, she had been gloomy and reserved with
her sister, but more than once closeted with Miss Cotgrave, who
had made her several long calls. Calls are sometimes very useful
in enlightening us as to the character and intentions of particular
friends who do not happen to be present, and Miss Cotgrave was
conscientiously anxious to disabuse Elsie's mind on the subject of
Fenton's attachment. For this benevolent purpose, the occurrence in the wood afforded excellent material. Elsie, who had
witnessed the accident from a distance, was at first unable to
move toward the spot, and afterward deterred by some pangs of
maidenly jealousy awakened by the passionate grief of her sister.

We do not like that others should display too much interest in those who ought to love us and us only; and the instinctive feeling of resentment is apt to extend itself even to the objects of such impertinent affection. So poor Elsie, whose brain was none of the clearest after that unhappy tumble, came at once to the conclusion that she must either have been deceived throughout, or that her young admirer had proved inconstant; and her uneasiness took the form of high displeasure at both parties concerned, with some share of the same feeling towards all the rest of the world, including her own silly self.

Fenton knocked at Mr. Lightbody's door, and Elsie ran and hid herself in the garden. Here she shed tears enough to have watered a heavier sorrow, and in the very tempest of her passion she saw her false love and her cruel sister going out as for a walk, engaged in earnest conversation. The thing was certain, and the blue eyes were proudly dried—to be swimming again the very next moment.

"Elsie! Elsie!" It was her father's voice; and summoning new resolution, she wiped away the intrusive tears and hastened to the house. In the keepin-room she encountered Mr. Poppleton and his youthful reverend. Mr. and Mrs. Lightbody sat by, but Mr. Poppleton was again the spokesman.

"Which of you is it?" asked the good man after brief salutation to the April-faced maiden; then checking himself, he added, "But that isn't it—are you the one that had the green string around her neck t'other day? That was the one we wanted."

Elsie answered mechanically, "Yes."

"Why you don't look so chirk as you did then. You ain't sick, be ye?"

This brought a mechanical "No."

"Oh! only a little peakin, eh! Well! now you see, we've come on particular business. Mr. Hammond stands in need of a helpmate; and after consulting with his friends, and also getting the consent and good-will of your honoured father, he wishes to know if you could be agreeable to undertake the journey of life with him,—that is, if you think you could pitch upon him for a husband?"

"Mr. Poppleton," began the blushing Mr. Hammond, as soon

as he could edge in a word, "you embarrass the young lady, sir!
Allow me a few minutes' conversation—"

"Mr. Hammond," rejoined the elder, with rather a severe air,
"missionaries and missionaries' wives must not be fancy-led like
the vain world. This young woman has been well brought up,
and showed her duty in all things, and now the only question
seems to *me* to be, whether she can make up her mind to renounce
vanity and folly, and spend the rest of her life in doing good."
And upon this text spoke Mr. Poppleton for something like half
an hour, aided very warmly now and then by Mr. Lightbody,
but uninterrupted by any body else. His discourse had so much
the air of a sermon that it would have seemed impertinent,—so
Mr. Hammond thought, we dare say,—to have attempted to refute
or modify any of its positions. Even a sermon must have an end,
however, and when the orator had gone over and over, and round
and round the subject till he felt satisfied with his exposition of it,
he turned to Mrs. Lightbody with a very complacent, "Well,
ma'am, what do *you* say?"

Mrs. Lightbody remembered, though she did not tell, that she
had for some time past observed certain almost intangible indications of a liking for somebody else, and she therefore referred the
matter to Elsie herself, only observing that a good minister's wife
was a great blessing to the people.

What was her surprise when Elsie, who had been gazing out
of the window, turned suddenly to her father, and gave an un-
conditional, and almost impetuous consent.

"Why, Elsie!" said Mrs. Lightbody.

"She's right!" said the deacon, rubbing his hands.

"I hope she'll be a burning"—began Mr. Poppleton. But Mr.
Hammond, looking at the agitated countenance of the beautiful
girl, motioned to his ally to cease, and taking her hand desired
her to compose herself, saying, stiffly enough, but yet kindly,
that he would give her no further trouble at present, but would
call again in a day or two.

And with the usual adieux these odd negotiators departed.

## VI.

Kissing the lips of unacquainted change.

THAT very evening, when the two fair sisters retired to their chamber, did Ruth, drawing encouragement from Elsie's tear-stained cheeks, open her mission—how different from the other!

It was a tale of such passionate protestation—such humble suing,—on the part of the hero of the hickory-nutting—that Elsie, stung with compunction for her blind precipitancy, called and thought herself the most wretched of human beings; and almost frightened her more placid sister by the vehemence of her sorrow. Fenton loved her then, after all; and she—what had she done! "Why, Elsie, dear!" said the soft-voiced Ruth, as the stricken-hearted girl sobbed upon her bosom, "what *can* be the matter? I used to think you liked Joe Fenton—"

"Oh! Ruth! I have promised—promised that odious old Poppleton—that hateful young minister,"—and here tears stopped the sad story.

"Promised what, dear?" said Ruth, who was a matter-of-fact little body.

"Oh! promised to be a missionary—to go and live in the woods —to marry that—oh dear! oh dear!"

"To marry that young clergyman! Why, Elsie! how can you call him hateful! He is as much handsomer than Joe Fenton as—"

"Handsome! I don't care for his being handsome! I hate him! I wish I had never seen him! Oh! that miserable nutting!" And her tears poured afresh.

Ruth sat in musing silence. She could not find it in her heart to condole with her sister upon the prospect of becoming the help-meet of so attractive à missionary; and she was unconsciously balancing in her own mind the various points of difference between Mr. Hammond and Joe Fenton, when Elsie suddenly started up.

"Ruth! why won't you take him yourself?"

"I !" said Ruth, bridling up a little, " why, because he has not asked me !"

" Oh ! but—dear, dear sister—you know we are so much alike that strangers never can tell us apart. Now do ! there's a dar-ling good girl ! do save me from all this misery ! I can never love him—I shall hate him—and that will be so wicked for a mis-sionary's wife !"

Ruth shook her head very discouragingly. She could not think of offering herself, even to a minister.

" Ah ! but you know, Mr. Poppleton only asked for the one that wore the green riband, and if you would just change with me, nobody would know the difference except father and mother ; and they would not tell. Oh ! Ruth, if you love me one bit you can't refuse ! You are just the very thing for a minister's wife ! so much better than poor me ! Dear, dear Ruth—won't you ? You have never loved any body else ; and I'm sure this young minis-ter is good as well as handsome. You don't know how kindly he spoke to me,"—and Elsie stopt for want of breath.

" You said just now that he was hateful," said Ruth, with her most demure air.

" Ah ! but I was thinking of poor Joe, then—I mean I was thinking how he loved me—you told me yourself, you know—oh ! I should be so miserable—but I never will marry him, and then father will be so angry !" And with a profusion of tears and kisses she besought her sister to say yes, but in vain. All that Ruth could be brought to promise was, that she would talk to her father and mother about it, though she could scarcely withstand the sobs which continued to burst from Elsie's heart long after she had fallen asleep.

Upon consulting with the higher powers, Mrs. Lightbody was soon persuaded into thinking with Elsie, that if Ruth would take her place, the young minister would never observe the differ-ence ; but Mr. Lightbody had the dignity of the cloth too much at heart to allow of this attempt at deception. He persisted in his opinion that since Elsie had made an engagement, she ought cer-tainly to fulfil it.

" And let Fenton take Ruth, if he's a mind to," concluded the old gentleman with his peculiarly solemn air. " Joe's a good

young man, and he's got a good farm too—that is—he will have
when it's cleared up—and Ruth will likely have a sight more of
worldly goods than Elsie, though she won't have a minister, to be
sure—I hold that a young woman that's got a minister hasn't got
much to wish for."

"But, father," said Elsie, who was almost writhing under this
business-like estimate of the matter,—"what will poor Joe say ?"

"Say! why that's pretty good! Didn't you tell me just now
that the reverend Mr. Hammond would just as leave marry one
as the other? Is Joe Fenton to set up to be more difficult than a
minister, I should like to know ?"

Yet Elsie did not desist in despair. She was accustomed to
victory upon easier terms, it is true, but she spared neither tears
nor coaxing until she brought her father to a compromise.

It was agreed that when Mr. Hammond paid the critical visit
both sisters should wear green ribands, and let the young divine
make a choice, which was to be considered final.


## VII.

Say that but once I see a beauteous star,
I may forget it for another star.


THE toilet of youth and beauty ought never to cost much time,
and the ordinary costume of the fair twins was simpler than the
simplest ; yet the reverend Mr. Hammond had been in the parlour for a long nervous half hour, and Mr. Lightbody had given
several Blue-Beard-like calls at the foot of the stairs, before Ruth
and Elsie made their appearance on the day of destiny. The
interval had been spent in the most minute and anxious comparison of every several ringlet—every article of dress—and particularly every knot and wave of the talismanic green riband.
When all was done they could scarce be sure each of her own
blushing image in the mirror, so perfect was the resemblance.

"But oh ! dear, dear Ruth !" said Elsie, "I am so afraid you
will not be able to speak like me ! Do try to be a little wild and

saucy! I fear that will betray us, after all. I can be as still as
you, but you will not talk, I know!"

"I will do my best, since I have promised," said Ruth, with
a sigh; "but oh! Elsie, if you were not such a dear, good sister—"

"Oh! come, come—don't let us wait a moment longer! There
is father calling again!" And she hurried her sister along till
they stood in the dreaded presence.

Mr. Hammond, who had fortunately or wisely left his Achates
at home this time, arose to receive the fair sisters as they entered
the room side by side. He cast his eyes wonderingly from one to
the other, and finding himself totally at a loss, gravely resumed
his seat with an air of painful embarrassment. It might embarrass a bolder man to find that he could not tell his betrothed
"from any other true-love."

"Which of these young ladies have I seen before?" said he at
last, with straightforward simplicity.

"You have seen us both!" exclaimed Elsie hastily.

The young man smiled, very quietly, and at once drew his
chair near Elsie's, with so evident a recognition of the voice and
manner that the poor child had much ado to restrain her tears.
She looked imploringly at Ruth, but Ruth could do nothing but
blush, and the catastrophe seemed inevitable, when Miss Cotgrave
came sailing into the room.

She made her best and most sweeping courtesy to the young
minister, and cast a very searching glance at our two agitated
damsels. The young lady's eye was more than piercing—it was
screwing—yet it was at fault now. Mr. Hammond was thrown
out too, for in the process of receiving the new guest, Ruth and
Elsie had changed their places, and Elsie, warned by past mis-
chance, was resolutely silent.

"Dear! how dark you *do* keep your room, Mrs. Lightbody,"
said Miss Cotgrave, who, being intuitively aware of a matrimonial cloud in the horizon, was determined to have more light on
the subject. "I declare, coming in out of the light I can scarcely
see any body!"

"The western sun shone in so dazzling"—Mrs. Lightbody said.
But Miss Cotgrave was not so to be baffled.

" Do *you* like the fashionable style of dark rooms, sir ?" said she, appealing to Mr. Lightbody.

Fashion ! at Deacon Lightbody's ! The word "dance" did not galvanize douce Davie Deans more severely than did this unlucky term our worthy friend.

" No, indeed !" he exclaimed, with solemn earnestness ; and in less than half a minute he had conscientiously withdrawn every curtain and thrown wide every blind, letting in the whole crimson flood of a gorgeous sunset, and adding an angelic radiance to the beautiful faces of his daughters.

" Why, Ruth ! I didn't know you !" exclaimed Miss Cotgrave ; " you and Elsie are more like each other than you are like your-selves !" Then in a lower tone to Elsie—" Poor Joe Fenton's shot, eh !"

A trained belle in a " fashionable" boudoir could not have fainted more gracefully than did our simple Elsie at these words. All was flutter, as is usual on such occasions, and nobody was half so frightened as poor Miss Cotgrave.

" Mercy on us ! what is the matter ? I wasn't in earnest—I only meant that he had got the bag to hold ! Elsie, Elsie ! don't ! I was only joking because you had given him the mitten !"

During the time occupied in giving voice to these choice figures of speech, Elsie's scattered wits had been recalled by the abun-dant aid of cold water, and when she seemed quite recovered, Miss Cotgrave took her leave, a good deal mortified by the awk-ward result of her humorous effort, yet overjoyed to have come into possession of a secret, and above all, anxious to get somebody to help her keep it.

The young divine had stood gravely aloof during this scene. Inexperienced as he was in the matter of female whims, he was not yet so blind as to need telling that emotion, and not the illness which Elsie tried to pretend, had in reality caused her swoon. So, like a good and sensible Timothy as he was, he took the readiest and simplest way to relieve his gathering perplexities.

" Father !" said he, approaching Mr. Lightbody, who sat twirling his thumbs in a paroxysm of fidgets at Elsie's perverse-ness, " you have kindly consented to entrust me with one of your daughters, and I had hoped that the one I had the pleasure of

seeing here before, was disposed to listen to me with some degree
of favour. If this is so, if the young lady does feel willing to
undertake the toils and hardships of a missionary life—will you
yourself bestow her upon me ? for I confess that the wonderful
resemblance between them leaves me entirely at a loss."

Mr. Lightbody gave a deep hem ! sensibly relieved.

"Come here, Ruth, my dear !" said he, drawing the blushing
damsel to him very gently, and with a manifest softening of the
aspect which he usually considered becoming ; " come here and
tell your father if you think you could learn to be happy with this
reverend gentleman," (his reverence was three-and-twenty,) "and
whether you are willing to make the sacrifices that a minister's
wife must make in this new country, and devote yourself to the
service of religion and the advancement of sound doctrine ?" He
paused for a reply, but none came. Perhaps Ruth was thinking
over these sacrifices, which form a standard topic on these occasions, though they are not, practically, very obvious, especially
to people who have been accustomed to a country life.

Taking silence for assent, her father placed her passive hand
in that of Mr. Hammond, and pronounced an emphatic blessing
on them both. And, when this was done, her mother embraced
her, and murmured in her ear some words of exhortation or
encouragement, and then gave place to Elsie, who, after her own
manner, kissed and cried, and whispered her thanks and blessings.
And then the minister, whose views did not seem to accord in all
respects with Mr. Poppleton's, (that gentleman would probably
have judged it superfluous to remain after the business was settled,) drew his gentle *fiancée* to the garden-door, and thence into
the garden, though it was already twilight, and there contrived to
make her understand his plans and prospects much better than he
could have done by proxy, even though that proxy had been Mr.
Poppleton.

It was after they had vanished, that our hero of the nutting-
party made his appearance upon the *tapis*, having been inspired
by Miss Cotgrave with an irresistible desire to know what was
really going on at Deacon Lightbody's. He could hardly have
"happened in" at a more fortunate juncture. Elsie, to be sure,
was "weeping-ripe," but the awful deacon was walking the floor

in a most complacent humour, and Mrs. Lightbody's mild eyes seemed to beam with unusual kindness.

Master Fenton was a man of few words, but those which he mustered for this occasion were very much to the purpose ; and if Mr. Lightbody did not experience the same swelling of the heart as when he bestowed Ruth upon a minister, he gave his darling Elsie to the young farmer with very good will, and a blessing which came warm from the heart.

There was not a second garden for Fenton and Elsie, but they were old acquaintance ; and, as the evening closed in, Mr. Lightbody rang the bell for family worship, and then, in the midst of happy hearts, reverently returned thanks for the manifold blessings of his earthly lot.

Mr. Hammond is fortunately settled in our neighbourhood, for the present at least ; and he has the ueatest little cottage in the wood, standing too under a very tall oak, which bends kindly over it, looking like the Princess Glumdalclitch inclining her ear to the box which contained her pet Gulliver. This cottage possesses among its recommendations that of being at the extremity of a charming walk through the forest, and this circumstance makes it especially precious to Elsie and Fenton, who are very attentive to the dominie's lady. Farmers cannot marry so speedily as ministers, but after next spring's business is finished, we shall, may be, have another wedding to record.

# AMBUSCADES.

"Loves's not a flower that grows on the dull earth;
  Springs by the calendar—must wait for sun—
  For rain—matures by parts—must take its time
  To stem—to leaf—to bud—to blow ; it owns
  A richer soil and boasts a quicker seed."

J. SHERIDAN KNOWLES.

TOM OLIVER is the hero of my story, and there is almost
enough of him to make two drawing-room heroes.  Tom is long,
and strong, and lithe enough to stand for a Kentucky Apollo; and
in his fringed hunting-shirt, with rifle in hand, and a dashing
'coon-skin cap overshadowing his dark eyes, he is no bad personification of the Genius of the West.  And this is paying the West
a great compliment ; for there is a wild grace and beauty about
Tom's whole appearance that is not to be found everywhere.

I know not whether it would be safe to say that Tom has made
his "hands hard with labour," for he is not particularly fond of
work ; but I may say he has made his " heart soft with pity," for
a gentler nature lives not.  Daring hunter as he is, he has found
time to be the most dutiful of sons ; and from his boyhood he was
the sole support and comfort of a widowed mother.  She depended upon him as if their relation had been reversed, and when the
poor soul came to die, she could bear no hand near her but his.
Night and day did he watch by her bedside, and the kind offices
of the neighbouring matrons came no nearer than the preparation
of such things as Tom required for his nursing.  His hand ad-
ministered the remedies, and offered the draught to the parched lip,
and smoothed the pillows, and fanned the fainting brow.  And
when the last dread moment came, the same kind and dear hand
was clasped in the chill embrace of the dying, and afterwards

closed with pious care the eyes that had so long looked upon him
with more than a mother's love.  Then and long afterwards,
Tom mourned for his poor old mother as if she had been a youthful bride.  He has a kind heart.

Tom's passion was hunting; and although this had been duti-
fully restrained while his mother required his services, when she
was gone he found relief in indulging it to the uttermost.  Whole
weeks would he be absent, and at length return with only the
skins of the deer and other animals that he had killed, and perhaps
a small supply of food for an interval of rest.  So expert was he
in woodcraft that this course secured him all that his simple mode
of life required.  The cottage that had been his mother's home
continued to be his; and the "forty" on which it stood was called
his farm, though I believe the deer roamed as freely there as any
where else in the forest.  He has shot foxes and raccoons from
his window.  Yet he was accounted rich, for his log house was a
good one and better furnished than most; and he had planted fruit
and made various improvements for his mother's sake, which he
would have been slow in making for his own; and, besides, he was
known for so able and ingenious a "hand" that his services were
much in request, and always commanded the highest price in the
market.  Such is our primitive estimate of the elements of worldly success, that Tom, take him all in all, was considered quite a
speculation in the matrimonial way.

But a roving hunter is no mark for "the blind boy's butt-
shaft."  Our damsels might have saved themselves the trouble
of curling their beau-killers, and slipping off their aprons as he
approached.  He never seemed to see them; but inquired, "Polly, where's your father?" or "Abby, does your mother want
some venison?" without taking off his cap or putting down his
rifle.  The girls had well nigh given him up as a hopeless case
before he announced his intention of travelling to see the world;
and, when this was known, it was guessed by shrewd mothers
that Tom meant to bring home a more "stylish" bride than any
which our humble bounds afforded.

Tom went first to "York State"—that being the natural bent
and limit of our travels—and after having been absent only
about three weeks, he came back to his own house very compo-

sedly during a violent storm, and got ready to go hunting again. Neighbours felt a good deal of curiosity to learn what had sent him back so soon, but he only said the East was not what it was cracked up to be, and went on his old course. Ere long he was missing again, and no one could tell anything of his intentions, or of the probable length of his absence. His nearest neighbour took care of his cow and pigs, for every one liked to do Tom a good turn; and nobody broke his windows or pulled the shingles off his roof to make fishing-lights or quail-traps, because he might come back any day, and would not be likely to " impeticos" such gratuities very kindly. The whole long winter passed, and nothing was seen or heard of Tom Oliver.

During this time, an event of unwonted importance gave a stir to our village—nothing less than the addition of two new families, and those not of a stamp likely to slip unnoticed into so small a community. Widows guided them both, and each boasted a young lady; but if the mistresses might be cited in proof that the genus "vidder" has many varieties, so no less might we quote damsels as specimens of the distinct orders that are observable in young ladyhood.

Mrs. Levering was a thrifty dame, with one grown up son and ever so many little ones, and one only daughter, a lovely girl of seventeen or so, who wrought day and night with the patience of the gentle Griselidis, and seemed to feel that she was but labouring in her vocation. Her mother, a most devout believer in the lawful supremacy of the stronger sex, had brought up Emma to think that she was born to work for " the boys ;" and so potent is habit, that the young girl, fair as she was, and worthy of a softer lot, had never learned to wish it otherwise. A plain house plainly furnished, and a moderate farm moderately stocked, formed the little all of the Leverings; and so completely were their time and attention absorbed by the cares of life, that Emma and her mother did not join the sewing society, nor the young man the hunting parties which alone constituted the winter's gayety. Yet everybody liked Emma, and many a wish was expressed that she would let her rosy cheeks be seen " somewhere else besides in the meetin'-house."

The other lady was a more marked person than any of the

Leverings. Mrs. Purfle, widow of the celebrated Doctor Purfle, who performed so many cures—time and place not specified—of diseases both before and since considered incurable—was somewhat past her prime, indeed had probably for some time been so. Yet she maintained much splendour of appearance; and having flourished as a milliner at the South, she had the advantage of possessing, in the remnants of her professional stores, more unmatched and unmatchable articles of finery than often find their way to this utilitarian West. She had also, as we may suppose, profited by the Doctor's professional researches; since she assured those of the young ladies whom she especially favoured, that washing spoils the complexion, and that her own somewhat shadowy hue was owing to her having discovered this cosmetic secret late in life. Add to all this that Mrs. Purfle is a woman of property, having a clear income of an hundred and fifty dollars per annum, (so says Rumour,) and a marriageable niece who is her decided heiress, and it will readily be imagined that the little green-blinded tenement which shelters Mrs. Purfle and her fair charge, was an object of no small interest in the eyes of the village.

Miss Celestina Pye, (called Teeny by her aunt, except on solemn occasions,) was scarcely taller than Mrs. Purfle's high-backed rocking-chair, but of a most bewitching *embonpoint*. Her complexion was of that kind which reminds one of a fat stewed oyster---white, soft, and unmeaning—probably a monument of the success of her aunt's hydrophobic plan. Her eyes were blue, what there was of them; her cheeks boasted each a spot of pink which looked like hectic; and her mouth was so pursed up that it seemed at first glance as if she must always have been fed with a quill. Yet upon proper inducement Miss Celestina could draw out her lips to a becoming simper, beyond which she never ventured, not having good teeth. She wore the longest bodice and the largest bustle that had ever been seen west of Detroit; and her curls were so innumerable that certain of the ruder beaux compared her to " an owl in an ivy-bush." In short the young lady had been brought up for a belle and a beauty, and both herself and Mrs. Purfle considered the work crowned in the result.

We have among us so few people that "live on their money," that we look up to such with an instinctive reverence. Whether Mrs. Purfle's income had been exaggerated (as many were inclined to suspect,) was a matter of frequent discussion; but all the world joined in paying her the same attention and deference as if its amount had been ascertained beyond a doubt. She was considered as a leader of the *ton* on all occasions, and being naturally of a gay as well as of a sentimental turn, she helped to enliven the village not a little.

One little peculiarity of Mrs. Purfle, only worth telling as it develops the tenderer elements of her character, has not yet been mentioned. Her morning-room—indeed, her only parlour—was fitted up in a style so unique that the visitor was naturally led to inquire as to the cause of Mrs. Purfle's partiality for a colour not usually much in favour with the ladies. To begin with the principal ornament, the lady herself—she sat always in a tall yellow rocking-chair, dressed in a buff gown and a cap trimmed with paradise ribbons. Nankeen slippers graced her feet, and these, by way of contrast, bore a meandering embroidery in straw-coloured worsteds. Her windows were draped with orange moreen; the cover of her work-table was a monument of her housewifely ingenuity, having been dyed with turmeric by her own thrifty fingers. Her pincushion, founded on a brick, and of course of respectable dimensions, was covered with well-saved triangles of yellow flannel, and edged with a tarnished gold lace. Yellow tissue-paper clothed the frames of the numerous coloured engravings which adorned the walls; and a splendid apron of the same hid the fire-place all summer, and was pinned before the book-shelf in winter. Upon Mrs. Purfle and all these golden accompaniments waited a little yellow boy, whom she had brought from the South with her, and whose name she had changed from Belzy to Brimstone, that he might be in keeping with the rest of the furniture.

The widow's preference for the colour of jealousy was not without a reason and a pertinent one, although her deceased lord had been a person of unsuspected constancy during the six months of their married life. There are some sentiments which can give tenderness even to yellow. Doctor Purfle had been settled in the

city of New Orleans and his wife's comfortable house only a single season, when he fell a victim to the prevailing fever. From
this time forward did his faithful relict vow herself to the most
odious of hues. " He was all yaller," she would pensively observe, " and I'll be yaller too !" " And, besides," she had been
known to add, when speaking to a confidential friend, " it came
very handy, for my yaller things hadn't sold as well as I expected."

Having been so happy in her married life, we shall excite no
surprise when we confess that Mrs. Purfle's darling object was to
secure a husband for her niece. Her own individual objects in
life were answered ; she had been married, she had changed her
name, (very advantageously too, for her own used to be Bore—
she always insists that those long tippets the ladies used to wind
round their necks were named after her,) she had kept her property, and also acquired in addition the Doctor's cupping-glasses,
his saddle-bags, and many other useful articles ; and now her sole
care was the fortunate disposal of the fair Celestina. Some years
had passed since the commencement of her efforts, and Miss Pye
did not seem any nearer to the goal than at first ; but Mrs. Purfle
was not discouraged, for she had, as she said, almost given up,
herself, when the Doctor came along, all in a minute like, and she
was married without any trouble at all. Hoping for some such
windfall, she and Miss Teeny persevered, and, meanwhile, amused
themselves as well as they could.

In the interest excited by these two new families—one so busy,
and the other so independent—we had almost forgotten Tom Oliver, when some observant eye espied a smoke issuing from his
chimney as calmly as if no interval had occurred in its owner's
housekeeping ; and the neighbour who peeped in to ascertain
whether there was a mortal and an honest tenant, found Tom
boiling his venison with potatoes, as usual, in a huge pot which
held at least a week's provision, and sent forth a savoury steam.

" Why, Tom ! is that you ?" said neighbour Brumbleback.

" Flesh and blood, and blue veins," was the laconic reply.

" When did you get home ?" pursued the inquirer.

" Just as the east was cracking for daylight."

" Where in the world have you been this time ?"

"In the world! Why, bless your soul! I've been to Saint Peter's."

"You don't! was he to hum?"

Tom looked up and laughed.

"Brumbleback," said he, "there ain't many saints in the army. They call a fort after Saint Peter, away off on the Mississippi river."

"What notion sent you there?"

"I went after my cousin, John Hanford."

"Do tell! was he a goin' to help you any?"

"I don't want any help. I only went to see him. He was at Kalamazoo, and he wrote me it was rather a busy place, and I thought I'd go out there and take a hand with the rest. You know I tried York State a while last summer?"

"Yes," said Brumbleback, "I know you did, and I expected you'd come back so big that a man couldn't touch you with a ten foot pole. But you didn't stay long enough to get uppish. What sent you back so soon? I've always wanted to know."

"Oh! I found it was no place for me. I went to see my uncle in Jefferson County, and he wanted me to stay with him in place of a son he'd lost; but when I came to try the woods, I gave it up at once. You never saw such mean hunting. I might walk all day without a sight. And there's no room to shoot when you do see any thing. I came within one of shooting the prettiest girl I ever laid eyes on. She was out in the woods looking for wintergreens. I never shall forget how she looked. I thought she was dead, but she had only fainted away, and when I saw she was coming to life, I ran like a *painter*.* I would not have met her eyes for the world. I sent some one else to see to her."

"And didn't you see her again?"

"Not I! I thought I had discovered that the East was no place for me, so I just gathered myself together, shook hands with my uncle, and made tracks westward. I wouldn't have taken the old man's stony farm for a gift. I can make five dollars here where I can one there."

"Well! and what took you to Kalamazoo?" said Brumbleback, who had never before found Tom so communicative.

* Panther.

"Why, John Hanford wrote me that they were going to have a bear-hunt out there, and that, besides, there was a good deal to do, so I thought I'd try my luck. When I got there I found a heavy rain had spoiled the bear-hunt, and my cousin had gone to St. Joseph's to keep a boarding-house. I went on to St. Joseph's, and there found that John had changed his mind, and started three days before for Chicago. I had got into the humour of travelling now, so I thought I'd go too and not give up since I'd come so far to see John. So off I went, but would you believe it! John had just started with a party to Rock River to see what was doing there. I was determined not to be distanced, so I gave chase again. At Rock River I missed him just as I had done before. He had had a better offer to go to Galena and work among the lead mines. I felt sure of him now, so I stayed a few days at Rock River to see what I could, and rest myself a little, and then started for Galena. Lo and behold! John was off to Wheat-Diggins, because he wanted to see a place where they never cut their corn, but turned in their hogs to fat themselves according to their own notion. I'd half a mind to give up, but I thought I'd like to see such curious work too, so off I streaked to Wheat-Diggins. Do you believe, John was off before I got there!"

"Well, perhaps; but you warn't fool enough to follow him any further?"

"Wasn't I! By that time I'd got so gritty, I'd have followed him to the Pacific, rather than have given up. He had gone over the prairies with a party of young men, and there was another party just ready to start, so I was glad of the chance to go with them—for I had never seen a real prairie—and a fine hearty set of fellows they were."

"How did you like the prairies?"

"Right well! There were seventy miles of the way without a house, so we camped out. One prairie that we crossed was twenty-six miles long, sometimes level as a floor, and then again rolling. At times we could see neither tree nor bush, but just a great lake like, frozen over and covered with snow—for it began to be cold by that time. There would be timber-patches that looked at first no bigger than your hand, but when you'd come up to 'em, you'd find they covered four or five acres, and sometimes fifty or an hundred. These patches looked exactly like islands. We camped in these for the sake of shelter and fire-wood. After supper we lay down and slept with our feet to the fire ; but we did not dare to sleep long, for fear of getting numb with the cold. So every hour or so we'd get up and wrestle a spell, and then lie down and take another nap. Oh ! we had grand times !"

" But what did you do for money ?"

" I didn't need much, for generally I couldn't get people to take pay for my lodging. They were glad to see any body from the settlements, and they would ask a great many questions ; and by talking round we generally found that I knew somebody they knew, and then they would never take a cent. They would give me a bit of paper with their name and where they lived, to give to their acquaintance when I went back. Once they did that when I did not know the man they asked about, but had only heard him preach. Yet when I reached St. Peter's, two thousand miles from home, I had only two dollars in my pocket. *But I found my cousin !*"

" Shy game, *I* tell ye !" said Brumbleback ; " but how did you get home ?"

" Oh, they were building a saw mill not far from there, and John engaged as a hand, and they offered me twenty dollars a month and my board, if I'd stay too. I did not let them know how low I was in pocket, but kept a stiff upper lip, and made as if I didn't care whether I worked or no. At length I told 'em if they'd give me thirty dollars, I'd stay. So they agreed, and I got enough to pay my passage home, buy a new suit of clothes at Chicago, and leave a nest-egg in my pocket after all."*

When Tom had finished his recital he inquired in his turn as to the course of things at home during their absence. He was duly informed of the accession to our population and many other interesting particulars. Brumbleback's account of the two new belles was not very fascinating. " The chunky one," said he, " is fixed off like a poppy-show, and never lets the draw-strings

---

* If Tom's yarn seems a tough one, I can only say it was taken down from his own lips, and preserved as being characteristic of the habits of the country.

out of her lips. T'other gal is likely enough, but the mother's a blazer! Whoever marries Emmy, had better look out for his ears. The mill-clack is nothing to the old woman's tongue."

Tom stayed at home long enough to clean his rifle and eat his dinner, and then went out hunting to rest himself after his journey. He was passing by a cranberry-marsh about half a mile from the village, when he heard, quite near him, the sound of feminine distress, loud and real. He dashed in among the tangled bushes, and found a young lady sticking in the half-frozen mud. It was Miss Celestina Pye, and she certainly had no drawstrings in her lips just then. Tom observed afterwards, (with less than his usual gallantry,) " that nothing but a pig in a gate ever beat her." He extricated her very ably—a lamentable figure—her dress torn by the inconsiderate briers, and her prim face unshaped by the agony of her terror. She had been searching for those choicest of cranberries which are found still on the bushes after the winter is past. The water in which they chiefly grow is often frozen over, deceptively enough, so that a plunge is not unusual. But Miss Pye's eastern fears of rattlesnakes were still in full force, and as soon as she found herself in the marsh, she jumped to the conclusion that she was bitten to death as a matter of course.

After her rescue occurred the difficulty of presenting such a figure on her walk through the village. Here Tom's natural politeness suggested a short cut, to facilitate which he took down a part of the rail-fence and pointed out to the young lady a path by which she might reach the back of her aunt's domain without betraying her disaster to the public.

During all this, it is not to be supposed that Miss Celestina, though her eyes were small and somewhat obscured by mud, had not managed to perceive that her deliverer was a young man, a stranger, and one whose splendid proportions and fine face would have commanded notice any where. She looked through her torn green veil and her multitudinous curl-papers (for she was cranberrying incog.) at our hero's dark eyes, and found herself very much in love, as was quite natural and proper under the circumstances.

That evening at sunset Tom presented himself at Mrs. Purfle's door with a buck nicely dressed, inquiring whether the lady wished to purchase.

"How much?" asked Mrs. Purfle.

"A dollar," said the hunter.

"That's too much," observed Mrs. Purfle. "It's more than you ought to ask, young man," she said, very solemnly, and with an air of reproof.

The deer weighed some sixty or seventy pounds—perhaps more. Tom moved onward.

"Can you let me have half of it for fifty cents?"

"Never cut," said Tom, who seldom wasted words in such cases.

Just then Miss Pye made her appearance. She was very smart, and her head quivered with subdivided ringlets. When she saw Tom with the venison at his feet, she took it for granted that he had called to inquire after her health, and that the game was an offering to her charms. What wonder that the advancing smile was a gracious one! Or what wonder that the corners of her mouth took a downward curve when Tom flung his buck upon his shoulder and walked off without looking at her!

"Why, aunt!" said Miss Teeny, dolefully, "that's the very one!"

"What one?" said Mrs. Purfle.

"Why the one that helped me out of the marsh! I dare say he came to see me. If I had had my other frock on he would have known me."

Now it was so well understood between Mrs. Purfle and her niece that a *beau* for the latter, (technically speaking,) was the one thing needful, that it was no longer ranked among subjects debateable. There was nothing to be said about it, even by Mrs. Purfle. So she stood and looked after Tom in silence, musing upon the ill-timed thriftiness that had driven so fine a young man from the vicinity of Miss Pye's attractions.

"Teeny!" she said at length, with her eyes still travelling down the street.—"Teeny! it is a long while since you called upon Emma Levering. Get your things, quick! and go down there!"

This speech began *moderato*, but the *crescendo* was so rapid

that the close was *prestissimo*.  Miss Pye, following the direction
of her aunt's eye, saw that Tom had stopped at Mrs. Levering's,
and she lost not a breath in getting her bonnet.

At Mrs. Levering's gate stood Mrs. Levering herself, her cap
border blown back by the chill wind, and her tongue in full activity, enlightening the young hunter's mind as to the true and
proper value of venison " out here in the woods."

" It costs you nothing at all," she said, " but just the powder
and ball it takes to shoot 'em, and that can't be much, for powder's only six shillings a pound, and as for shot, you can put in
old buttons or any thing."

Tom was looking at the speaker with an eye that said as plainly as eye could speak, "Have you almost done ?"   But he waited,
for he was too civil to walk off while a lady was speaking, and it was
difficult to catch a moment when Mrs. Levering was *not* speaking.

Miss Pye, with the first breath she could command, asked for
Emma, and Mrs. Levering called her.   Tom was taking the opportunity to move off, but ere he had shouldered his burthen he
caught sight of a face that charmed him to the spot.   Had he indeed seen it before ?   Miss Teeny, scarce greeting Emma, turned
at once to the handsome hunter, and in her choicest terms thanked
him for his assistance in extricating her from her perilous situation.

Tom could with difficulty be induced to comprehend what she
meant, for it was not easy to recognize in the rainbow-tinted
speaker the muddy heroine of the morning.   And then he seemed
to feel himself in " a scrape," and to be puzzled for a suitable
reply to so much gratitude.

" I thought I never *should* have got out !" said Miss Teeny,
rolling up her little eyes with a pathetic expression of self-pity.

" Oh !" said Tom, " I've got a cow out of there before now."

Tom meant simply that he had done a much more difficult
thing than the helping of a young lady out of the marsh—but the
illustration was not fortunately chosen.   Yet Miss Celestina forbore to notice the error, and only said very graciously that her
aunt would take the venison.

" Venison !" said Emma ; " oh, mother, poor Jack said he
thought he could eat some venison if he could get it."

" He shall have it and welcome," said Tom, throwing the deer saddlewise on the rail of the little porch, and turning away quickly. In vain did the widow and Miss Teeny call after our retreating hero. He barely raised his cap from his brow as he passed, and then, clearing the ground with a hunter's stride, disappeared round the first corner, before the trio had recovered from their astonishment.

"Very odd!" exclaimed Miss Celestina Pye, "when aunt said she would take it."

"Odd, indeed!" responded Mrs. Levering, "when he wouldn't look at anything less than a dollar just now!"

Emma said nothing, but busied herself in preparing some of the venison for her sick brother, with possibly an occasional recollection of the gallant huntsman.

From the period of Tom's return from the expedition to the Mississippi, all his friends remarked a change in his appearance and habits. Not only was his dress more cared for, but his way of living was essentially civilized; and his manner lost that tinge of untameableness which had formerly characterized it. He attended the singing-school regularly, and often escorted home some of the fair ones who brightened these evening gatherings. He never indeed went so far as to volunteer a call, but he would sometimes accept an invitation to a tea party, though he generally amused himself on such occasions by playing with the dog, or with the baby if there was no dog. He was seldom caught looking at a young lady; but if he did look at any one, it was at Miss Celestina Pye. She even thought that she had discovered the costume which best pleased him, for he never looked at her so much as when she was dressed in her buff calico with large purple sprigs. So she used to put on this dress very frequently, with a suitable accompaniment of thready curls and gay ribbons.

Emma Levering all this time, the mere drudge of the most thrifty and exacting of mothers, was in a manner forgotten by all. She was the only pretty girl in the village circle that Tom Oliver never was seen to look at, although he was unceasing in his attentions to her sick brother, whom he supplied with the choicest game the woods afforded. Tom was an odd fellow, and everybody but Miss Pye and Mrs. Purfle thought that he was resolved to be an old bachelor.

About these days, Mrs. Purfle, who was of an active and enterprising turn of mind, and something of a diplomatist withal,
thought proper to give a large party—no unusual expedient to
enhance one's importance, and to make one's acquaintance
coveted.  Everybody was invited and great preparation made,
though there was unfortunately no possibility of enlarging the
small parlour, nor any of the suite of apartments of which that
capped the climax.  But if our good lady had been initiated into
the fashionable notion of a " feed," she could not have provided
more bounteously for those who were to be squeezed within her
walls.  Tom had a note of course; and he was further favoured
with a P. S., asking if he could " as well as not" provide Mrs.
Purfle with game for the occasion.  What he sent would have
made the fortune of a city supper ; and, in addition to this, there
were days' works of cake, and pies, and custards, not to speak of
an unspeakable variety of minor adjuncts.  The very gathering
of the cups and saucers, and plates, and knives, and spoons, was
a serious business.  In the country it is still customary to provide
for as many guests as you invite—another proof that we are
behind the age.

Two o'clock came, and with it a good portion of the company.
Even from the neighbouring settlements whole wagon-loads were
imported, whose bustling Sunday clothes filled Mrs. Purfle's yellow parlour, borrowed chairs and all.  At first the silence was
prodigious; then would be heard an occasional burst of giggle,
quickly smothered ; but gradually rose a continuous hum, which
swelled ere long into an undistinguishable clatter, enlivened ever
and anon by such explosions of laughter as are heard only at the
West.  During all this time Tom Oliver did not make his appearance.  It grew dusk—three candles were lighted on the mantelpiece, in front of a great many black profiles ; the tea (secretly
put back) was at length made—Miss Pye's eyes were anything
but auspicious—when in came Tom, dressed in his Chicago suit,
and looking handsomer than ever.  Oh, how the room brightened
in Miss Celestina's eyes !  It was as if all three of the candles
had been snuffed at once !

Our bashful hero had scarcely time to cast a glance about him
(over the heads of most of the company) when he was called

upon by Mrs. Purfle to lead the way into "the other room," as
the kitchen was modestly denominated. Tom had not ascertained
who was and who was not present, so he gave his hand, at a venture, to Miss Polly Troome, the blacksmith's tall daughter, gal-
lantly handing her to the long tea-table, and seating her opposite
to a promising bowl of apple-sauce. Other ladies were soon
seated, and when every corner of the board (and they were many,
since no two tables in the neighbourhood matched in size or
shape,) was filled, it became the duty of the beaux to play the
part of waiters, which devoir was performed with various grace
by the various youths concerned. A roast pig was to be carved
and a huge chicken-pie distributed; bowls of pickles, and plates
of hot biscuits were to be handed about; and, worse than all, a
ceaseless succession of cups of tea required all the skill and
discretion of the *preux chevaliers*. Some scalding there was, but
not serious; much pretty shrieking, and not a little unrefined
laughter. Miss Pye's new blue silk apron was the recipient of a
saucer of pudding; old Mrs. Spindle made her usual disparaging
remarks about the strength of tea, in an audible whisper; poor
little Brim was trodden upon and tumbled over by everybody
—but upon the whole, the party presented the true party aspect,
saving and excepting some few conventional prejudices as to the
dress of the company and the nature of the refreshments.

But in the midst of the feast a blank occurred—felt more particularly by one of the gay assemblage, yet perceived by numerous others. Tom Oliver was missing. What could this mean?
Was he preparing something characteristically odd, to help along
the general hilarity? This was thought of, but conjectures died
away after a while, for the young hunter appeared no more.
The usual amusements went on; all sorts of forfeits were played
—" scorn" and " criminal," and whatever gives an excuse for
some little romping and kissing, but all was begun and finished
without Tom. This was like a sprinkling of cold water, for Tom
had become a general favourite with the young people.

But it is time to account for our hero. It had been whispered
about that Emma Levering could not come, on account of the illness of her brother, but no one thought of the circumstance in
connection with Tom's disappearance. Yet it was to the busy

widow's that he had gone from the gay assembly, and there, while all was gayety at Mrs. Purfle's grand party, he was already established as a watcher for the night, while the weary family had gone quietly to bed, trusting to his well-known reputation as a nurse. This was the last thing his young companions would have guessed, yet it was the most natural thing in the world for Tom to think of. We hardly think that the fair face of Emma had any share in originating the benevolent impulse—at least there is no testimony to this effect—but we doubt not there was a sympathy for her overtasked condition. Tom was a practical man, and Mrs. Levering's exactions were notorious. If he had but known what pity is akin to, we think he might perhaps have eschewed it; but Tom read no poetry.

This generosity, however, was like much that passes for such —it was at the cost of another. Tom cared nothing about the party, but poor Miss Teeny felt that all her pains had been thrown away, since the handsome hunter had slighted the occasion so cruelly. When she had heard what called him away, she was disposed to be vexed with her unpretending neighbour; but she very soon ascertained that Emma had been sent to bed immediately on Tom's arrival, so that they had scarcely even met. So she was encouraged again, feeling sure that her own attractions must be victorious in fair field. Much did she walk for her health during that rainy spring, and numerous were the errands which took her to Mrs. Brumbleback's, the way to whose house lay directly past Tom's gate. Yet she found the huntsman very hard to encourage. If he was standing by his door when she passed, he was very apt to go in and shut it without waiting to bow to her; and if he happened to be at his well, he would go on drawing water without once turning his head. It was very odd that he should be so bashful.

Tom's well was a model of a well—for a new country we mean. It was curbed at the top with a cut from a hollow button-wood tree, about four feet in diameter on the inside, and perfectly smooth, inside and out. This curb rested on a layer of plank some two feet within the ground, and from this floor downward the well was built of brick in the neatest manner, and the clear water filled it almost to the platform. It was partly roofed over, and provided with a great trough of white wood *au naturel*, well befitting the beauty of the whole structure.*

This was an object of just pride to the owner, for it was the work of his own hands, and he had been the fortunate finder of the tree which had afforded curbs for several wells in the neighbourhood. It was placed near his cottage under the shadow of an elm which chanced to grow just in the right place.

To this well came Tom one afternoon just as the sun was setting, driving a pair of " two-year-olds," and singing very audibly and in no bad taste, " Some love to roam," which he had caught from Mr. Russell's own lips as that " vocalist" passed, like a musical meteor, through our far-away state. He was just executing " A life in the woods for me !" with an attempt at the original cadenza, when he looked over his beautiful well-curb and saw—

Mercy on me—what an exclamation, Tom ! How would that sound at " the East ?"

It was Miss Celestina Pye, standing on the planks, and looking upward with a piteous glance.

" Oh, Mr. Oliver ! I'm so scar't ! I'm almost out of my senses !"

And in her distraction she adjusted her curls, and threw back her green veil.

" What's scar't you this time ?" said Tom, with odious coolness.

" Why, I thought I heard a bull ! I'm sure I thought I did ; and if you only knew how 'fraid I am of a bull ! Aunt says I ought never to walk out alone, I'm so timid !"

" I should think she was right," observed Tom, drily.

" And now," continued Miss Celestina Pye, " how I am to get out of this place—I'm sure I don't know."

" How did you get in ?"

" Oh ! I was so frightened, you see, that I climbed over that low place by the trough. I'm afraid you'll have to lift me out ! I feel so very weak."

" Wait a moment," said Tom ; and Miss Pye waited a good

* A well precisely similar to Tom's may be seen near the door of an inn, some twelve miles west of Detroit, on the Grand River road.

many moments, expecting the return of her squire. By and bye, when she had begun to find the well rather chilly, she heard a footstep.

"Oh! here you are at last," said she.

"Yes, here I be!" answered Brumbleback's gruff voice, "and here's my ox-chain for you to climb up by," and he lowered the ox-chain, looped, having the ends fastened outside. "There! you can climb up by that, easy enough!" observed this squire of dames; "you needn't be afeared, for it would bear five ton."

"But where's Mr. Oliver?" asked the doleful Celestina.

"He's off! he thought he heard something in the wheat field, and he told me to help you out."

Miss Pye's walk homeward was not a pleasant one; she was a little damp and dreadfully crestfallen; but Mrs. Purfle assured her that she was certain Tom "felt so" he could not venture to take her out, for fear of letting her down the well.

The oil of her aunt's flattery served once more to trim the lamp of hope in Miss Teeny's heart; aunt had gone through it all, and surely she ought to know. So Miss Pye refreshed her array, and sat down to her knitting, Mrs. Purfle thinking it probable, "considering all things," that Tom would call.

Miss Teeny had picked up the lamp-wick with a pin several times, and begun to yawn pretty frequently, when she heard Tom's ringing laugh as he passed the window. He *was* coming, after all!

Alas! he had only been to carry a brace of prairie-hens to Jack Levering. Miss Celestina Pye put her curls in twenty-two papers, and then went desperately to bed.

With the morning light, however, came a ray of mental illumination. That song! the gallant hunter was fond of music! Miss Teeny had something called a piano, which, though lacking several important strings, still was capable of an atrocious noise which passed with some for music. This had never yet been brought to bear upon Tom; but the summer was coming and such a resource must no longer be neglected. Among the poetical scraps in Miss Pye's album was the following—

Music hath charms to soothe the savage *beast*—

How much more then one who only hunted such animals!  So
the tinkling torment was put in requisition, and Mons Meg herself could scarcely have been more noisy.  "Oh! come with
me!"  "Meet me by moonlight!"  "Leave me not!" were the
pathetic adjurations which now arrested the attention of the pass-
ers-by; but, as ill-luck would have it, just about that time Tom
got a habit of going to town by the back street.  However, the
weather had now become pleasant, and Mrs. Purfle happening to
be in the garden at the time he usually passed, politely invited
him in, saying that Celestina had been tuning up the piano quite
nice.  Tom could not refuse, and once in, he underwent the
whole without flinching.  Miss Pye's voice was not exactly a
*contralto*, indeed it was puzzling to determine the class; since
what there was of it was so strained and filtered through a very
small mouth, and a most miserably pinched nose, that it resembled
the chirping of a mouse in a cheese.  But the accompaniment
was loud enough to make up for that.  This was extemporaneous
entirely, but when she confined her bass to the key-note, she made
out pretty well for uninstructed ears.  It was only when she became enthusiastic and branched out into involuntary chromatics,
that it grew absolutely unendurable.  This pass had been nearly
attained when Tom asked for "Fare thee well!"  This not being on Miss Teeny's list, he was about taking his leave when she
volunteered "Faithless Emma."  Tom sat down again, heard
the song through, asked a repetition, and then seized his cap resolutely.

"Are you going to singing-school to night?  *I* am," said Miss
Teeny, all in a breath.

"I don't know whether I shall or no," said stony-hearted Tom,
and he bolted rather unceremoniously.

"Well, I declare!" said Mrs. Purfle, "that fellow is the hard-
est to manage!"

The fact is, that the tactics of Mrs. Purfle and Miss Pye ought
to have brought Tom down long before; but he was like Wel-
lington at Waterloo, and did not know when he was beaten.  He
must have borne a charmed life, to walk unharmed within point-
blank range of such formidable artillery; but we are unable to
furnish our readers with the recipe.  Gay's sweet ballad says,

" *Love* turns the balls that round me fly,
 Lest precious tears should fall from Susan's eye."

But Tom had as yet paid Love no homage, and we well know that wicked power does nothing for nothing. Our conjectures as to Tom's safeguard point indeed toward that bewitching face which his rifle had so nearly marred, but would a roving hunter remember one look so long?

But Miss Pye's ammunition was not yet exhausted. The very next Sunday saw her, laced almost to extinction, on her way to meeting, arrayed in her most seducing paraphernalia, her face white and her hands shining purple through their lace gloves, from the energy with which she had striven to be delicate. She had seen a belle faint in public at " the East;" she had observed the solicitude of her attendant knight; and she did not know why such things might not be done by some people as well as others. So she took her seat on the women's side of the narrow passage which divides the two rows of benches in our school-room, determined to find the vulnerable part in Tom's heart, if indeed there was one—which she began to doubt.

This mode of parting the rougher from the gentler sex in public, prevails wherever seats are common property—the why is not so easy to determine. If designed to prevent stray thoughts, it is quite a mistake, for by this arrangement eyes are left at full liberty, nay, are placed under a sort of necessity for encountering. If to secure attention to the speaker, it is still more unfortunate, for the deadly cross-fire from the sides is far more effective than the scattering fire from the platform. But it suited Miss Teeny's purpose, for it brought her face to face with her indomitable enemy.

She had done her work so effectually at home that there was little to be done in meeting. The fainting had very nearly come off in earnest, and her face began to look deadly blue very soon after the commencement of the sermon. At length she fell back on the desk before which she was sitting.

All was now confusion and dismay, for we are not accustomed to such things. Mrs. Purfle bustled about, and called upon Mr. Oliver to help her take her niece in the open air. But the minister,

with a solemn air of reproof, just then requested the congregation
to sit down, adding, in an authoritative and awful manner,

"Deacon Grinderson! will you help that young woman out?"

So poor Teeny was carried out, not very gracefully, by Deacon
Grinderson and a young clodpole whom he summoned to his aid;
and it required but very little water dashed in her face to bring
her to her senses, and particularly to the sense that it was "no
go," as Tom would have said if he had understood the affair.

"Now cut her binder, and she'll do," said Deacon Grinderson's
assistant, borrowing a figure from the wheat field, as was quite
natural, seeing that Miss Teeny's contour, exclusive of the sup-
plementary bustle, was not unlike that of a stout sheaf. But
there was very little spirit in her just now.

We know not that Miss Teeny could ever have been inspired,
even by the powerful afflatus of her aunt's flattery, to make
another attempt at so inaccessible a heart; but, ere long, fate
threw in her way an opportunity which skill could scarcely have
commanded. She had succeeded in reducing herself by sighing,
pickles, and silk braid, to something nearer a sentimental outline,
when our part of the country was enlightened by a visit from a
nephew of Dr. Purfle's, whom his lady had known at the South
—a decided genius, and one of the universal kind. This individual had had the misfortune to lose both his feet by exposure at
the North, and he would have been at his wits' end for a living
if those wits had been only as comprehensive as the wits of common people. But he managed to live very much at his ease,
having a man to wait on him and supply the only deficiency of
which he had ever been conscious. Mr. Ashdod Cockles came
among us in the character of an artist, having his wagon loaded
with wax-figures, puppets, magic-lanterns, and all those temptations which the pockets of western people, lank as they are,
always find irresistible—including a hand-organ of course; and
he put up at Mrs. Purfle's.

Most exhilarating were the preparations, which now filled everybody's mouth. The village ball-room was to be the scene of
the grand exhibition of Mr. Cockles' glory; and the stairs which
led to that honoured chamber were well worn during that day of
ceaseless bustle and excitement. Not that the common eye was

permitted to get even a glimpse of the mysteries within, for a thick curtain was suspended inside, so that the assistants could pass in and out a hundred times without one's getting a single peep. But the boys and idlers still thought they *should* see something; so there they stayed from morning till night—scarcely taking time to eat.

But while all promised so fair for the multitude, what was the surprise and grief of Mr. Ashdod Cockles to find that one of his wax figures, nay, the one of all others that he could worst spare, had been completely crushed by the superincumbent weight of the hand-organ. The Sleeping Beauty! That *she* should have been lost! What is a wax-work without a Sleeping Beauty! Dire was the disappointment of Mr. Cockles, and loud his lamentations, (in private,) and much did he try to make his factotum acknowledge that he had erred in the packing. Nick knew his business too well for that; but he nevertheless condescended to suggest a remedy—viz.: that Mr. Cockles should induce some pretty girl of the village to be dressed in the glittering drapery of the crushed nymph, and perform the part for that night only. This seemed the more feasible that the figure was to be covered up in bed, and the performance would thus involve no fatigue. So it only remained to obtain the handsome face, and touching this delicate point Mr. Cockles consulted Mrs. Purfle.

"Miss Emmy's the prettiest!" said Brim, who stood by grinning from ear to ear.

"Get out, Brim!" said Mrs. Purfle, accompanying the hint with a resounding box on the ear; "get out! you're a fool!"

Then turning to the artist with a bland smile, she communicated to him in a whisper her belief that Celestina would undertake the part, if she was properly requested.

"Ahem!" said Mr. Ashdod Cockles, who was troubled with a cold; "ahem! yes, ma'am—but it would be asking quite too much of your niece. I think we had better—"

"Not at all, not at all!" insisted the lady; "Teeny is so obliging she'll not think anything of it. I'll ask her at once."

"But," persisted Mr. Cockles, fidgeting a good deal, "she is really quite too short for the character. A taller figure—"

"Oh! you forget she is to be conveyed under the quilt! I'll manage all that," said the zealous diplomatist, "I'll dress her, and everything."

And she left the room and returned in a very short time with Miss Pye's unhesitating consent. So Mr. Cockles could not but be very much obliged; and Mrs. Purfle, in the highest spirits, sent Brim off at once to Mr. Oliver's, to tell him he must be sure to come to the exhibition. "And Brim," she added, "if you tell him a word about you know what, I'll skin ye!" A favourite figure of speech of Mrs. Purfle's.

"What exhibition?" said Tom, who had but just returned from the woods.

"Oh, every thing in the world!" said Brim, who was as much excited as any body; "and Miss Teeny—" but here he thought of his skin, and no persuasions of Tom could extort another word on that point, though he was fluent on the main subject.

The evening came at last, and the weather chanced to be pleasanter than it generally is on great occasions. The ball-room was elegantly fitted up with suspended crosses of wood stuck with tallow candles,—rather drippy, but you must keep out of their way,—(I have seen gentlemen's coats completely iced with sper-maceti, which, if more genteel, is also more destructive.) Instead of glass cases, a screen or medium of dark-coloured gauze was interposed between the eye and the wax figures, in order to pro-duce the requisite illusion. The puppets and the magic-lantern came first in order, and so great was the delight of the spectators that it would seem that any after-show must have been an anti-climax; but the experienced Mr. Cockles knew better. It was not until all this was done, that he ordered Nick to draw aside the baize which had veiled the grand attraction. Great clapping and rapping ensued, and it was some time before Mr. Cockles could venture to begin, this being a part of the exhibition in which he expected to shine personally.

"This, ladies and gentlemen," he began, at the upper end of the room, "this is the New Orleans beauty; she was engaged to be married to two gentlemen at once, and to avoid the torments of jealousy, they settled it between 'em, and first shot her and then each other through the heart! and they're all buried in one tomb; and I should have had the tomb too, only it was rather heavy to carry."

Every body crowded to this interesting sight.

"This," continued the exhibiter, in a high-toned and theatrical voice, waving at the same time a gilded wand, which excited much admiration, "is the celebrated Miss M'Crea and her murderers, from likenesses taken on the spot by an eye-witness."

A shudder ran through the throng at this announcement, and the grinning Indians were closely scrutinized, and the fierceness and many evil qualities of their race commented on in an under tone.

"Here is a revolutionary character, ladies and gentlemen," Mr. Cockles went on, as his familiar edged him along on his wheel-chair; and he pointed to a stumpy old man in a blue coat faced with red, who brandished a wooden sword as high as the ceiling would allow.

"This was one of my forefathers," observed the orator, with no little swell; "my great-great-grandfather, or some such relation. He was a man by the name of Horatio Cockles, that cut away the bridge at Rome just as the British was coming across it. You've all heard of Rome, I suppose?"

A murmur of assent went round; and one man observed, "I was born and brought up within five *mile* of it, but I never heard tell o' that 'ere feller!"

"Ay, yes! maybe not," said Mr. Cockles, quite undisturbed, "but do you understand history?"

The objector was posed, and the orator proceeded.

"This is Lay Fyett, and this is Bonypart, with a man's head that he has just cut off with his sword. He used to do that whenever he got mad."

A shudder, with various exclamations.

"But here," said Mr. Cockles, drawing aside with a flourishing air, a mysterious-looking curtain, which had excited a good deal of curiosity during the evening, "this here is the Sleeping Beauty. Her infant daughter got broke a-coming."

And there lay a female figure, in whose well-rouged cheeks and dyed ringlets no one recognized the heiress of Mrs. Purfle's

worldly substance. Even the eyebrows, which nature had left
white, were entirely altered by the experienced skill of the artist,
who had felt himself at liberty to put them on where he thought
they would look best, the original ones being invisible by candle-
light. A very elegant cap, full trimmed with artificial flowers,
had been arranged by Mrs. Purfle; and the sky-blue pillow
fringed with gold, and the purple quilt which belonged to the
character, made altogether a very magnificent affair, though Mr.
Ashdod Cockles had not thought it prudent to suspend more than
a single candle within the chintz curtains and the gauze blind.

Just as the concealing screen had been withdrawn, and while
a buzz of admiration was still in circulation, Tom Oliver, who
had been in no haste to obey Mrs. Purfle's hint, made his way
into the room. He took a momentary glance at the attractions
which lined the walls, and then sought the object which now fixed
the eager crowd. It took a good look to satisfy him; but with
the help of Brim's hint and certain potent recollections, the truth
came upon him at once; and with a very audible " pshaw !" he
turned on his heel and made for the door. The string by which
the Sleeping Beauty's candle was suspended passing along near
the ceiling, caught Tom's cap in his hasty retreat, and ruin ensued. In an instant Miss Teeny's gay head-dress was all in a
blaze, and one whole side of her curls was burnt off before the
cruel flames could be smothered. Tom was among the most active in endeavouring to repair the mischief he had done, and then,
much mortified, darted out of the room. As his evil stars must
have decreed, he met Emma Levering at the top of the stairs,
and if ours were of the fashionable single-flight order, broken
bones would have certainly ensued. But most fortunately there
was a saving platform, which received Tom and his victim, in
time to prevent so serious a catastrophe. As it was, however,
the pretty Emma was a good deal hurt, and to Tom's eager questions she could only answer with a burst of tears. So Tom, without ceremony, caught her up in his arms, and ran with her to her
mother's, which was not far distant; and then, after more apologies than he ever made before in the whole course of his life,
he took his leave, and hid his head beneath his own roof.

Before Emma's bruises got well, it was all over with Tom.

The barriers about his heart seemed to have been fractured by
the fall ; and Cupid is not slow in making the most of such advantages.   Tom Oliver forgot to hunt, but occupied his time instead, in building an addition to his house, and putting a new fence
about his door-yard.   What arguments he may have found necessary to overcome Emma's resentment against him, we are not
informed ; but we are assured that it was not until he was obliged
to own she had wounded his heart that he mustered courage to
tell her that he came very near being beforehand with her, away
off in Jefferson County.   The fact of their betrothment became
known in due time by the lamentations of Mrs. Levering, who
thought it very unkind in Emma to be willing to leave her for
any body else.   Few of the neighbours could conscientiously
agree with her in this view of Emma's choice.   Most people
thought it very natural ; and Emma succeeded in reconciling her
mother to the change by the suggestion that Tom could fill the
place which Jack's ill-health prevented him from taking.

Miss Pye's ringlets were a long time growing, during which
interval she remained much at home, in rather low spirits.   Emma is benevolently waiting until the fair Celestina is presentable,
in order that she may stand bridesmaid, at her own urgent request.   Mrs. Purfle is understood to have been so much discouraged by the ill success of her efforts in behalf of her niece,
that she declares it her fixed determination to let her take her
chance in future.   This resolve, if adhered to, gives hopes that
history may yet record a happy termination of all Miss Pye's
anxieties ; since, whether in town or country, no labour is more
apt to defeat itself than that which has for its object the acquisi-
tion of the grand desideratum—a husband.

# OLD THOUGHTS ON THE NEW YEAR.

" Il mondo invecchia
  E invecchiando intristisce."

TASSO'S " AMINTA."

The world is growing older
  And wiser day by day:
Every body knows beforehand
  What you're going to say !
We used to laugh and frolic ;
  Now we must behave !
Poor old Fun is dead and buried—
  Pride dug his grave.

FREE TRANSLATION.

THERE are doubtless many new things to be said about the
New Year, if one had wit enough to think of them ; but an' if
it be not so, may we not think over our last year's thoughts, or
those which pleased us ten years ago ?   It is certain that Providence sends us this holiday season, with all its stirring influences,
once every year ; and doubtless intends it should be enjoyed by
thousands who never had an original thought in their lives.   So
we will write down our roving fancies as they rise, and leave
them to be woven into the fire-light reveries of just such comfortable people.

   " What does 'holiday' mean, George ?" said we once to a
shouting urchin of some seven years standing, as he was tossing
up his cap and huzzaing at the thought of a vacation.   " What
does ' holiday' mean ?"

   He stopped, looked serious, and then replied

   " Why—I don't know—but—I always thought it was because
the boys holla so when they are let out of school."

   We predicted on the spot that George would write a dictionary if he lived long enough.   A decidedly etymological genius, and quite original ; for he owed but little to books, to our certain knowledge.

We cannot hope to make as lucky a guess on the origin of the New Year festival ; but we will venture to say, nothing could be more natural than the disposition to observe this way-mark on life's swift-rolling course.   In proof of this, the practice of noticing anniversaries has prevailed from the earliest times.   It is only in these wondrously wise days, that the notion has arisen that it is being too minute and vulgar to recognize occasions so revered by our fathers :

> " We take no note of time save by its loss,"

in another sense than that of the poet.   We are disposed to " cut " holidays, as we do other antiquated worthies.   Then again the young and gay, in the levity of their hearts, think it tedious to mingle with their joyance any touch of old-time remembrances. We admit that the New Year, though a season for placid and hopeful smiles, is scarcely one for laughter ; yet we might (under privilege of our gravity,) inquire whether an element of sobriety may not sometimes be profitable, even in our pleasure.   The bereaved and sorrowful tell us that the habit of commemorating particular days only makes more striking the chill blanks in the social circle ; pointing out the vacant chair ; recalling the missing voice, already but too keenly remembered.   This is true ; but while sorrow is yet new and fresh, what is there that does *not* bring up the beloved ?   And after the great Consoler has done his blessed office, and grief is mellowed into sadness, do we not attach a double value to whatever awakens most vividly the cherished memory ?

Gifts and keepsakes and little surprises used to be a pretty part of the holiday season ; and in Europe the New Year is still the time of all others for *cadeaux,* and *souvenirs,* and *gages d'amitié,* and *gages d'amour.*   But the increase of luxury and the cultivation of pride have almost spoiled all these pleasant things for us. I fear we have leavened such matters with the commercial spirit. Presents are made a sort of traffic, or a device of ostentation. When emulation begins, sentiment is lost.   The moment we ad-

mit the idea that our generosity or our splendour will attract admiration ; the moment we think that our friend, if poor, will receive our new-year gift as payment for some past kindness, or, if
rich, that he will be sure to give something still more elegant in
return, the present is degraded into an article of merchandise.
Indeed, costliness is no proper element of a mere present, since a
symbol is all we want.

In England the celebration of New Year is almost lost in that
of Christmas, which is a high and universal festival ; whether
kept exactly in accordance with its true meaning and intent we
shall not here stop to inquire. Be this as it may, its approach
arouses " the fast-anchor'd isle" to its very heart. Even thread-
bare court-gaiety receives an accession of something like sentient
life ; and maids of honour new furbish their languid smiles, and
gentlemen-in-waiting pocket their scented 'kerchiefs, no longer
needed to veil inadmissible yawns. If high life brighten, how
much more the common folk, always so wisely ready to be
pleased ! The housekeeper spends her evenings for six weeks
stoning " plums" in preparation for prelatic mince-pies and national puddings. Huge sirloins of beef jostle at the corners of the
streets. The confectioner gives an additional touch of enchant-
ment to his sparkling paradise, which needed not this to make it
irresistible to the longing eyes that linger round it, unconsciously
endowing each individual temptation with the dazzling beauty
of the whole, and so really coveting all, though wishing only for
a modest portion. Christmas taxes all the invention of all the
artists in Pleasure's train for the production of novelties and ex-
cellences in their several departments, and as there is not time
for a renewal of energy before New Year, they blend the two
occasions, and rejoice double tides. Even the poet, though not
always in the way when money is to be made, finds his services
now in request, and enjoys the farther delight of hearing his darling verses chanted by the far-sounding throat of the street-singer :
true fame this, and not posthumous, like that of most poets.
Verses like those which follow, married to airs well deserving
such union, awaken the Queen's subjects earlier than they like
on Christmas morning :

" The moon shines bright
And the stars give a light
A little before 'tis day,
And bid us awake and pray.
Awake ! awake ! good people all !
Awake and you shall hear  .  .  .

The life of Man
Is but a span,
    And cut down in his flower.
We're here to-day and gone to-morrow ;
    We're all dead in an hour.

" O teach well your children, men,
    The while that you are here ;
It will be better for your souls
    When your corpse lie on the bier.

" To-day you may be alive, dear man,
    With many a thousand pound ;
To-morrow you may be dead, dear man,
    And your corpse laid under ground ;
With a turf at your head, dear man,
    And another at your feet ;
Your good deeds and your bad ones
    They will together meet.
God bless the ruler of this house
    And send him long to reign ;
And many a happy Christmas
    May he live to see again.

" My song is done, I must be gone ;
    I can stay no longer here ;
God bless you all, both great and small,
    And send you a jovial New Year."

So runs a " Christmas carol," entitled " Divine Mirth," bought
in the streets of London not many years ago.   But we are like
our transatlantic neighbours—letting Christmas swallow up New
Year.   To return from these " specimens of English poetry."

We KNICKERBOCKERS date our New-Year festivities from our
honoured Dutch progenitors ; and it should be considered treason
even to propose the discontinuance of such time-honoured com-
memorations.   Among the innovations of the day, few try our
patience more severely than those pseudo-refinements upon plea-

sure, which have been devised by the little great and the meanly
proud of our land, who in their agonizing efforts after a superiority
to which neither nature nor education has given them a claim,
hesitate not to sacrifice much for which they will never offer an
equivalent to society.   An adherence to ancient usages belongs
to those who are accustomed to the enjoyments of wealth, and
covet the heightening power of association; who feel their position to be secure, and therefore enjoy it with dignity, and make
no feverish efforts at display.   These still keep up the social
round on the first day of the year, with its cordial greeting, its
hospitable welcome, and its whole-souled *abandon*, symbolical at
least of a forgetting of all causes of feud, and a renewing of ancient good-will, however interrupted.   There is a primitive relish
about these things to those who understand them; but to the
merely fashionable, who think only of the quantity of plate which
it is possible to exhibit on the occasion, the splendour and costliness of the refreshments, and above all, the number of *stylish*
names which may be enrolled among the hundreds of unmeaning
visiters, it is *caviare* indeed.   Their spirit is a profane one; it
fancies that money will buy every thing.

We would not insist upon the full adherence to primitive customs; since that would include rather more stimulus than accords
with our notions of propriety; and we have heard too that the
KNICKERBOCKER practice of presenting each guest with a shield-
like " cookie," though an excellent one for the bakers, was wont to
prove rather inconvenient to some thorough-going visiters, who
were in danger of meeting with the fate of the damsel of old,
who was crushed under the weight of gifts somewhat similar.
Tradition informs us that the Dutch Dominies, who were especial
favourites, used to be obliged to leave whole pyramids of splendid
cookies—suns, moons, General Washington, Santa-Claus, and all
—at the houses of tried friends, to be sent for next morning.   We
would not ask so minute an observance of the customs of Nieuw-
Amsterdam, but we plead for the main point, the festival, with
the hearty, social feeling that gives value to it.   This may be
unfashionable in some quarters, but it is human, and gives occasion for one of the too few recognitions of a common nature and
a common interest.   But, strange power of fancy ! here we are

carried back to all the bustle and excitement of a New-Year's
day in the city. What a contrast to the realities around us!
This bright, soft-singing wood fire, crackling occasionally with
that mysterious sound which the good vrouws call "treading
snow," and which they hold to foretell sleighing; the cat coiled
up cozily on the hearth-rug, fast asleep; even the sounds which
but just reach the ear when the ground is dry and bare, now
hushed by the thick covering of snow out of doors; now and
then a low, black sled moving silently along the road ; and still
more seldom a solitary foot-passenger, with his rifle or his axe
on his shoulder; how can we imagine to ourselves the thronging
crowds that make the very stones resound under the thousand vehicles and quick trampling feet in the great thoroughfares ? Not
Imagination but Memory lends her aid in this instance; Memory,
never more faithful than when she recalls to the emigrant the
home-scenes of former days. Yet we ought hardly to call her
faithful, for she always reverses rules in her pictures, placing her
brightest tints in the back-ground. Brilliant lights, with only
shadow enough to bring them out, characterize her distant views,
and this is no true perspective, though we are prone to put faith
in it. We must not use such views for *studies*.

Far removed from all the pleasurable associations of this period,
we too hail the New Year, but not with the old feeling. We wish
each other a "happy new year" as usual, but there is a touch
of sadness in our greeting. Our new homes have not yet the
warmth of the old; there is a chill hanging about them still,
especially at these seasons when we recall the warm grasp of
early friends. The young only are thoroughly gay here. They
dwell not on the past ; they trouble not their heads about the
future. They have an ever-welling fount of happiness within ;
while we, their elders, are compelled to dig deep, and sometimes
even then strike no vein. To them, sport in the wilds is as good
as sport any where else. They skate, they slide, they run races ;
they take the hill-side with their rough, home-made sleds, and
they ask nothing better. This for the younger scions. Those a
step more advanced, get up shooting-matches, or dancing-matches ;
pleasure on a more dignified scale. We will not describe that
vile form of the shooting-match, wherein a poor turkey is tied to

a post, to be mangled in cold blood by the boobies of the neighbourhood ; those who never fired a shot in their lives taking the lead ; as
when a number of lawyers are to speak on the same side, those
who are not expected to hit at all are placed first. This is a cruel,
unmanly, un-western sport, and should be scorned by the forester.
He has been driven to it by the unnatural lack of all decent and
proper amusement. The true shooting-match, when conducted
on the large scale, affords famous sport. Two parties, matched
and balanced as nearly as may be in skill and numbers, and each
commanded by a leader chosen on account of his general qualifications, social as well as sporting, set out at break of day, in
different directions ; it makes but little difference which way,
since game is plenty at all points. A time and place of rendezvous are appointed, and certain kinds of game prescribed as
within the rules ; and each party, collectively or severally, as
circumstances may require, makes as wide a search as time will
allow, and brings down as many deer, partridges, quails, etc., as
possible ; horses being in attendance to bear home the fortune of
the day. At the place appointed the whole is examined, counted
and judged, according to the rules and rates agreed on, and
umpires then award the palm of victory. "To the victors belong
the spoils" of course ; so the vanquished furnish the evening's
entertainment, except that the game is common property. This
makes no contemptible New Year's day for the young men ; and
choice game is not despised as the substantial part of the supper.
which succeeds or rather divides what we mentioned awhile ago
—a dancing-match.

This, we should think, must be more laborious even than the
shooting-match ; at least it is more like steady, serious, unremit-
ting work. Two in the afternoon is not too soon to begin, nor six
in the morning too late to finish. Now if this be not a trial of
strength, what is ? It proves so ; for only the most resolute hold
out through the whole time. Even they would doubtless flag
were it not for the supper at which we have hinted above, of
which (to their honour be it spoken) our rustic damsels are not
too affected to be willing to partake with good will and without
mincing. They dance " the old year out and the new year in,"
sometimes ; but usually the ball closes the sports of New-Year's

day, and you may see them as the sun is rising on the second day of the year, sleigh-load after sleigh-load, going home as merry as larks, under the care of their stout beaux, not half so tired as a city belle is after walking through a cotillon.

Sometimes the snow is so fine that a grand sleigh-ride takes the place of the grand hunt on this day. As many as possible are engaged, and they go off some fifteen or twenty or thirty miles, with as many strings of bells as can be raised for the occasion, and have an impromptu supper and dance, and return home by moonlight. One indispensable condition of such a party is an exact pairing—an Adam and Eve division of the company; so that if a single nymph or swain be missing before the day arrives, and no one is found to supply the vacancy, the counterpart shares the misfortune, and remains at home. We have known companies where an approach to this rule—a belle to every beau—would have been convenient, and saved some sour looks. Here it is all in good faith, and the appropriation very strict, for the time being; and particular attention or graciousness to more than one of the party is contrary to etiquette. The pairs speak of each other as "my mate," with all the gravity imaginable.

After all, these are the people who taste the true sweets of pleasure, strictly so called. They enjoy themselves freely and heartily, caring nothing for what those very dignified and rather dull people who call themselves "the world" may think of their dress or their dancing. It would not give them a moment's concern to be told that people a hundred miles off thought them half savages. And nothing would be so odious to them as the ceremony, the constraint, the clatter, and the stupidity of many an unmeaning fashionable party. They would hardly believe you if you should tell them that people really do get together at great cost and trouble to look at each other's dresses and a decorated supper-table, and go home again. "What! no music! no dancing! no nothing! Awful! I'd ruther spin wool all day!"

To those of us who have done with all these things; whose "dancing days are over," and who are studying the difficult art of "growing old gracefully," the coming of another year brings reflection, if not sadness. "What shadows we are, and what shadows we pursue!" Who can stand upon the verge of another

era, without emotion ?    Who does not feel, as this change passes
before him, something of the awe that thrilled the veins of him who
saw "an image" but "could not discern the form thereof?"
How little can we guess of this turning leaf in our destiny !    If
the heart be light, we read on the dim scroll words of soft and
sweet promise, traced by the ready fingers of Hope.    If there be
a cloud on the spirit, we can discern only characters gloomy as
any that remain of memory's writing ; while perhaps that Eye
from which nothing is hidden, sees Death sweeping with his dark
wing all that fond imagination had presented to our view, leaving
our part in this life's future, one chill blank.    Blessed be God that
our eyes are "holden !"    To HIM who has controlled the past in
love and mercy, we may safely commit the future.

# THE SCHOOLMASTER'S PROGRESS.

MASTER WILLIAM HORNER came to our village to keep school when he was about eighteen years old : tall, lank, straight-sided, and straight-haired, with a mouth of the most puckered and solemn kind.   His figure and movements were those of a puppet cut out of shingle and jerked by a string ; and his address corresponded very well with his appearance.   Never did that prim mouth give way before a laugh.   A faint and misty smile was the widest departure from its propriety, and this unaccustomed disturbance made wrinkles in the flat skinny cheeks like those in the surface of a lake, after the intrusion of a stone.   Master Horner knew well what belonged to the pedagogical character, and that facial solemnity stood high on the list of indispensable qualifications.   He had made up his mind before he left his father's house how he would look during the term.   He had not planned any smiles, (knowing that he must " board round"), and it was not for ordinary occurrences to alter his arrangements ; so that when he was betrayed into a relaxation of the muscles, it was " in such a sort" as if he was putting his bread and butter in jeopardy.

Truly he had a grave time that first winter.   The rod of power was new to him, and he felt it his "duty" to use it more frequently than might have been thought necessary by those upon whose sense the privilege had palled.   Tears and sulky faces, and impotent fists doubled fiercely when his back was turned, were the rewards of his conscientiousness ; and the boys—and girls too—were glad when working time came round again, and the master went home to help his father on the farm.

But with the autumn came Master Horner again, dropping among us as quietly as the faded leaves, and awakening at least

as much serious reflection.   Would he be as self-sacrificing as
before, postponing his own ease and comfort to the public good ?
or would he have become more sedentary, and less fond of cir-
cumambulating the school-room with a switch over his shoulder?
Many were fain to hope he might have learned to smoke during
the summer, an accomplishment which would probably have
moderated his energy not a little, and disposed him rather to
reverie than to action.   But here he was, and all the broader-
chested and stouter-armed for his labours in the harvest-field.

Let it not be supposed that Master Horner was of a cruel and
ogrish nature—a babe-eater—a Herod—one who delighted in
torturing the helpless.   Such souls there may be, among those
endowed with the awful control of the ferule, but they are rare
in the fresh and natural regions we describe.   It is, we believe,
where young gentlemen are to be crammed for college, that the
process of hardening heart and skin together goes on most vigor-
ously.   Yet among the uneducated there is so high a respect for
bodily strength, that it is necessary for the schoolmaster to show,
first of all, that he possesses this inamissible requisite for his place.
The rest is more readily taken for granted.   Brains he *may* have
—a strong arm he *must* have : so he proves the more important
claim first.   We must therefore make all due allowance for Master Horner, who could not be expected to overtop his position so
far as to discern at once the philosophy of teaching.

He was sadly brow-beaten during his first term of service by
a great broad-shouldered lout of some eighteen years or so, who
thought he needed a little more " schooling," but at the same
time felt quite competent to direct the manner and measure of his
attempts.

" You'd ought to begin with large-hand, Joshuay," said Master
Horner to this youth.

" What should I want coarse-hand for ?" said the disciple, with
great contempt ; " coarse-hand won't never do me no good.   I
want a fine-hand copy."

The master looked at the infant giant, and did as he wished,
but we say not with what secret resolutions.

At another time, Master Horner, having had a hint from some
one more knowing than himself, proposed to his elder scholars to

write after dictation, expatiating at the same time quite floridly,
(the ideas having been supplied by the knowing friend,) upon the
advantages likely to arise from this practice, and saying, among
other things,

"It will help you, when you write letters, to spell the words
good."

"Pooh!" said Joshua, "spellin' ain't nothin'; let them that
finds the mistakes correct 'em. I'm for every one's havin' a
way of their own."*

"How dared you be so saucy to the master?" asked one of
the little boys, after school.

"Because I could lick him, easy," said the hopeful Joshua,
who knew very well why the master did not undertake him on
the spot.

Can we wonder that Master Horner determined to make his
empire good as far as it went?

A new examination was required on the entrance into a second
term, and, with whatever secret trepidation, the master was obliged
to submit. Our law prescribes examinations, but forgets to provide for the competency of the examiners; so that few better
farces offer, than the course of question and answer on these occasions. We know not precisely what were Master Horner's
trials; but we have heard of a sharp dispute between the inspectors whether a n g e l spelt *angle* or *angel*. *Angle* had it, and
the school maintained that pronunciation ever after. Master
Horner passed, and he was requested to draw up the certificate
for the inspectors to sign, as one had left his spectacles at home,
and the other had a bad cold, so that it was not convenient for
either to write more than his name. Master Horner's exhibition
of learning on this occasion did not reach us, but we know that
it must have been considerable, since he stood the ordeal.

"What is Orthography?" said an inspector once, in our presence.

The candidate writhed a good deal, studied the beams overhead
and the chickens out of the window, and then replied,

"It is so long since I learnt the first part of the spelling-book,

* Verbatim.

that I can't justly answer that question. But if I could just look
it over, I guess I could."

Our schoolmaster entered upon his second term with new courage and invigorated authority. Twice certified, who should dare
doubt his competency ? Even Joshua was civil, and lesser louts
of course obsequious ; though the girls took more liberties ; for
they feel even at that early age, that influence is stronger than
strength.

Could a young schoolmaster think of feruling a girl with her
hair in ringlets and a gold ring on her finger ? Impossible—and
the immunity extended to all the little sisters and cousins ; and
there were enough large girls to protect all the feminine part of
the school. With the boys Master Horner still had many a battle, and whether with a view to this, or as an economical *ruse*,
he never wore his coat in school, saying it was too warm. Perhaps it was an astute attention to the prejudices of his employ-
ers, who love no man that does not earn his living by the sweat
of his brow. The shirt-sleeves gave the idea of a manual-labour
school in one sense at least. It was evident that the master
worked, and that afforded a probability that the scholars worked
too.

Master Horner's success was most triumphant that winter. A
year's growth had improved his outward man exceedingly, filling
out the limbs so that they did not remind you so forcibly of a
young colt's, and supplying the cheeks with the flesh and blood
so necessary where moustaches were not worn. Experience had
given him a degree of confidence, and confidence gave him
power. In short, people said the master had waked up ; and so
he had. He actually set about reading for improvement ; and
although at the end of the term he could not quite make out from
his historical studies which side Hannibal was on, yet this is readily explained by the fact that he boarded round, and was obliged to read generally by firelight, surrounded by ungoverned children.

After this, Master Horner made his own bargain. When
school-time came round with the following autumn, and the teacher presented himself for a third examination, such a test was pronounced no longer necessary ; and the district consented to en-

gage him at the astounding rate of sixteen dollars a month, with the understanding that he was to have a fixed home, provided he was willing to allow a dollar a week for it. Master Horner bethought him of the successive "killing-times," and consequent dough-nuts of the twenty families in which he had sojourned the years before, and consented to the exaction.

Behold our friend now as high as district teacher can ever hope to be—his scholarship established, his home stationary and not revolving, and the good behaviour of the community insured by the fact that he, being of age, had now a farm to retire upon in case of any disgust.

Master Horner was at once the pre-eminent beau of the neighbourhood, spite of the prejudice against learning. He brushed his hair straight up in front, and wore a sky-blue riband for a guard to his silver watch, and walked as if the tall heels of his blunt boots were egg-shells and not leather. Yet he was far from neglecting the duties of his place. He was beau only on Sundays and holidays; very schoolmaster the rest of the time.

It was at a "spelling-school" that Master Horner first met the educated eyes of Miss Harriet Bangle, a young lady visiting the Engleharts in our neighbourhood. She was from one of the towns in Western New York, and had brought with her a variety of city airs and graces somewhat caricatured, set off with year-old French fashions much travestied. Whether she had been sent out to the new country to try, somewhat late, a rustic chance for an establishment, or whether her company had been found rather trying at home, we cannot say. The view which she was at some pains to make understood was, that her friends had contrived this method of keeping her out of the way of a desperate lover whose addresses were not acceptable to them.

If it should seem surprising that so high-bred a visiter should be sojourning in the wild woods, it must be remembered that more than one celebrated Englishman and not a few distinguished Americans have farmer brothers in the western country, no whit less rustic in their exterior and manner of life than the plainest of their neighbours. When these are visited by their refined kinsfolk, we of the woods catch glimpses of the gay world, or think we do.

> " That great medicine hath
> With its tinct gilded—"

many a vulgarism to the satisfaction of wiser heads than ours.

Miss Bangle's manner bespoke for her that high consideration which she felt to be her due. Yet she condescended to be amused by the rustics and their awkward attempts at gaiety and elegance ; and, to say truth, few of the village merry-makings escaped her, though she wore always the air of great superiority.

The spelling-school is one of the ordinary winter amusements in the country. It occurs once in a fortnight, or so, and has power to draw out all the young people for miles round, arrayed in their best clothes and their holiday behaviour. When all is ready, umpires are elected, and after these have taken the distinguished place usually occupied by the teacher, the young people of the school choose the two best scholars to head the opposing classes. These leaders choose their followers from the mass, each calling a name in turn, until all the spellers are ranked on one side or the other, lining the sides of the room, and all standing. The schoolmaster, standing too, takes his spelling-book, and gives a placid yet awe-inspiring look along the ranks, remarking that he intends to be very impartial, and that he shall give out nothing *that is not in the spelling-book*. For the first half hour or so he chooses common and easy words, that the spirit of the evening may not be damped by the too early thinning of the classes. When a word is missed, the blunderer has to sit down, and be a spectator only for the rest of the evening. At certain intervals, some of the best speakers mount the platform, and " speak a piece," which is generally as declamatory as possible.

The excitement of this scene is equal to that afforded by any city spectacle whatever ; and towards the close of the evening, when difficult and unusual words are chosen to confound the small number who still keep the floor, it becomes scarcely less than painful. When perhaps only one or two remain to be puzzled, the master, weary at last of his task, though a favourite one, tries by tricks to put down those whom he cannot overcome in fair fight. If among all the curious, useless, unheard-of words which may be picked out of the spelling-book, he cannot find one which the scholars have not noticed, he gets the last head down by some quip or catch. "Bay" will perhaps be the sound; one scholar spells it " bey," another, " bay," while the master all the time means " ba," which comes within the rule, being *in the spelling-book.*

It was on one of these occasions, as we have said, that Miss Bangle, having come to the spelling-school to get materials for a letter to a female friend, first shone upon Mr. Horner. She was excessively amused by his solemn air and puckered mouth, and set him down at once as fair game. Yet she could not help becoming somewhat interested in the spelling-school, and after it was over found she had not stored up half as many of the schoolmaster's points as she intended, for the benefit of her correspondent.

In the evening's contest a young girl from some few miles' distance, Ellen Kingsbury, the only child of a substantial farmer, had been the very last to sit down, after a prolonged effort on the part of Mr. Horner to puzzle her, for the credit of his own school. She blushed, and smiled, and blushed again, but spelt on, until Mr. Horner's cheeks were crimson with excitement and some touch of shame that he should be baffled at his own weapons. At length, either by accident or design, Ellen missed a word, and sinking into her seat, was numbered with the slain.

In the laugh and talk which followed, (for with the conclusion of the spelling, all form of a public assembly vanishes,) our schoolmaster said so many gallant things to his fair enemy, and appeared so much animated by the excitement of the contest, that Miss Bangle began to look upon him with rather more respect, and to feel somewhat indignant that a little rustic like Ellen should absorb the entire attention of the only beau. She put on, therefore, her most gracious aspect, and mingled in the circle; caused the schoolmaster to be presented to her, and did her best to fascinate him by certain airs and graces which she had found successful elsewhere. What game is too small for the close-woven net of a coquette ?

Mr. Horner quitted not the fair Ellen until he had handed her into her father's sleigh ; and he then wended his way homewards, never thinking that he ought to have escorted Miss Bangle to her uncle's, though she certainly waited a little while for his return.

We must not follow into particulars the subsequent intercourse
of our schoolmaster with the civilized young lady.    All that
concerns us is the result of Miss Bangle's benevolent designs
upon his heart.    She tried most sincerely to find its vulnerable
spot, meaning no doubt to put Mr. Horner on his guard for the
future ; and she was unfeignedly surprised to discover that her
best efforts were of no avail.    She concluded he must have
taken a counter-poison, and she was not slow in guessing its
source.    She had observed the peculiar fire which lighted up his
eyes in the presence of Ellen Kingsbury, and she bethought her
of a plan which would ensure her some amusement at the expense of these impertinent rustics, though in a manner different
somewhat from her original more natural idea of simple coquetry.

A letter was written to Master Horner, purporting to come
from Ellen Kingsbury, worded so artfully that the schoolmaster
understood at once that it was intended to be a secret communication, though its otensible object was an inquiry about some
ordinary affair.    This was laid in Mr. Horner's desk before he
came to school, with an intimation that he might leave an answer in a certain spot on the following morning.    The bait took
at once, for Mr. Horner, honest and true himself, and much
smitten with the fair Ellen, was too happy to be circumspect.
The answer was duly placed, and as duly carried to Miss Bangle
by her accomplice Joe Englehart, an unlucky pickle who " was
always for ill, never for good," and who found no difficulty in
obtaining the letter unwatched, since the master was obliged to
be in school at nine, and Joe could always linger a few minutes
later.    This answer being opened and laughed at, Miss Bangle
had only to contrive a rejoinder, which being rather more particular in its tone than the original communication, led on yet
again the happy schoolmaster, who branched out into sentiment,
" taffeta phrases, silken terms precise," talked of hills and dales
and rivulets, and the pleasures of friendship, and concluded by
entreating a continuance of the correspondence.

Another letter and another, every one more flattering and encouraging than the last, almost turned the sober head of our poor
master, and warmed up his heart so effectually that he could
scarcely attend to his business.    The spelling-schools were re-

membered however, and Ellen Kingsbury made one of the merry
company ; but the latest letter had not forgotten to caution Mr.
Horner not to betray the intimacy, so that he was in honour
bound to restrict himself to the language of the eyes, hard as it
was to forbear the single whisper for which he would have given
his very dictionary.   So their meeting passed off without the explanation which Miss Bangle began to fear would cut short her
benevolent amusement.

The correspondence was resumed with renewed spirit, and
carried on until Miss Bangle, though not over-burdened with
sensitiveness, began to be a little alarmed for the consequences
of her malicious pleasantry.   She perceived that she herself had
turned schoolmistress, and that Master Horner, instead of being
merely her dupe, had become her pupil too ; for the style of his
replies had been constantly improving, and the earnest and manly
tone which he assumed promised any thing but the quiet, sheepish
pocketing of injury and insult, upon which she had counted.   In
truth, there was something deeper than vanity in the feelings
with which he regarded Ellen Kingsbury.   The encouragement
which he supposed himself to have received, threw down the
barrier which his extreme bashfulness would have interposed
between himself and any one who possessed charms enough to
attract him ; and we must excuse him if, in such a case, he did
not criticise the mode of encouragement, but rather grasped
eagerly the proffered good without a scruple, or one which he
would own to himself, as to the propriety with which it was ten-
dered.   He was as much in love as a man can be, and the
seriousness of real attachment gave both grace and dignity to his
once awkward diction.

The evident determination of Mr. Horner to come to the point
of asking papa, brought Miss Bangle to a very awkward pass.
She had expected to return home before matters had proceeded
so far, but being obliged to remain some time longer, she was
equally afraid to go on and to leave off, a denouement being
almost certain to ensue in either case.   Things stood thus when
it was time to prepare for the grand exhibition which was to close
the winter's term.

This is an affair of too much magnitude to be fully described

in the small space yet remaining in which to bring out our veracious history. It must be " slubber'd o'er in haste,"—its important preliminaries left to the cold imagination of the reader—
its fine spirit perhaps evaporating for want of being embodied in
words. We can only say that our master, whose school-life was
to close with the term, laboured as man never before laboured in
such a cause, resolute to trail a cloud of glory after him when
he left us. Not a candlestick nor a curtain that was attainable,
either by coaxing or bribery, was left in the village ; even the
only piano, that frail treasure, was wiled away and placed in one
corner of the rickety stage. The most splendid of all the pieces
in the " Columbian Orator," the " American Speaker," the——
but we must not enumerate—in a word, the most astounding and
pathetic specimens of eloquence within ken of either teacher or
scholars, had been selected for the occasion ; and several young
ladies and gentlemen, whose academical course had been happily
concluded at an earlier period, either at our own institution or
at some other, had consented to lend themselves to the parts and
their choicest decorations for the properties, of the dramatic portion of the entertainment.

Among these last was pretty Ellen Kingsbury, who had agreed
te personate the Queen of Scots, in the garden scene from
Schiller's tragedy of " Mary Stuart ;" and this circumstance ac-
cidentally afforded Master Horner the opportunity he had so long
desired, of seeing his fascinating correspondent without the presence of peering eyes. A dress-rehearsal occupied the afternoon
before the day of days, and the pathetic expostulations of the
lovely Mary—

> Mine all doth hang—my life—my destiny—
> Upon my words—upon the force of tears !—

aided by the long veil, and the emotion which sympathy brought
into Ellen's countenance, proved too much for the enforced prudence of Master Horner. When the rehearsal was over, and
the heroes and heroines were to return home, it was found that,
by a stroke of witty invention not new in the country, the harness
of Mr. Kingsbury's horses had been cut in several places, his
whip hidden, his buffalo-skins spread on the ground, and the sleigh

turned bottom upwards on them. This afforded an excuse for the master's borrowing a horse and sleigh of somebody, and claiming the privilege of taking Miss Ellen home, while her father returned with only Aunt Sally and a great bag of bran from the mill—companions about equally interesting.

Here, then, was the golden opportunity so long wished for! Here was the power of ascertaining at once what is never quite certain until we have heard it from warm, living lips, whose testimony is strengthened by glances in which the whole soul speaks or—seems to speak. The time was short, for the sleighing was but too fine ; and Father Kingsbury, having tied up his harness, and collected his scattered equipment, was driving so close behind that there was no possibility of lingering for a moment. Yet many moments were lost before Mr. Horner, very much in earnest, and all unhackneyed in matters of this sort, could find a word in which to clothe his new-found feelings. The horse seemed to fly—the distance was half past—and at length, in absolute despair of anything better, he blurted out at once what he had determined to avoid—a direct reference to the correspondence.

A game at cross-purposes ensued ; exclamations and explanations, and denials and apologies filled up the time which was to have made Master Horner so blest. The light from Mr. Kingsbury's windows shone upon the path, and the whole result of this conference so longed for, was a burst of tears from the perplexed and mortified Ellen, who sprang from Mr. Horner's attempts to detain her, rushed into the house without vouchsafing him a word of adieu, and left him standing, no bad personification of Orpheus, after the last hopeless flitting of his Eurydice.

" Won't you 'light, Master ?" said Mr. Kingsbury.

" Yes—no—thank you—good evening," stammered poor Master Horner, so stupified that even Aunt Sally called him " a dummy."

The horse took the sleigh against the fence, going home, and threw out the master, who scarcely recollected the accident; while to Ellen the issue of this unfortunate drive was a sleepless night and so high a fever in the morning that our village doctor was called to Mr. Kingsbury's before breakfast.

Poor Master Horner's distress may hardly be imagined. Disappointed, bewildered, cut to the quick, yet as much in love as
ever, he could only in bitter silence turn over in his thoughts the
issue of his cherished dream; now persuading himself that Ellen's
denial was the effect of a sudden bashfulness, now inveighing
against the fickleness of the sex, as all men do when they are
angry with any one woman in particular. But his exhibition
must go on in spite of wretchedness; and he went about mechanically, talking of curtains and candles, and music, and atti-
tudes, and pauses, and emphasis, looking like a somnambulist
whose "eyes are open but their sense is shut," and often surprising those concerned by the utter unfitness of his answers.

It was almost evening when Mr. Kingsbury, having discovered,
through the intervention of the Doctor and Aunt Sally the cause
of Ellen's distress, made his appearance before the unhappy eyes
of Master Horner, angry, solemn and determined; taking the
schoolmaster apart, and requiring an explanation of his treatment
of his daughter. In vain did the perplexed lover ask for time to
clear himself, declare his respect for Miss Ellen and his willing-
ness to give every explanation which she might require: the
father was not to be put off; and though excessively reluctant,
Mr. Horner had no resource but to show the letters which alone
could account for his strange discourse to Ellen. He unlocked
his desk, slowly and unwillingly, while the old man's impatience
was such that he could scarcely forbear thrusting in his own hand
to snatch at the papers which were to explain this vexatious mystery. What could equal the utter confusion of Master Horner
and the contemptuous anger of the father, when no letters were
to be found! Mr. Kingsbury was too passionate to listen to reason, or to reflect for one moment upon the irreproachable good
name of the schoolmaster. He went away in inexorable wrath;
threatening every practicable visitation of public and private
justice upon the head of the offender, whom he accused of having
attempted to trick his daughter into an entanglement which should
result in his favour.

A doleful exhibition was this last one of our thrice-approved
and most worthy teacher! Stern necessity and the power of
habit enabled him to go through with most of his part, but where

was the proud fire which had lighted up his eye on similar occasions before ?   He sat as one of three judges before whom the unfortunate Robert Emmet was dragged in his shirt-sleeves, by two fierce-looking officials ; but the chief judge looked far more like a criminal than did the proper representative.   He ought to have personated Othello, but was obliged to excuse himself from raving for " the handkerchief ! the handkerchief !" on the rather anomalous plea of a bad cold.   " Mary Stuart" being " i' the bond," was anxiously expected by the impatient crowd, and it was with distress amounting to agony that the master was obliged to announce, in person, the necessity of omitting that part of the representation, on account of the illness of one of the young ladies.

Scarcely had the words been uttered, and the speaker hidden his burning face behind the curtain, when Mr. Kingsbury started up in his place amid the throng, to give a public recital of his grievance—no uncommon resort in the new country.   He dashed at once to the point ; and before some friends who saw the utter impropriety of his proceeding could persuade him to defer his vengeance, he had laid before the assembly—some three hundred people, perhaps—his own statement of the case.   He was got out at last, half coaxed, half hustled ; and the gentle public only half understanding what had been set forth thus unexpectedly, made quite a pretty row of it.   Some clamoured loudly for the conclusion of the exercises ; others gave utterance in no particularly choice terms to a variety of opinions as to the schoolmaster's proceedings, varying the note occasionally by shouting, " the letters ! the letters ! why don't you bring out the letters ?"

At length, by means of much rapping on the desk by the president of the evening, who was fortunately a " popular" character, order was partially restored ; and the favourite scene from Miss More's dialogue of David and Goliah was announced as the closing piece.   The sight of little David in a white tunic edged with red tape, with a calico scrip and a very primitive-looking sling ; and a huge Goliah decorated with a militia belt and sword, and a spear like a weaver's beam indeed, enchained every body's attention.   Even the peccant schoolmaster and his pretended letters were forgotten, while the sapient Goliah, every time that he rais-

ed the spear, in the energy of his declamation, to thump upon the
stage, picked away fragments of the low ceiling, which fell con-
spicuously on his great shock of black hair.  At last, with the
crowning threat, up went the spear for an astounding thump,
and down came a large piece of the ceiling, and with it—a shower of letters.

The confusion that ensued beggars all description.  A general
scramble took place, and in another moment twenty pairs of eyes,
at least, were feasting on the choice phrases lavished upon Mr.
Horner.  Miss Bangle had sat through the whole previous scene,
trembling for herself, although she had, as she supposed, guarded
cunningly against exposure.  She had needed no prophet to tell
her what must be the result of a tête-à-tête between Mr. Horner
and Ellen ; and the moment she saw them drive off together, she
induced her imp to seize the opportunity of abstracting the whole
parcel of letters from Mr. Horner's desk ; which he did by means
of a sort of skill which comes by nature to such goblins; picking the lock by the aid of a crooked nail, as neatly as if he had
been born within the shadow of the Tombs.

But magicians sometimes suffer severely from the malice with
which they have themselves inspired their familiars.  Joe Englehart having been a convenient tool thus far, thought it quite time
to torment Miss Bangle a little ; so, having stolen the letters at
her bidding, he hid them on his own account, and no persuasions
of hers could induce him to reveal this important secret, which
he chose to reserve as a rod in case she refused him some inter-
cession with his father, or some other accommodation, rendered
necessary by his mischievous habits.

He had concealed the precious parcel in the unfloored loft
above the school-room, a place accessible only by means of a
small trap-door without staircase or ladder ; and here he meant
to have kept them while it suited his purposes, but for the untime-
ly intrusion of the weaver's beam.

Miss Bangle had sat through all, as we have said, thinking the
letters safe, yet vowing vengeance against her confederate for not
allowing her to secure them by a satisfactory conflagration ; and
it was not until she heard her own name whispered through the
crowd, that she was awakened to her true situation.  The sagacity

of the low creatures whom she had despised showed them at once that the letters must be hers, since her character had been pretty shrewdly guessed, and the handwriting wore a more practised air than is usual among females in the country. This was first taken for granted, and then spoken of as an acknowledged fact.

The assembly moved like the heavings of a troubled sea. Every body felt that this was every body's business. " Put her out !" was heard from more than one rough voice near the door, and this was responded to by loud and angry murmurs from within.

Mr. Englehart, not waiting to inquire into the merits of the case in this scene of confusion, hastened to get his family out as quietly and as quickly as possible, but groans and hisses followed his niece as she hung half-fainting on his arm, quailing completely beneath the instinctive indignation of the rustic public. As she passed out, a yell resounded among the rude boys about the door, and she was lifted into a sleigh, insensible from terror. She disappeared from that evening, and no one knew the time of her final departure for " the east."

Mr. Kingsbury, who is a just man when he is not in a passion, made all the reparation in his power for his harsh and ill-considered attack upon the master ; and we believe that functionary did not show any traits of implacability of character. At least he was seen, not many days after, sitting peaceably at tea with Mr. Kingsbury, Aunt Sally, and Miss Ellen; and he has since gone home to build a house upon his farm. And people *do* say, that after a few months more, Ellen will not need Miss Bangle's intervention if she should see fit to correspond with the umquhile schoolmaster.

# HALF-LENGTHS FROM LIFE.

## CHAPTER I.

### OPERATIVE DEMOCRACY.

"A theme of perilous risk
Thou handlest, and hot fires beneath thy path
The treacherous ashes nurse."

"Can't you let our folks have some eggs?" said Daniel Webster Larkins, opening the door, and putting in a litttle straw-coloured head and a pair of very mild blue eyes just far enough to reconnoitre; "can't you let our folks have some eggs? Our old hen don't lay nothing but chickens now, and mother can't eat pork, and she a'n't had no breakfast, and the baby a'n't drest, nor nothin'!"

"What is the matter, Webster? Where's your girl?"

"Oh! we ha'n't no girl but father, and he's had to go 'way to-day to a raisin'—and mother wants to know if you can't tell her where to get a girl?"

Poor Mrs. Larkins! Her husband makes but an indifferent "girl," being a remarkable public-spirited person. The good lady is in very delicate health, and having an incredible number of little blue eyes constantly making fresh demands upon her time and strength, she usually keeps a girl when she can get one. When she cannot, which is unfortunately the larger part of the time, her husband dresses the children—mixes stir-cakes for the eldest blue eyes to bake on a griddle, which is never at rest— milks the cow—feeds the pigs—and then goes to his "business," which we have supposed to consist principally in helping at raisings, wood-bees, huskings, and such like important affairs; and

" girl" hunting—the most important and arduous, and profitless of all.

Yet it must be owned that Mr. Larkins is a tolerable carpenter, and that he buys as many comforts for his family as most of his neighbours. The main difficulty seems to be that " help" is not often purchasable. The very small portion of our damsels who will consent to enter anybody's doors for pay, makes the chase after them quite interesting from its uncertainty ; and the damsels themselves, subject to a well known foible of their sex, become very coy from being over-courted. Such racing and chasing, and begging and praying, to get a girl for a month ! They are often got for life with half the trouble. But to return.

Having an esteem for Mrs. Larkins, and a sincere experimental pity for the forlorn condition of " no girl but father," I set out at once to try if female tact and perseverance might not prove effectual in ferreting out a " help," though mere industry had not succeeded. For this purpose I made a list in my mind of those neighbours, in the first place, whose daughters sometimes condescended to be girls ; and, secondly, of the few who were enabled by good luck, good management, and good pay, to keep them. If I failed in my attempts upon one class, I hoped for somenew lights from the other. When the object is of such importance, it is well to string one's bow double.

In the first category stood Mrs. Lowndes, whose forlorn loghouse had never known door or window ; a blanket supplying the place of the one, and the other being represented by a crevice between the logs. Lifting the sooty curtain with some timidity, I found the dame with a sort of reel before her, trying to wind some dirty, tangled yarn ; and ever and anon kicking at a basket which hung suspended from the beam overhead by means of a strip of hickory bark. This basket contained a nest of rags and an indescribable baby ; and in the ashes on the rough hearth played several dingy objects, which I suppose had once been babies.

" Is your daughter at home now, Mrs. Lowndes ?"

" Well, yes ! M'randy's to hum, but she's out now. Did you want her ?"

"I came to see if she could go to Mrs. Larkins, who is very
unwell, and sadly in want of help."

"Miss Larkins! why, do tell! I want to know! Is she sick
agin? and is her gal gone? Why! I want to know! I thought
she had Lo-i-sy Paddon! Is Lo-i-sy gone?"

"I suppose so. You will let Miranda go to Mrs. Larkins, will
you?"

"Well, I donnow but I would let her go for a spell, just to
'commodate 'em. M'randy may go if she's a mind ter. She
needn't live out unless she chooses. She's got a comfortable
home, and no thanks to nobody. What wages do they give?"

"A dollar a week."

"Eat at the table?"

"Oh! certainly."

"Have Sundays?"

"Why no—I believe not the whole of Sunday—the children,
you know—"

"Oh ho!" interrupted Mrs. Lowndes, with a most disdainful
toss of the head, giving at the same time a vigorous impulse to
the cradle, "if that's how it is, M'randy don't stir a step! She
don't live nowhere if she can't come home Saturday night and
stay till Monday morning."

I took my leave without farther parley, having often found this
point the *sine qua non* in such negotiations.

My next effort was at a pretty-looking cottage, whose overhanging roof and neat outer arrangements, spoke of English
ownership. The interior by no means corresponded with the
exterior aspect, being even more bare than usual, and far from
neat. The presiding power was a prodigious creature, who looked like a man in woman's clothes, and whose blazing face, orna-
mented here and there by great hair moles, spoke very intelligi-
bly of the beer-barrel, if of nothing more exciting. A daughter
of this virago had once lived in my family, and the mother met
me with an air of defiance, as if she thought I had come with an
accusation. When I unfolded my errand, her *abord* softened a
little, but she scornfully rejected the idea of her Lucy living with
any more Yankees.

"You pretend to think everybody alike," said she, "but when

it comes to the pint, you're a sight more uppish and saucy than
the ra'al quality at home; and I'll see the whole Yankee race
to ——"

I made my exit without waiting for the conclusion of this com-
plimentary observation; and the less reluctantly for having observed on the table the lower part of one of my silver teaspoons, the
top of which had been violently wrenched off. This spoon was
a well-remembered loss during Lucy's administration, and I knew
that Mrs. Larkins had none to spare.

Unsuccessful thus far among the arbiters of our destiny, I
thought I would stop at the house of a friend, and make some inquiries which might spare me farther rebuffs. On making my
way by the garden gate to the little library where I usually
saw Mrs. Stayner, I was surprised to find it silent and uninhabit-
ed. The windows were closed; a half-finished cap lay on the
sofa, and a bunch of yesterday's wild-flowers upon the table. All
spoke of desolation. The cradle—not exactly an appropriate adjunct of a library scene elsewhere, but quite so at the West—
was gone, and the little rocking-chair was nowhere to be seen. I
went on through parlour and hall, finding no sign of life, save the
breakfast-table still standing with crumbs undisturbed. Where
bells are not known, ceremony is out of the question; so I penetrated even to the kitchen, where at length I caught sight of the
fair face of my friend. She was bending over the bread-tray,
and at the same time telling nursery-stories as fast as possible, by
way of coaxing her little boy of four years old to rock the cradle
which contained his baby sister.

" What *does* this mean ?"

" Oh! nothing more than usual. My Polly took herself off
yesterday without a moment's warning, saying she thought she had
lived out about long enough; and poor Tom, our factotum, has
the ague. Mr. Stayner has gone to some place sixteen miles off,
where he was told he might hear of a girl, and I am sole representative of the family energies. But you've no idea what capital bread I can make."

This looked rather discouraging for my quest; but knowing
that the main point of table-companionship was the source of
most of Mrs. Stayner's difficulties, I still hoped for Mrs. Larkins,

who loved the closest intimacy with her "help," and always took them visiting with her. So I passed on for another effort at Mrs. Randall's, whose three daughters had sometimes been known to lay aside their dignity long enough to obtain some much-coveted article of dress. Here the mop was in full play ; and Mrs. Randall, with her gown turned up, was splashing diluted mud on the walls and furniture, in the received mode of these regions, where "stained-glass windows" are made without a patent. I did not venture in, but asked from the door, with my best diplomacy, whether Mrs. Randall *knew* of a girl.

"A gal ! no ; who wants a gal ?"

"Mrs. Larkins."

"She ! why don't she get up and do her own work ?"

"She is too feeble."

"Law sakes ! too feeble ! she'd be able as anybody to thrash round, if her old man didn't spile her by waitin' on——"

We think Mrs. Larkins deserves small blame on this score.

"But, Mrs. Randall, the poor woman is really ill and unable to do anything for her children. Couldn't you spare Rachel for a few days to help her ?"

This was said in a most guarded and deprecatory tone, and with a manner carefully moulded between indifference and undue solicitude.

"My gals has got enough to do. They a'n't able to do their own work. Cur'line hasn't been worth the fust red cent for hard work ever since she went to school to A——."

"Oh ! I did not expect to get Caroline. I understand she is going to get married."

"What ! to Bill Green ! She wouldn't let him walk where she walked last year !"

Here I saw I had made a misstep. Resolving to be more cautious, I left the selection to the lady herself, and only begged for one of the girls. But my eloquence was wasted. The Miss Randalls had been a whole quarter at a select school, and will not live out again until their present stock of finery is unwearable. Miss Rachel, whose company I had hoped to secure, was even then paying attention to a branch of the fine arts.

"Rachel Amandy !" cried Mrs. Randall at the foot of the lad-

der which gave access to the upper regions—" fetch that thing
down here!  It's the prettiest thing you ever see in your life!"
turning to me.   And the educated young lady brought down a
doleful-looking compound of card-board and many-coloured wa-
ters, which had, it seems, occupied her mind and fingers for some
days.

"There!" said the mother, proudly, "a gal that's learnt to
make sich baskets as that, a'n't a goin' to be nobody's help, I
guess!"

I thought the boast likely to be verified as a prediction, and
went my way, crestfallen and weary.   Girl-hunting is certainly
among our most formidable " chores."

## CHAPTER II.

### INTRODUCTIONS AND REMINISCENCES

> " Ah ! what avails the largest gifts of heaven
>      When drooping health and spirits go amiss ?
>      How tasteless then whatever may be given !
>      Health is the vital principle of bliss,
>      And exercise of health."

THUS unsuccessful, it was for rest more than for inquiry that I turned my steps toward Mrs. Clifford's modest dwelling—a house containing only just rooms enough for decent comfort, yet inhabited by gentle breeding, and feelings which meet but little sympathy in these rough walks. Mrs. Clifford was a widow, bowed down by misfortune, and gradually sinking into a sort of desperate apathy, if we may be allowed such a term—a condition to which successive disappointments and the gradual fading away of long-cherished hopes, will sometimes reduce proud yet honourable minds. The apathy is on the surface, but the smouldering fires of despair burst forth at intervals, in spite of their icy covering. Exertion had long since been abandoned by this unfortunate lady, and she sat always in her great arm-chair, seeming scarce alive to common things, yet starting in agonized sensitiveness when the tender string of her altered fortunes was touched by a rude hand. This total renunciation of effort had done its work upon her mind and body. Mrs. Clifford had become a mere mountain in size, while her pale face and leaden eye told of anything but health and enjoyment. She read incessantly, seeking that " oblivious antidote " in books, which coarser natures are apt to seek in less refined indulgences. She lived in a world of imagination until she had insensibly become unfit for a world of reality. Who can find anything charming in common life, after a full surrender of the mind to the excitements of fiction ? Who ever relished common air after a long draught of exhilarating gas ?

To the looker-on, this poor lady, broken down and dispirited
as she was, seemed to have much left for which to be grateful.
Her two daughters and their manly brother were patterns of duty
and devoted affection.   Through the whole sad period of the
downfall of their fortunes, and the gradual withdrawal, from
various causes, of almost the very means of existence, Augustus
Clifford shrank from nothing which promised advantage to his
mother's condition.   While she had yet an income, he was her
very efficient and accurate man of business; and when the "misfortunes" of banks, and the assiduity of "defaulters" had made
this office a sinecure, he turned his hand to the plough, and was
the "patient log-man" of a poverty-stricken household.   He had
seen with unavailing distress the sad decay of his mother's energies, and done all that a son may, to avert the ill consequences
of her indolent habits; but finding matters only growing worse,
he had left home at the urgent entreaty of his sisters, a few
weeks before the time when our story commences, to seek employment in the city, where abilities like his are so much more in
request than in the woods.

Of the two daughters, Rose, the elder, was in feeble health,
and, though gentle and unassuming, and much beloved at home,
not particularly attractive elsewhere.   She was said to have
been crossed in love, and her subdued and rather melancholy
manner seemed to confirm the report.   But Anna Clifford had
beauty and grace of a rare order, though in a style not always
appreciated by those who admire that fragility of form which is so
coveted by our own fair countrywomen.   She was taller than
most women, but so beautifully proportioned that this would not
occur to you until you saw her measured with others.   Magnificent is the epithet for her beauty; and much intercourse with
polished society had given a free and finished elegance to her
manners, while it had detracted nothing from the truth and simplicity of her character.   Born to fortune, and having the further
advantages of connections high in place, it is not surprising that
she should have found many admirers.   Indeed we have the satisfaction of knowing that our forest judgment of her charms had
been borne out by the homage rendered to our fair neighbour by
various young men of acknowledged taste who had bowed at her

shrine in happier days.  But it may not be so easy to believe
that her heart was still her own.  Perhaps the careless gayety of
her spirits had proved her shield, since all passion is said to be
serious.  However this may be, she declared she would not
marry till thirty, adding, with the deep determination of twenty-
one, and also with the tone which befits the inheritrix of certain
prejudices, that then the happy man should be neither a Yankee,
a Presbyterian, nor a widower.

We have omitted to mention that these our friends were from
England—one forgets that friends are foreigners.  Mrs. Clifford,
whose income at home had diminished from various causes, was
attracted to this country by the far higher interest to be obtained
on money ; and during some years that she resided in one of the
great cities, her expectations of increased income were more than
realized, and she and her family had enjoyed all that the best
American circles afforded to the wealthy and the accomplished of
whatever land.  When the dark days came, and Mrs. Clifford
found herself left with scarcely a pittance, the "West"—then an
El Dorado—offered many attractions to the sanguine mind of
Augustus, and he persuaded his mother to withdraw, while yet
she might be able to purchase a little land where land is almost
given away.  What had been the result of this enterprise, we
have already seen.  Mrs. Clifford was too old to bear transplanting.  A high aristocratic pride was the very soul of her being.
In the present condition of her circumstances, she felt not only
inconvenience—that was unavoidable under a complete revulsion
of habits—but degradation ; an idea which common sense and
self-respect should have scouted.  And the very thing that should
have made present sacrifices easy, served but to embitter them.
The Cliffords had expectations from England, on the demise of
some long-lifed uncle or aunt; a fortune, of course, since an
English legacy always passes for a fortune, an involuntary compliment, I suppose, to the well-known wealth of our magnificent
mother.  However, the Cliffords said "expectations," which we
will leave to be limited, or unlimited, by the imagination of the
reader.

This much by way of introduction—an indispensable ceremony, always attended with some awkwardness.  Our present one

has been circumstantial and minute, after the fashion of the country, *e. g.:*

"Miss Wiggins, let me make you acquainted with an uncle of His'N, just come down from Ionia county, the town of Freemantle, village of Breadalbane—come away up here to mill, (they ha'n't no mills yet, up there.)  Uncle, this is Miss Wiggins, John Wiggins's wife, up yonder on the hill, t'other side o' the mash—you can see the house from here.  She's come down to meetin'."

# CHAPTER III.

### "THE HARROWS."

In brave poursuitt of honourable deede,
There is I know not what great difference
Between the vulgar and the noble seede—
Which unto things of valorous pretence,
Seem to be borne by native influence.

THIS same introduction has unavoidably called for so many
words, that we must hasten over some minor points in the character and situation of our young friends. It would require a
long story to express fully the difficulties under which these
sweet girls laboured, in trying to soften for their mother a lot
which they could cheerfully have endured themselves. Mrs.
Clifford's habits were imperative, her prejudices immoveable.
All that had yet occurred had failed to make her perceive that it
was necessary to do without everything but the bare requisites
of subsistence ; and to keep this sad necessity from her eyes had
been the constant study of her children. She had, indeed, no
idea of their efforts and sacrifices, or of the real condition of the
household.

" Where is the silver chocolate-pot, Anna ?" Mrs. Clifford inquired one morning at breakfast.

" You, know, mamma, the handle was loose, and I took it to
the village."

" But what a length of time it has been gone ! Pray inquire
for it ! I do so hate this earthen thing !"

The poor lady would have been without chocolate, and without
tea also, if the *chocolatière* had not been transferred, at least *pro.
tem.* to the possession of our village dealer-in-all-things. But
the idea of such a transaction would almost have crazed her ;
and she had so far lost the train of cause and effect, that she
thought the last bank-note brought in by Augustus had sufficed

for six weeks' family expenses. The girls never gathered courage to enlighten their mother's views as to pecuniary matters, though they were sometimes obliged to run away to hide their tears when she would remark the meanness of their dress, and fear they were contracting habits which would unfit them to enjoy better fortune. Anna Clifford and her sister, forced by suffering to learn a premature prudence, often wished, in the grief of their hearts, that no prospect of an inheritance had prevented their mother from accommodating her ideas to her present condition. This "waiting for dead men's shoes" is proverbially enervating to the character.

When I entered the little parlour, I was somewhat startled by the sight of two rough-looking men, one fanning himself with his hat, the other drumming on the table with his long, black, horny nails, and both taking a deliberate survey of the apartment and all that it contained. In the accustomed chair sat Mrs. Clifford, a purple spot on each cheek, and a look of helpless anger in her eye, while her daughters, one on either side of her, stood, pale as death, gazing on these strange guests.

"Well! I guess we may as well levy, if you've nobody to stay judgment," said the straw hat, who seemed to be principal. "Mr. Grinder told us the money or the things. That's the hang of it. No mistake. Turn out what you like, or we'll take what *we* like. No two ways about it! You ha'n't hid nothing, have ye? If you have, you'd better rowst it out at once't! We've a right to sarch."

Mrs. Clifford gasped for breath.

"Who sent you here?" she said.

"Oh! we're for Grinder. That bill, you know. Your son there confessed judgment. I s'pose he thought levyin' time would never come. We want a hundred dollars, or goods to that amount. You've got a good deal more than the law allows—now what'll you turn out? Come, be lively, gals, for we can't wait!"

This was said quite facetiously.

"Couldn't you grant a little time, till we can hear from my brother?" said Anna, who seemed more self-possessed than her mother or Rose.

"Can't go it! No fun in waitin'. Hearin' from him won't do no good, unless he sends money. Do you expect money?"

"Yes—that is—we hope—"

"Ha! ha! hope starved a rattlesnake! We can't eat nor drink hope. Come, Woodruff, they a'n't a goin' to turn out any thing but talk. Go ahead!"

Our poor friends were overwhelmed, but seeing no present remedy, they could only sit quietly looking on while the officers proceeded to execute this trying process of law. I must do Mr. Beals and his assistant the justice to say that, allowing for their rude natures, they were not wilfully insulting, but performed their duty with as few words as possible. Indeed, nothing can be more foreign to the character of the men of this country than any thing like intentional rudeness to a woman. We must not blame them for not respecting feelings which they could not understand.

When they had departed, Mrs. Clifford's pride came to the rescue. In reply to the words of sympathy which one cannot help offering in such cases, she said it was a thing of no importance at all. "My son will come or send before these people actually proceed to sell our property! It can never be that the very furniture of my house is to be taken away by a low person like Grinder! I cannot imagine why Augustus does not write! I expected he would have sent us funds long ago!"

It would have been unavailing to convince the poor lady that her son might not probably find it very easy to pick up money, even in the city, in these times; so we turned the discourse gradually to other things. I stated the purpose of my long walk and its ill success; and after some attempts at conversation—laboured enough when all hearts were full of one subject, and that, one that did not bear handling—I invited Mrs. Clifford with her daughters to remove to our house until Augustus should return.

The old lady's manner was stately enough for Queen Elizabeth. She thanked me very graciously, but felt quite too sad, as well as too infirm, she said, to think of quitting home. And with this reply I was about to take my leave, when Anna, suddenly turning to her mother, declared she should like very much to accept the invitation.

It was as easy to read high displeasure in the countenance of the mother as most painful surprise in that of the gentle Rose. But Anna, though her cheek was flushed and her lip quivering with emotion, persisted in her wish.

" You will return with me now ?"

" Not just now, but this evening."

And I promised to send.

\*        \*        \*        \*        \*        \*        \*

" What *must* you have thought of me ?" said the dear girl as I welcomed her. " But you could not suppose for a moment that I really coveted a visit when my poor mother's heart was so cruelly wrung! Ah no! it was a lucky thought that struck me when you said Mrs. Larkins wanted a servant. It flashed upon me that in that way I might earn a pittance, however small, on which mamma and Rose can subsist until we hear from Augustus. You see what these horrid debts come to, and we are absolutely without present resources. Ah! I see what you are going to say; but do not even speak of it! Mamma would rather die, I believe! Only get me in at Mrs. Larkins', and you shall see what a famous maid I'll make! I have learned *so* much since we came here! And I have arranged it all with Rose, that mamma shall never discover it. Mamma is a little deaf, you know, and does not hear casual observations, and Rose will take care that nobody tells her. Poor Rose cried a good deal at first, but she saw it was the best thing I could do for mamma, so she consented. She can easily do all that is needed at home, while my strong arms"—and here she extended a pair that Cleopatra might have envied, so round, so graceful, so perfect—" my strong arms can earn all the little comforts, that are every thing to poor mamma! Won't it be delightful! Oh, I shall be so happy! There is only one sad side. My mother will think—till Augustus returns—that I have selfishly flown from her trials." And at the thought she burst into tears, for the remembrance of her mother's displeasure weighed sorely upon her.

I have not thought it necessary to record the various interruptions which I could not help making to this plan. Anna's warmth overpowered all I could say, and she succeeded in convincing my reason at least, if not my feelings, that it was the best thing for

the present. Her eyes did not allow of close application to the
needle, and the uncertainty of that most laborious of all ways of
earning a poor living, was a further objection. In the country
few persons undertake needlework as a business. Sometimes a
widow with children, or a wife whose husband frequents the tavern, earns a scanty and ill-paid addition to her means in this way,
and with such it seems hardly right for the young and healthy
to interfere. But "girls" are universally in request, and get as
well paid and much better treated than schoolmistresses, with far
less wearing employment. I knew that at Mrs. Larkins' Anna
would meet with decent treatment, and be sure of a punctual dollar per week; since Mr. Larkins hates mixing griddle-cakes too
much ever to lose a girl for want of this essential security.

The thing was settled, and all I could do was to procure the
introduction.

Mrs. Larkins was at first a little afraid of "such a lady" for
a help, but after a close and searching examination, she consented to engage Miss Clifford for a week.

I left Anna in excellent spirits, and, during several evening
visits which she contrived to make me in the course of this her
first week of servitude, she declared herself well satisfied with
her situation, and only afraid that Mrs. Larkins would not care
to retain one who was so awkward about many things required in
her household. But she must have underrated her own skill, for
on the Saturday evening, Mr. Larkins put into her hands a silver
dollar, with a very humble request for a permanent engagement.

The spending of that dollar, Anna Clifford declared to me was
the greatest pleasure she could remember.

## CHAPTER IV.

### CHARACTERISTICS.

That maid is born of middle earth,
And may of man be won.

THAT blessed privilege of the state of " girlhood" in the country—the undisturbed possession of Sunday—not falling to the lot
of Miss Clifford, she could only snatch a moment to visit her mother and sister, and deposit with the latter the various little matters which were the fruit of her first earnings.  She went, however, in high spirits.  " Poor Rose will be so happy !" she said.

When she returned, a cloud sat on her beautiful brow, and her
cheeks bore the marks of much weeping.  " Mamma received
me very coldly," she said ; " she thinks I am enjoying myself
with you !  But I must bear this—it is a part of my duty, and I
thought I had made up my mind to it.  'Twill be but a little
while !  When Augustus comes, all will be well again."

Strong in virtuous resolution, Anna returned to her toil.  Another week or two passed, and the Larkinses continued to esteem
themselves the most fortunate of girl-hunters.  Anna's active habits, strong sense, and high principle, made all go well ; and the
influence which she soon established over the household, was such
as superior intellect would naturally command, where there was
no idea of difference of station.   Mrs. Larkins would have thought
the roughest of her neighbours' daughters entitled to a full equal-
ity with herself ; and she treated Miss Clifford with all the additional respect which her real superiority demanded.   It has been
well said that the highest intellectual qualifications may find employment in the arrangements of a household ; and our friends
the Larkinses, young and old, if they had ever heard of the doctrine, would, I doubt not, have subscribed to it heartily, for they
will never forget Miss Clifford's reign.   Without dictating, like
good Mrs. Mason, in the Cottagers of Glenburnie, (whose benefits,

I have sometimes thought, must have been harder to bear than other people's injuries,) she continued to introduce many excellent improvements, and indeed a general reform throughout. The beds were shielded from public view ; the family ablutions were no longer performed in an iron skillet on the hearth, or a trough under the eaves ; and Mrs. Larkins solemnly burnt the willow switch which had hitherto been her only means of government, declaring the children never required it under Miss Clifford's excellent management. Thus encouraged by her success in the process of civilization, Anna told me laughingly that she did not despair of the highest step—to induce Mrs. Larkins to boil corned beef instead of frying it, and Mr. Larkins to leave off tobacco. And far from feeling degraded by her labours, she said she was quite raised in her own opinion by the discovery of her power of being useful.

I own I suspected a little the solidity of this boast of independence. We sometimes say such things for a double purpose—as a boy passing through a church-yard at night whistles partly to show he is not afraid and partly to keep up his courage. Anna's position with regard to the people with whom she lived, was indeed, as we have said, one of decided superiority. To see her maid well drest and at leisure every afternoon, seated in the "keepin'-room" ready to be introduced to any one who should call ; to give her always the lady-like title of "Miss," and to share with her whatever was laborious or unpleasant in the daily business—this Mrs. Larkins considered perfectly proper in all cases, and to Miss Clifford she gladly conceded more in the way of respectful observance. But in this vulgar world, spite of all that philosophers have said and poets sung, there lurks yet a certain degree of prejudice, which makes real independence not one of the cheap virtues.

> All lots are equal, and all states the same,
> Alike in merit though unlike in name.

Yet if we look for a recognition of this truth any where out of the woods, we shall probably be frowned upon as very wild waifs from dream-land—visionaries, who, in this enlightened age, can still cling to the antiquated notion, that theory should be the mould

of practice. So, in my pride of worldly wisdom, I took upon me
to doubt whether my friend Anna was indeed the heroine she
thought herself. The matter was not long doubtful.

Among the gentlemen who had been disposed to play the agreeable to Miss Clifford, was a certain Captain Maguire, an Irish
officer, who had met her in Montreal. From Anna herself one
would never have learned that her beauty had found a solitary
adorer; but the tender and unselfish Rose could not help boasting
a little, in her quiet way, of the triumphs of her sister's charms.
She had thought well of the Captain's pretensions, and rather
wondered that his handsome person and gallant bearing had not
made some impression upon Anna, who was the object of his devoted attention.

" But Anna thought him a coxcomb," she said, " and never
gave him the least crumb of encouragement; so, poor fellow ! he
gave over in despair."

Now, as it would happen, just at the wrong time, this unen-
couraged and despairing gentleman chanced to be one of a party
who made a flying pilgrimage to the prairies ; and being thus far
favoured by chance, he took his further fate into his own hands,
so far as sufficed to bring him to the humble village which he had
understood to be shone upon temporarily by the bright eyes of
Miss Clifford. He went first to her mother's, of course, and during a short call, ascertained from the old lady that her youngest
daughter was on a visit to us. The Captain was not slow in
taking advantage of the information, and he was at our door
before Rose had at all made up her mind what should be done in
such an emergency.

I was equally embarrassed, since one never knows on what
nice point those things called love affairs may turn. However, I
detained the Captain, and wrote a note to Miss Clifford. What
was my surprise when a verbal answer was returned, inviting
Captain Maguire and myself to Mrs. Larkins'. There was no
alternative, so I shawled forthwith ; but I really do not know how
I led the young gentleman through the shop into the rag-carpeted
sitting-room of Mrs. Larkins. The scene upon which the door
opened must have been a novel one for fashionable optics.

Anna Clifford, with a white apron depending from her taper

waist, stood at the ironing-table, half hidden by a clothes-frame already well covered with garments of all sizes. Mrs. Larkins occupied her own, dear, creaking rocking-chair; holding a little one in her lap, and jogging another in the cradle, while blue-eyed minims trotted about or sat gravely staring at the strangers.

"Get up, young 'uns!" said Mrs. Larkins, hastily, as Captain Maguire's imposing presence caught her eye, and Miss Clifford came forward to welcome him; "Jump up! clear out!" And as she spoke she tipped one of the minims off a chair, offering the vacated seat to the gentleman, who, not noticing that it was a nursing-chair, some three or four inches lower than usual, plumped into it after a peculiar fashion, a specimen of bathos far less amusing to the young officer than to the infant Larkinses, who burst into a very natural laugh.

"Shut up!" said the mother, reprovingly; "you haven't a grain o' manners! What must you blaat out so for?" Then turning to the Captain with an air of true maternal mortification, she observed, "I dare say you've noticed how much worse children always behave when there's company. Mine always act like Sancho! How do you do, sir, and how's your folks?"

This civility was delivered with an indescribable drawl, and an accent which can never be expressed on paper.

Captain Maguire replied by giving satisfactory assurance of his own health; but having a large family connection and no particular home, perhaps thought it unnecessary to notice the second branch of Mrs. Larkins' inquiry.

Miss Clifford meanwhile asked after friends in Montreal and elsewhere, and entertained her dashing beau with all the ease and grace that belonged to the drawing-rooms in which they had last met. It was most amusing to note the air with which Anna ran over the splendid names of her quondam friends, and contrast it with the puzzled look which would make itself evident, spite of "power of face," in the countenance of her visitor. Never was man more completely mystified.

At the very first pause, Mrs. Larkins, who was particularly social, and who had seemed watching a chance to "put in," asked the Captain, with much earnestness, if he knew "a man by the name of Maguire," who had been in "Canady" in the last war.

" Was he any relation to the Captain ?  He used to peddle some among the sojers around Montreal and those parts."

The Captain declared he did not recollect the gentleman, but he had hundreds of Irish cousins, and thought it highly probable that Mrs. Larkins' friend might be one of them.

" Oh ! he wasn't an Irishman at all !  He was a very respectable man !" said the lady.

" Ah then !" remarked the Captain, with perfect gravity, " I'm quite sure he can't be one of my cousins !"

And Mrs. Larkins gravely replied, " No, I dare say he wasn't; but I thought I'd ask.  What are you a cracklin' so between your teeth ?" continued she, addressing Daniel Webster.

" Oh ! the bark of pork," replied the young gentleman.

" *Rind*, Webster," said Anna ; " you should say *rind*."

" Well ! rind, then," was the reply.

Mr. Larkins now brought in a huge armful of stove-wood, which he threw into a corner with a loud crash.

" Will there be as much wood as you'll want, Miss Clifford ?" said he.

" Yes—quite enough, thank you," said Anna, composedly ; " I have nearly finished the ironing."

At this, the Captain, with a look in which was concentrated the essence of a dozen shrugs, took his leave, declaring himself quite delighted to have found Miss Clifford looking so well.

We were no sooner in the open air than he began—and I did not wonder—

" May I ask—will you tell me, Madam, what is the meaning of Miss Clifford's travestie ?  Is she masquerading for some frolic ?  or is it a bet ?—for I know young ladies do bet, sometimes—"

" Neither, sir," I replied.  " Miss Clifford is, in sad and sober earnest, filling the place of a servant, that she may procure the necessaries of life for her family.  More than one friend would gladly offer aid in an emergency which we trust will be only temporary, but Miss Clifford, with rare independence, prefers devoting herself as you have seen."

" Bless my soul ! what a noble girl !  What uncommon spirit and resolution !  I never heard anything like it !  Such a splen-

did creature to be so sacrificed!" These and a hundred other enthusiastic expressions broke from the gay Captain, while I recounted some of the circumstances which had brought Mrs. Clifford's family to this low ebb; but as he pursued his trip to the
prairies the next morning without attempting to procure another
interview with the lady he so warmly admired, I came to the
conclusion—not a very uncharitable one, I hope—that Anna had
shown her usual acuteness in the estimate she had formed of his
character.

Perhaps the Captain thought his pay too trifling to be shared
with so exalted a heroine. But we must not complain, for his
mystified look and manner at Mrs. Larkins' affords us a permanent income of laughter, which is something in these dull times;
and I have learned, by means of his visit, that there is one really
independent woman in the world.

## CHAPTER V.

### DARKNESS AND LIGHT.

Time and tide had thus their sway,
Yielding, like an April day,
Smiling noon for sullen morrow,
Years of joy for hours of sorrow.

As levying day had come before it was expected, so selling day, the time so dreaded by the affectionate daughters, came duly on, and no tidings yet of Augustus. Many letters had been forwarded to his address in New York, and no answers arriving, the anxiety of the family had been such as almost to drown all sense of the hopeless, helpless destitution which now seemed to threaten them. Being alone at this time, and wishing that whatever it was possible to do might be done properly for Mrs. Clifford, I took the liberty of sending for a neighbour, that is, a country neighbour—one who lived " next door about four miles off "—a gentleman well versed in the law, though not practising professionally.

Mr. Edward Percival, this friend of ours, came into this country—then a land of promise indeed—some seven years since. Having inherited a large tract of wild land, he chose to leave great advantages behind him for the sake of becoming an improver—a planter—a pioneer—what not? There must be some marvellous witchery in the idea of being a land-holder, if we may judge by the number of people who undertake this wild, rough life without the slightest necessity. Englishmen seem to be peculiarly attracted by the idea of unlimited shooting—a privilege so jealously monopolized by the great in their own country; but with our own citizens this is usually a matter of small interest. Be the spell what it may, we shall not wish to see it reversed while it brings us neighbours like Mr. Percival.

He came, he saw, he conquered—and Cæsar's victory must

pale by comparison, for Mr. Percival overcame a sheriff, and obtained an extension of time.  I say he came—that was a matter
of course, seeing he was sent for by a lady.  He saw—but I am
sadly afraid it was not the sight either of Mrs. Clifford or myself
that enlisted his sympathies so completely.  He saw two very
lovely young ladies—for Anna had easily obtained a furlough for
a day that she might comfort her mother and sister under their
trials.  And Mr. Edward Percival, though no beau, was made
of " penetrable stuff," and felt his heart strangely moved by the
unaffected sensibility and dutiful solicitude of those two sad-heart-
ed daughters.  By what particular course of strategy he conquered Sheriff Beals I have never learned, but I have understood
there is but one avenue to law-hardened hearts, and I suppose
some knowledge of the profession had endued Mr. Percival with
the acumen required for discovering this covered way.

The result was that Mrs. Clifford retained her fine old chased
gold watch, with its massive hook and crested seal, with several
other "superfluities" on which the law had laid its chill grasp ;
and the two Miss Cliffords, though they did not fall at Mr. Percival's feet to thank him for his intervention, looked as if they
could have done so ; and the gentleman himself, as he took his
leave, gave utterance to some consoling expressions, which fell
with strange warmth from lips usually very guarded.  So all
was well thus far.

But Augustus came not.  Anna returned to her householdry,
Mrs. Clifford to her reading, and Rose to her round of anxious
cares and painful economy.  Another week wore away—another
mail reached our Thule, and brought no tidings from the lost one.
Agonizing apprehensions were fast assuming the form of certain-
ties, and even Anna was yielding to despair, when Mr. Percival,
who had not failed to acquaint himself with the condition of
things, announced his intention of going to New York, and
offered his services in making the requisite inquiries after young
Clifford.

We have not been informed what urgent business called Mr.
Percival eastward, but conclude it to have been something sudden
and pressing, as he had returned from New York but a few weeks
before.

The suspense of our unhappy friends was destined to be lengthened out yet another week; but we need not detain our readers
proportionally.   At the end of that period then, after Mrs. Clifford
and her daughters had renounced all thoughts but one, Mr.
Percival returned, bringing with him the long-lost son and brother; or, rather, what might seem more the shadow than the
substance of the gallant youth who had left us some three months
before.

Poor Augustus—his heart wrung, and his brain on the rack
when he left us—had been seized with a fever, so violent in its
symptoms, that no hotel at Buffalo would receive him, through
fear of infection.   Other lodging places presenting the same difficulty, he was at last placed with a poor coloured woman, on the
outskirts of the town; poverty, and perhaps a better motive, indu-
cing her to overlook the danger.   Here he was nursed, with the
tenderness so characteristic of that kind-hearted race, through a
course of typhus fever; and from the first he had never been
long enough himself to give the address of his friends.   Tracing
him as far as Buffalo by means of the steamboat's books, Mr.
Percival had found no difficulty in discovering the place of his
retreat.   The invalid was beginning to sit up a little, and had
written a few lines to his mother by the mail of that very day.

Need we say that our friends forgot even grinding poverty for
awhile ?

Home, and the attentions of those we love, have wondrous restorative powers.   Augustus gained strength rapidly, and exulted
in the change as only those who have

Long endured
A fever's agonies, and fed on drugs,

can exult, in the sunshine and the breeze.   The exhilaration of
his spirits amounted almost to delirium.   He would recount again
and again the kindness of his dark nurse, and in happy oblivion
of the narrowness of circumstances which drove him from home,
reiterate his schemes of gratitude to poor dear Chloe—schemes
devised on a scale better befitting past than present fortunes.   As
the exquisite sense of recovery subsided, however, care reasserted

her empire, and poor Augustus gradually sank into his former condition of premature gravity.

Here, again, Mr. Percival's affairs seemed to favour our young friend strangely; for while Augustus had been gaining strength and losing spirits, that gentleman made the discovery that he was in pressing want of an assistant in his business. He had great tracts of land in far-away counties, calling for immediate attention; there was a great amount of overcharged taxes which must be argued down (if possible) at various offices; he had distant and very slippery debtors—in short, just such a partner as Augustus Clifford would make was evidently indispensable; and, Augustus got well.

Anna had come home to help nurse her brother, but with such positive promise of return, that Mr. Larkins did not go girl-hunting, but mixed griddle-cakes and dressed the children unrepiningly during the interregnum. When Augustus recovered, the secret of the weekly dollar was confided to him, and Anna prepared for going back to her " place." The brother was naturally very averse to this, and laboured hard to persuade her that he should now be able to make all comfortable without this terrible sacrifice. But she persisted in fulfilling her engagement, and, moreover, declared that it really was not a sacrifice worth naming.

" Look at your hands, dear Anna!" said Rose.

" Oh! I do look at them—but what then? Of what possible use are white satin hands in the country? I should have browned them with gardening, if nothing else; and when once Uncle Hargrave's money comes, a few weeks' gloving will make a lady of me again."

" But Mr. Percival, I am sure—" Rose tried to whisper, but Anna would not hear her, and only ran away the faster.

By and by, Uncle Hargrave's legacy did come, and whether by a gloving process or not, it was not long before Anna's hands recovered their beauty. Mrs. Larkins lost the best " help" she ever had, and Anna at length told all to her mother, who learned more by means of this effort of her daughter, than all her misfortunes had been able to teach her.

The legacy, like many a golden dream, had been tricked out by the capricious wand of Fancy. In its real and tangible form.

far from enabling Mrs. Clifford to return to city splendour, it proved so moderate in size that she was obliged to perceive that a comfortable home even in the country would depend, in some degree, on economy and good management. Certainty being thus substituted for the vague and glittering phantom which had misled her, and helped to benumb her naturally good understanding, she set herself about the work of reform with more vigour than could have been anticipated; and an expression of quiet happiness again took possession of faces which had long been saddened by present or dreaded evils.

Strange to say, Mr. Edward Percival, by nature the most frank, manly, straightforward person in the world, seems lately to have taken a manœuvring turn. After showing very unmistakable signs of an especial admiration of Mrs. Larkins' "girl," he scarce ventures to offer her the slightest attention. At the same time, his interest in the ponderous mamma is remarkable, to say the least. Hardly a fine day passes that does not see a certain low open carriage at Mrs. Clifford's door, and a grave but gallant cavalier—handsome and well-equipped—soliciting the old lady's company for a short drive. This is certainly a very delicate mode of mesmerizing a young lady, but it is not without effect. Anna does not go to sleep—far from it! but her eyelids are observed to droop more than usual, and choice flowers, which come almost daily from the mesmerizer's green-house, are very apt to find their way from the parlour vase to the soft ringlets of the lovely sleep-waker. What these signs may portend we must leave to the scientific.

Mr. Percival came from the very heart's core of Yankeeland; he may say with Barlow,

All my bones are made of Indian corn—

he is a conscientious Presbyterian, and he has been four years a widower. All these disabilities have been duly represented to Miss Clifford; nay—I will not aver that they may not even have been wickedly dwelt upon—thrown in her teeth, as it were, by one who loves to tease such victims; and I have come to the conclusion, which Anna herself suggested to me the other day, hiding at the same time her blushing face on my shoulder, after a confidential chit-chat, " There certainly is a fate in these things."

## AN EMBROIDERED FACT.

ALL the stories in this volume are from the life—either in facts
or characters, or both ; but the one which succeeds is as nearly
a transcript of actual reality, as could well be without giving
names and dates.  The ride and its object—the suspicion—the
pursuit—the arrest—and the denouement—were described to
me by the hero himself, ere yet the memory of the toilsome winning of his beautiful bride had lost any of its freshness.

What the phrenologists call " approbativeness" is an excellent
development, but we may have it too full.  People born without it
are intolerable—those who have a superabundance, pay dearly
enough for being agreeable.  They win, without conscious effort,
—instinctively, as it were,—" golden opinions" from those with
whom they associate ; and too good a reputation is sometimes a
severe tax in more ways than one.  As with other luxuries, it
costs a good deal to support it.  One of our friends got rid of his,
inadvertently.  We have the story from himself, only adding some
explanations of our own.

George Elliott had, from his childhood, been the model of all excellence among his own family.  His parents had other children,
and they all did very much as they pleased, not having set out
with a character to support.  They did not always please to prefer what was wisest ; and then they were sure of a lecture, to
which George's prudence and self-government afforded the text.

George must have been really a good fellow, for his brothers
loved him in spite of his position ; and as for his sisters, they
thought no mortal man, and hardly even Thaddeus of Warsaw, approached him in excellence.  He was, in truth, less spoiled by this
general homage than was to be expected.  The shape of his head
was not improved by the cultivation of a faculty which shows it-

self in squaring out the head just on each side the crown ; but
his black hair hid the superfluity, and the ceaseless good humour
that beamed from his eyes, joined to a fine ruddy complexion and
white teeth, made him an Adonis in the eyes of all the young ladies of the neighbourhood.   Not a house but was open to him—
not a mamma but smiled upon him.   He was already " well to
do," and such qualities as his promised constant bettering.

But here, again, George experienced the disadvantage of being too well liked.   The invariable welcome which awaited him,
the capital footing on which he stood with the mammas and papas,
and the fear that whenever he should select a special partner, it
would be at the expense of a large amount of friendship and attention, had kept him undecided until five-and-twenty ; and, we fear,
a little too well satisfied with himself to promise uncommonly well
as a husband.

Among his perfections,—in his father's eyes, at least,—was a
strict and energetic attention to matters of business.   He was the
factotum in every affair requiring peculiar skill and discretion.
He travelled, he negotiated, he advised.   Never was there an
eldest son on whose indomitable prudence a father could rely so completely.   Was a hard thing to be said, George must say it—because George could say it without hurting any body's feelings.
Was a slippery debtor to be approached, George was the messenger; and if it proved necessary to follow the "defaulter" to
Texas, he never flinched, and generally returned with man or
money.   We will not say that such trusts were always agreeable ; indeed, we have already hinted that our friend sometimes
found his reputation rather costly.   But developments are fate,
and his " approbativeness" kept on growing.

Once upon a time, when affairs called George from home, he
was about to pass the night in a village, about sixty-five miles
from his father's residence.   There was no one to visit, for he
knew none but the gentleman with whom his business lay ; and
he strolled out after tea, as men will when they have nothing else
to do, not exactly seeking adventure, but in a mood of mind to be
well pleased with any thing that should occur, to help off the
evening.   He paced the bank of the noisy little " privilege" that
turned the grist-mill, the carding machine and the trip hammer,

which formed the wealth of the village, until the light had faded to that pleasant gray which we poetically call dusk ; and he was about returning to the inn to read the newspaper over again, when a wild-looking girl, with a shawl over her head, accosted him.

" They want you, up yander," she said, in a mumbling and embarrassed tone.

George's eyes followed the direction of the thick red finger, and rested upon a pretty cottage on the side of a hill, at no great distance.

" Who wants me ?   There must be some mistake."

The girl stood perfectly still, staring straight forward.

" Who is it that wishes to see me ?" repeated George.   " Whom were you told to ask for ?"

" You're the one," said the messenger, confidently.   " I've forgot the name."

" Was it Elliott ?" asked George.

" Yes," said the messenger ; " they want you right off."

Musingly did George follow the girl up the hillside, perfectly convinced of the impracticability of getting any thing more out of her, and tolerably certain that he could not be the person in requisition.   Why did he go then ?   We have already said that he was born to oblige, and also that he found the Templeville hotel somewhat dull.

The clumsy-footed emissary turned into a little court, full of spring flowers, and passing through a porch shaded to perfect darkness by climbing plants, opened a door on the right.   The room thus disclosed was a pretty rural parlour, on the sofa of which lay a young girl in a white wrapper, with an elderly lady sitting by her side.

" Here he is," said the girl ; " I've fetched 'um."

The young lady started—the elder screamed outright.

" Who is this ?" said the more ancient, turning to the girl with an annihilating frown, and seeming entirely to forget that the young man *might* be innocent, and was therefore entitled to decent treatment.

" I perceive there has been some mistake, madam," began our discomfited incomparable.

" Mistake !   Oh yes, I dare say !" muttered the guardian,

.vith a most unbelieving air. Then turning to the stupid maid, she proceeded to scold her in an under tone, but with inconceivable rapidity and sharpness, while George stood most uneasily waiting the result. He felt inclined to disappear at once, but that course seemed liable to further misconstruction; and he was, moreover, rather attracted by the invalid, who, though embarrassed, lost not her ladylike self-possession.

"The girl is newly come to us, and quite ignorant," she said, in rather a deprecatory tone. "She was sent for our physician, and must have mistaken you—"

"Oh, very likely," interrupted the elder lady, who forgot to scold the maid as soon as the young lady ventured to speak to George. "Doctor Beasley, with his bald head and one eye, is exceedingly like this gentleman! Quite probable that Hetty mistook the one for the other!"

The air of incredulity with which this was said could not be mistaken; but the implication was one which it was impossible to notice under the circumstances; and George concluded that the only course left for him was to make his bow and leave his character behind him.

As he turned, with his hat in his hand, a letter fell from it to the floor, unobserved by him in his embarrassment. He had not cleared the porch, when the maid ran after him with it.

"Here, Mister, they say they don't want none of yer letters."

George looked in his hat, found he must have dropt a letter, and took it, though it was now too dark to examine it. Here was a new confirmation of the evident suspicions of the lady-dragon as to some designs upon her fair charge.

Is it singular that a conviction began to dawn upon his mind that the said charge must possess considerable attractions?

"Don't touch that thing upon the table," says grandmamma, to the little one who is quietly playing on the floor.

"No, grandma," says the youth, and immediately leaves his play to get up and walk round and round the table, trying to reach the prohibited article.

George the prudent slept little that night. The young lady's eyes and voice, the delicate and languid grace of her figure, as she lay extended in evident feebleness on the sofa, rather unhinged his philosophy ; and he was, besides, not a little troubled by the recollection of the spiteful air of the duenna, and the probability that the error had cost the fair invalid some discomfort. Altogether, there was food for reverie ; and a hasty, unrefreshing morning slumber had not made amends for a wakeful night, when he was aroused by the breakfast bell.

Inquiries respecting the people of the cottage elicited only the interesting information, that there was " an oldish woman, and a young gal," which added little to George's knowledge. The innkeeper guessed they were " pretty likely folks," but couldn't say, as they had not been there long.

George went home, but said nothing of his adventure. He said he did not think it worth while. But he thought it worth while, two weeks afterwards, to travel the sixty-five miles which lay between his home and Templeville, just to try whether the landlord might not have discovered something beyond the interesting facts before ascertained as to the " young gal" and her duenna.

But the innkeeper had added nothing to his store of information on this point, except the conclusion that the people on the hill were " fore-handed folks," and that there was a man who came once in a while to see them and brought them lots of things.

" A man !" said George.   " Ah yes," (very unconcernedly, of course ;)  " of what age—about ?"

" Oh, he always comes in the evening, and is off again early in the morning.   Their help guesses he's an uncle or something."

Not much enlightened, even yet, George adopted the desperate resolution of trying boldly for an acquaintance.  He judged it absolutely necessary to inquire after the health of the invalid. So, writing a civil card of inquiry, he walked up to the pretty cottage, and, after reconnoitering a little, rapped at the door, and awaited the coming of the stupid maid, with a trepidation quite new to his quiet and well-assured frame of mind.

What was his dismay when the aunt herself, with a face of iron, opened the door.

George was completely at a loss for the moment.  The card was in his hand, but he could not offer it to the lady, so he stammered out something of his wish to inquire after the health of the family, and to express his regret for the misunderstanding on the former occasion.

Rigid was the brow with which the careful dame heard this announcement, and wiry were the muscles which held the door half shut, as if defying a forty-young-man power of getting in without consent of the owner.

"We're all quite well, I thank you," she said, closing her lips as tightly as possible as soon as she had communicated the information.

George stood still, and the lady stood as still as he. She looked at the distant hills, and he at the door which had once disclosed to him the reclining figure in white. At length, finding it in vain to attempt wearying the grim portress into an invitation to enter this enchanted castle, he turned off in despair, when the young lady came through the gate, as if just returning from a walk.

George darted towards her, but the elder lady scarce allowed time for a word.

"Come, Julia," she said, "it is quite time you came in."

The young lady looked at George with a scarce perceptible smile, and, such a comical expression, that their acquaintance seemed ripened in a moment.

"I must say good morning," said she, in a rather low tone, but so decidedly, that George, perceiving any attempt for a longer interview to be hopeless, put his card into her hand and departed —not without a secret vow that he would yet baffle the duenna.

The sixty-five miles seemed rather long this time, and his father remarked upon the difficulties which he must have encountered, to account for a two days' absence, and such a worn-out air. Yet all this time George persuaded himself that it was not *worth while* to mention his new acquaintance. He, with his old head upon young shoulders,—pattern of nice young men!—to find himself interested in a chance acquaintance—to be suspected by an ancient lady of designs upon her niece, and what was worse, to be conscious of a strong desire to furnish some foundation for such suspicions! Oh, it was too much! Pattern people find it so hard to come down to a neighbourly level with common, erring mortals! George found it easier to learn to perform the Templeville trip in the space of twenty-four hours, although it was, in

reality, pretty good work for twice that time.  In truth, it began
to be necessary for him to take Templeville in his way to any
point of the compass ; and, at last, chance, or some other power
that favours the determined, gave him an unexpected advantage.

It was the elder lady's turn to be an invalid, and, while she
was, perhaps, enjoying an interview with the veritable Dr. Beasley, his former unwitting representative espied the now blooming
cheeks of the young lady among other roses in a pretty little
arbour in the garden.

" The garden walls are high, and hard to climb," said Juliet
once ; and the pretty Julia of our story might have said much
the same thing of the picket fence which separated her from her
new friend.  But George was on the other side of it before she
could have had time to quote the line.

Could two young people, who met in this romantic sort of way,
in these unromantic times,—and after many a momentary interview, cut short by the cares of a duenna, too,—fail to find some
very particular subjects of conversation ?   We ask the initiated,
not pretending to be *au fait* in these matters.   However this may
be, it must have been that very visit that enlightened George
Elliott as to the young lady's position.

She was the prospective heiress of a bachelor uncle, who, in
consequence of a violent prejudice against matrimony, had vowed
all practicable vengeance in case she ventured to engage herself
before the mature age of twenty-five, full six years of which were
yet to come.   A very liberal provision, which this same odd uncle
allowed to the elder lady, Mrs. Roberts, who was his sister only
by marriage, was made dependent upon the same point.

Now, the natural consequence of all this was, first, an irresistible inclination on Julia's part to fall in love, just for the sake of
seeing whether her uncle would keep his word ; and, secondly,
from the extreme prudence of the aunt leading her to take up
her residence in a region of clodhoppers, an inevitable proclivity
of the damsel to fancy the very first tall, dark-eyed, personable
youth who should come in her way.   We are not sure that Julia
told George all this.   We give it merely as a comment of our
own, by way of *avis au lecteur.*

The garden interview was prolonged until the ruddy-fingered

serving-maid was sent to seek Miss Julia ; and as George was, on that occasion, put behind a thicket of lilacs for the moment, we infer that a considerable degree of intimacy had by this time been established between the young people.

Peaches were like little green velvet buttons when George was first mistaken for Dr. Beasley, and before they were ripe, he had learned to think it a small matter to ride one hundred and thirty miles in twenty-four hours, for the sake of spending an hour or two in the cottage garden at Templeville, and occasionally getting a cup of tea from the unwilling fingers of Mrs. Roberts.

He had, in the mean time, become the object of much remark at home. He had always been fond of a good horse, and rather celebrated for his equestrian skill ; but people began to call him a jockey now,—so many fine animals did he purchase, and so many did he discard again after only one trial on the Templeville road. The difficulty of breaking the subject at home had become greater with every visit, and our mirror of prudence had nearly persuaded Julia that her uncle's fortune was of no sort of consequence, and a six year's probation quite out of the question, before he could resolve to tell his father that he was about to marry a penniless young lady and her not very agreeable aunt— Mrs. Roberts being, of course, to be taken (fasting) with her niece.

While the disclosure was yet to make, a letter came for Mr. George Elliott, postmarked " Templeville," and directed in a prodigious scrawl with a very fine pen—a young-lady-like attempt at disguise which could not but draw attention at a country post-office, if any body could have suspected so prudent a youth of clandestine proceedings. This epistle, being opened, was found to contain only a few lines, most cautiously worded, to inform Mr. George Elliott that suspicions of treachery and fears of consequent calamity made a friend of his very miserable. Further specifications, diplomatically urged, gave Mr. Elliott to understand that the uncle was expected, and that there was reason to suppose he had been induced to plan a sudden removal of the cottagers to a far distant and (of course) inaccessible part of the country.

The rising sun of the next morning saw Elliott " making tracks" for Templeville, most literally ; for the fierce pace of his gallant steed indented itself upon the moist soil in a striking man-

ner.   He must reach there in the afternoon at all hazards; and,
although he had more than once performed the same feat before,
he was now so anxious lest some accident should cause delay,
that he pushed on with unwonted vehemence.   He had twice
changed horses, and had passed through a small village about
twenty miles from Templeville, when the people on the road noticed that he was closely pursued by two horsemen in fiery haste.

George rode like the Wild Huntsman, and his pursuers were
nearly as well mounted.   At every point they inquired how far
the maker of those dashing tracks was in advance of them, and
their breathless questions were always answered in such terms as
induced them to hope their chase was nearly at an end.   They
spared neither whip nor spur, therefore; but their horses were
not so well used to that rate of travel, and one of them gave out
entirely just as they entered Templeville, with our tired hero full
in sight.

George reached the tavern, and went, as was his wont, immediately to the stables, to see his horse cared for.   He examined
several stalls before he chose one, and was giving his directions
to the ostler when he was rather roughly accosted by two persons, who took their places on either side of him, and began in
very aggressive style asking him various questions.   Our prudent friend was not, we regret to say, a member of the peace society; and he responded to these inquiries in a way which
threatened difficulties in the pursuit of knowledge.

The crowd increased every moment.   The whole town of
Templeville seemed congregated in the stable-yard.   " There he
is!" "That's him!" "That's the chap!" "I'd know him for a
thief, anywhere!" were the cheering exclamations that met Elliott's ear on every side.

Not to dwell unnecessarily on particulars, we may say at once
that the elder of these gentlemen had been robbed of a pocket-
book, containing a large sum of money, and that circumstances
favoured the idea that the thief had taken the Templeville road.
George's hard riding pointed him out as the delinquent; and his
having gone into several stalls on his first arrival, led the bystand-
ers to suppose he had been seeking for a place to secrete his booty.

We need not notice Elliott's indignant denials of the charge.

The old gentleman took very little notice of them, indeed. He rather advised him (as a friend) to give up the pocket-book at once, without attempting to deceive a person of his astuteness. George, who was anxious beyond every thing to be on his way to the cottage, and who, likewise, felt exceedingly unwilling to call upon his only acquaintance in the village, knowing that would be to insure a faithful report of the whole affair at home, offered to submit to a search, provided it might be performed in private and without unnecessary delay. To this, after some consultation, the old gentleman agreed; and the landlord, (who, by the way, disclaimed all knowledge of the accused, except that he had made a great many inquiries as to the people at the cottage,) was showing the way through the crowd to an inner room, when George encountered Mr. Henderson, the person to whom he was known.

All chance of escaping recognition was now at an end, and it became evident to George Elliott that, in addition to the loss of consideration by an imprudent marriage, he must expect a good deal of hard joking on the subject of hard riding. The gaping crowd, commenting audibly upon every point of his physiognomy and equipment, and agreeing, *nem. con.*, that he had state prison written upon his face if ever a fellow had, was nothing, compared with the keen sense of mortification which came with every thought of home. Julia's power, however, was irresistible; and George, perceiving that Mr. Henderson knew his accuser, requested an introduction, which was accordingly performed, to the great discomfiture of the old gentleman, who became unpleasantly sensible that his wild goose chase had led him a great way from his lost money, ruined a fine horse, and brought him into very unpleasant circumstances with a young gentleman, who, upon close examination, did not look half so much like a gallows-bird as he had supposed.

"Upon my word and honour, sir," said the old gentleman, wiping his forehead with an air of the greatest perplexity, "I am extremely sorry for this mistake. If I can make you any amends, this gentleman, Mr. Henderson, will answer for me, that I shall be happy to offer any atonement in my power."

George, of course, disclaimed any such wish, and, only anxious to see Julia, he shook hands with his accuser and hurried off.

Before he shut the door, the old gentleman stopped him. "Will you do me the favour to tell me, before we part, what possible inducement you could have for riding at such a pace?"

George laughed, said he was fond of fast riding, and disappeared.

    \*      \*      \*      \*      \*      \*      \*

Julia, in tears, and all the despair of nineteen, met George with the intelligence that her aunt, after appearing to favour them, must have played them false, and induced the uncle to insist upon an immediate change of residence.

"To-morrow morning," she said, "we are to leave here, for ever. My uncle has already arrived, and we should have set off this evening, but for the circumstance of his having been robbed on his way hither."

"Robbed?" said George.

"Yes. He is now in pursuit of the thief, and will not probably return before night."

As Julia said this, sobbing all the time as if her little heart would break, not for her uncle's loss, but her own woes, the door opened, and George's new acquaintance walked in.

"Hey-day, hey-day, here's a pretty affair! This is the nice youth that has persuaded you to throw away your bread and butter, is it?"

Then, coming nearer, and taking a better look at George, who had thrown off the India-rubber overcoat which western men are wont to wear when showers are probable, he burst into a hearty laugh as he recognized the object of his former suspicions.

"So it wasn't my pocket-book you wanted, sir?" said he.

"No, sir," said George, glad of so good an opening for his suit, "No, sir; it is your niece, without any pocket-book at all."

"Will you take her without?"

"With all my heart and soul!"

"In one year from this time I will not object, on those terms," said the old gentleman.

But he probably thought he owed some reparation for his hasty accusation, for, when the year was out, George got the niece and the pocket-book too; but he could not regain his reputation as the mirror of prudence. We have never heard, however, that this detracted materially from his happiness.

# BITTER FRUITS FROM CHANCE-SOWN SEEDS.

IN an attempt at mere fiction, I should scarcely have ventured upon the invention of a chain of circumstances so improbable as those which form the groundwork of the following sketch.   We accept the axiom that Truth is often stranger than fiction ; yet the mind instinctively refuses sympathy when fiction ventures too far beyond the bounds of our own experience or observation. Men are usually supposed to be actuated by sufficient motives, and by those which correspond, in some degree, with the springs of action in their kind at large ; and where we see a striking departure from this general rule, we are apt to class the erratic somewhere in the many-graded list of the insane—a list which has, of late years, been made, by some speculators, long and wide enough to include Rousseau and Byron, as well as the most fiendish murderer, and any divine who ventures to look over the pale of his church.

Those who are acquainted with the peculiar tone of society in the new country may not, perhaps, find my characters unnatuarl ; but it can hardly be expected that others would not doubt the truth of a description which supposes such deep-seated enmity towards those who had committed no offence, and such intolerable wrongs suffered without a possibility of legal redress.   In ancient feudal times, small excuse served when the superior chose to vent his evil passions upon those whom Fate had rendered subject to his caprice.   At this day, in the newly settled part of the Western country, the feudality is reversed ; and it is the inferior who has it in his power, by means of an unenlightened or corrupt public sentiment, (referring always with more or lese distinctness to brute force,) to lord it over any one who, by an inconvenient integrity, or an unpopular refinement, is rendered obnoxious to those who are more disposed to resent than to imitate what pretends to superiority. Thus much for the probability of what may naturally be expected to shock the credulity of the reader.

As to the main facts of the case—the character of the Codding-ton family—their adoption of the young girl—the unprovoked enmity of the Blanchards—their threats and plots—the catastrophe to which they contributed—and the unsatisfactory result of the effort to obtain justice—these were all communicated to me circumstantially, (by an intelligent friend who had resided near the spot where the occurrences took place,) as a sort of psychological problem which, even in that country it was not easy to solve. The same friend afterwards sent me a newspaper published in the same county, in which various details were given, to which details was appended a public protest of the aggrieved party, with other matters touching the case—all which remained uncontradicted so far as I have ever heard.

I should not have occupied so much time with these explanatory remarks, but for objections which have been made to the probability of my story. The old man, though sketched from life, is introduced here arbitrarily, to supply what was wanting as to the origin of the young girl who exhibited traits so remarkable. Nothing of her parentage has reached me ; but it seems natural to suppose that a soul which partook of the passionate and poetic energy of a Sappho, must have been moulded by no common lot. One can scarcely imagine the descendant of a line of sober farmers, kindling into a love as ideal as that of Petrarch, and pouring out her feelings in poetic measures like an Improvisatrice, in a mental climate too frigid to call into life any but irrepressible germs of genius. Smothered fire there must have been somewhere, among our Julia's rough ancestry. I have supposed it to descend to her through the old Indian-killer, from the more genial and impulsive South.

## CHAPTER I.

Eyes which can but ill define
  Shapes that rise about and near,
Through the far horizon's line
  Stretch a vision free and clear:
Memories feeble to retrace
  Yesterday's immediate flow,
Find a dear familiar face
  In each hour of long ago.—MILNES.

IN wandering through the woods where solitude seems to hold
undivided reign, so that one learns to fancy companionable qualities in the flowers, and decided sympathetic intelligence in the
bright-eyed squirrel, it is not uncommon to find originals odd
enough to make the fortune of a human menagerie, such as will
doubtless form, at no distant day, a new resource for the curious.
If any of the experimental philosophers of the day should undertake a collection of this nature, I recommend the woods of the
West as a hopeful field for the search. Odd people are odder in
the country than in town, because there is nothing like collision
to smooth down their salient points, and because solitude is the
nurse of reverie, which is well known to be the originator of many
an erratic freak. There is a foster relationship, at least between
solitude and oddity, and nowhere is this more evident than in the
free and easy new country. A fair specimen used to thrive in a
certain green wood, not a thousand miles from this spot; a veteran
who bore in his furrowed front the traces of many a year of hard-
ship and exposure, and whose eyes retained but little of the twink-
ling light which must have distinguished them in early life, but
which had become submerged in at least a twilight darkness,
which scarce allowed him to distinguish the light of a candle.
His limbs were withered, and almost useless; his voice shrunk to
a piping treble, and his trembling hands but imperfectly performed
their favourite office of carrying a tumbler to his lips. His tongue

alone escaped the general decay; and in this one organ were concentrated (as it is with the touch in cases of blindness,) the potency of all the rest.  If we may trust his own account, his adventures had been only less varied and wonderful, than those of Sinbad or Baron Munchausen.  But we used sometimes to think distance may be the source of deception, in matters of time as well as of space, and so made due allowance for faulty perspective in his reminiscences.

His house was as different from all other houses, as he himself was from all other men.  It was shaped somewhat like a beehive ; and, instead of ordinary walls, the shingles continued in uninterrupted courses from the peak to the ground.  At one side was a stick chimney, and this was finished on the top by the remnant of a stone churn; whether put there to perform the legitimate office of a chimney-pot, or merely as an architectural ornament, I cannot say.  It had an *unique* air, at any rate, when one first espied it after miles of solitary riding, where no tree had fallen, except those which were removed in making the road.  A luxuriant hop-vine crept up the shingles until it wound itself around this same broken churn, and then, seeking further support, the long ends still stretched out in every direction, so numerous and so lithe, that every passing breeze made them whirl like greenrobed fairies dancing hornpipes about the chimney, in preparation for a descent upon the inhabitants below.

At the side opposite the chimney, was a sort of stair-case, scarcely more than a ladder, leading to the upper chamber, carried up outside through lack of room in the little cottage ; and this airy flight was the visible sign of a change which took place in the old man's establishment, towards the latter part of his life. A grand-daughter, the orphan of his only son, had come to him in utter destitution, and this made it necessary to have a second apartment in the shingled hive ; so the stairs were built outside as we have said, and Julia Brand was installed in the wee chamber to which it led.  She was a girl of twelve, perhaps, at this time, and soon became all in all to her aged relative.  But we will put her off for the present, that we may recall at more length our recollections of old Richard Brand.  The race of rough old pioneers, to which he belonged, was fast passing away ; and emigration and improvement are sweeping from the face of the land, every trace of their existence.  The spirit by which they were animated has no fellowship with steamboats and railroads ; their pleasures were not increased  but diminished by the rapid accession of population, for whom they had done much to prepare the way.  The younger and hardier of their number felt themselves elbowed, and so pressed onward to the boundless prairies of the far West ; the old shrunk  from contact with society, and gathered themselves, as if to await the mighty hunter in characteristic fashion.  Old Brand belonged to the latter class.  He looked ninety ; but much allowance must be made for winter storms and night-watches, and such irregularities and exposure as are sure to keep an account against man, and to score their demands upon his body, both within and without.

We have said that the house had a wild and strange look, and the aspect of the tenant of the little nest was that of an old wizard. He would sit by the side of the door, enjoying the sunshine, and making marks on the sand with the long staff which seldom quitted his feeble hands, while his favourite cat purred at his feet, or perched herself on his shoulder, rubbing herself against his grey locks, unreproved.  Weird and sad was his silent aspect ; but once set him talking, or place in his hands his battered violin, and you would no longer find *silence* tiresome.  One string was generally all that the instrument could boast ; but that one, like the tongue of the owner, performed more than its share.  It could say,

> Hey, Betty Martin, tip-toe, tip-toe,
> Hey, Betty Martin, tip-toe fine :
> Can't get a husband to please her, please her,
> Can't get a husband to please her mind !

as plain as any human lips and teeth could make the same taunting observation ; but if you ventured to compare the old magician to Paganini, "Humph!" he would say, with a toss of his little grey head, " ninny I may be, but pagan I a'n't, any how ; for do I eat little babies, and drink nothing but water ?"

Nobody ever ventured to give an affirmative answer to either branch of this question; so the old man triumphed in the refutation of the slander.

Directly in front of the door by which old Brand usually sat, was a pit, four or five feet deep, perhaps, and two feet in diameter at the top, and still wider at the bottom, where it was strewn with broken bottles and jugs. (Mr. Brand had, by some accident, good store of these.) This pit was generally covered during the day, but for many years the platform was at night drawn within the door, with all the circumspection that attended the raising of a draw-bridge before a castle gate in ancient times.

"Is that a wolf-trap?" inquired an uninitiated guest. An explosion of laughter met this truly *green* question.

"A wolf-trap! O! massy! what a wolf-hunter you be! You bought that 'ere fine broadcloth coat out of bounty money, didn't ye? How I should laugh to see ye where our Jake was once, when he war'n't more than twelve year old! You'd grin till a wolf would be a fool to ye! I had a real wolf-trap then, *I* tell ye! There had been a wolf around, that was the hungriest critter you ever heard tell on. Nobody pretended to keep a sheep, and as for little pigs, they war'n't a circumstance. He'd eat a litter in one night. Well! I dug my trap plenty deep enough, and all the dirt I took out on't was laid up o' one side, slantindicler, up hill like, so as to make the jump a pretty good one; and then the other sides was built up close with logs. It was a sneezer of a trap. So there I baited and baited, and watched and waited; but pigs was plenty where they was easier come at, and no wolf came. By-and-by our old yellow mare died, and what does I do but goes and whops th' old mare into the trap. 'There!' says I to Jake, says I, 'that would catch th' old Nick; let's see what the old wolf 'll say to it.' So the next night we watch'd, and it war'n't hardly midnight, when the wolf come along to go to the hog-pen. He scented old Poll quick enough; and I tell ye! the way he went into the trap war'n't slow. It was jist as a young feller falls in love; head over heels. Well! now the question was, how we should kill the villain; and while we was a consultin' about that, and one old hunter proposin' one thing, and another another, our Jake says to me, says he, 'Father,' says he, 'I've got a plan in my head that I know'll do! I'll bang him

over the head with this knotty stick.'   And before you could say
Jack Robinson, in that tarnal critter jump'd, and went at him.
It was a tough battle, *I* tell ye!   The wolf grinned; but Jake he
never stopped to grin, but put it on to him as cool as a cowcumber,
till he got so he could see his brains, and then he was satisfied.
' Now pull me out !' says little Jake, says he, ' And I tell ye what!
if it *a'n't* daylight, I want my breakfast !'   And Jake was a show,
any how !   What with his own scratches and the spatters of the
wolf's blood, he look'd as if the Indians had scalped him all over."

" But what is *this* hole for ?" persisted the visiter, who found
himself as far from the point as ever.

" Did you ever see a Indian ?" said the wizard.

" No! oh yes ; I saw Black Hawk and his party, at Washington ——"

" Black Hawk ! ho, ho, ho! and Tommy Hawk too, I 'spose !
Indians dress'd off to fool the big bugs up there !   But *I* mean
*real* Indians—Indians at home, in the woods—devils that's as
thirsty for white men's blood as painters !*   Why, when I come
first into the Michig*an*, they were as thick as huckleberries.
We didn't mind shooting 'em any more than if they'd had four legs.
That's a foolish law that won't let a man kill an Indian !   Some
people pretend to think the niggers haven't got souls, but for my
part I *know* they have; as for Indians, it's all nonsense !   I was
brought up right in with the blacks.   My father own'd a real
raft on 'em, and they was as human as any body.   When my
father died, and every thing he had in the world wouldn't half
pay his debts, our old Momma Venus took mother home to her
cabin, and done for her as long as she lived.   Not but what we
boys helped her as much as we could, but we had nothing to begin with, and never had no larnin'.   I was the oldest, and father
died when I was twelve year old, and he hadn't begun to think
about gettin' a schoolmaster on the plantation.   I used to be in
with our niggers, that is, them that used to be ours ; and though
I'd lick'd 'em and kick'd 'em many a time, they was jist as good
to me as if I'd been their own colour.   But I wanted to get some
larnin', so I used to lie on the floor of their cabins, with my head
to the fire, and so study a spellin'-book some Yankees had gi'n

* Panthers.

me, by the light of the pine knots and hickory bark.   The Yankee people was good friends to me too, and when I got old enough,
some on 'em sent me down to New Orleans with a flat, loaded
with flour and bacon.

   " Now in them days there was no goin' up and down the Mississippi in comfort, upon 'count of the Spaniards.   The very first
village I came to, they hailed me and asked for my pass.   I told
'em the niggers carried passes, but that I was a free-born American, and didn't need a pass to go any where upon airth.   So I
took no further notice of the whiskerandoes, till jist as I turn'd the
next pint, what should I see but a mud fort, and a passel of sojers
gettin' ready to fire into me.   This looked squally, and I come to.
They soon boarded me, and had my boat tied to a tree and my
hands behind my back before you could whistle.   I told the boy
that was with me to stick by and see that nothing happened to the
cargo, and off I went to prison ; nothing but a log-prison, but
strong as thunder, and only a trap-door in the roof.   So there I
was, in limbo, tucked up pretty nice.   They gi'n me nothing to
eat but stale corn bread and pork rinds ; not even a pickle to
make it go down.   I think the days was squeez'd out longer, in
that black hole, than ever they was in Greenland.   But there's
an end to most everything, and so there was to that.   As good luck
would have it, the whiskerando governor came along down the
river and landed at the village, and hearin' of the Yankee, (they
call'd me a Yankee 'cause I was clear white,) hearin' that there
was a Yankee in the man-trap, he order'd me before him.   There
he jabber'd away, and I jabber'd as fast as he did ; but he was a
gentleman, and gentlemen is like free-masons, they can understand each other all over the world.   So the governor let me go,
and then he and the dons that were with him, walk'd down with
me to my craft, and gave me to understand they wanted to buy
some o' my fixins.   So I roll'd 'em out a barrel of flour, and flung
up a passel of bacon, till they made signs there was enough, and
then the governor he pull'd out his gold-netted purse to pay me.
I laughed at him for thinkin' I would take pay from one that had
used me so well ; and when he laid the money upon a box slily,
I tied it up in an old rag and chucked it ashore to him after I
pushed off ; so he smil'd and nodded to me, and Peleg and I we

took off our hats and gi'n him a rousin' hurrah, and I thought
that was the last I should see on him.   But lo and behold! when
I got to New Orleans, there was my gentleman got there before
me, and remitted all government costs and charges, and found
buyers for my perduce and my craft, and like to have bought
me too.   But I lik'd the bush, so I took my gun and set off afoot
through the wilderness, and found my way home again, with my
money all safe.   When I come to settle with the Yankees, there
was a good slice for me and mother, so I come off to buy a tract
in the Michigan.   I come streakin' along till I got to the Huron
river, and undertook to swim that with my clothes on and my
money tied round my neck.   The stream was so high that I come
pretty near givin' up.   It was 'pull devil, pull baker,' with me,
and I was glad to ontie my money and let it go.   That was before
these blessed banks eased a fellow of his money. so slick, and you
had to carry hard cash.   So mine went to the bottom, and it's
there yet for what I know.   I went to work choppin' till I got
enough to buy me an eighty; and I bought and sold fourteen
times before I could get a farm to suit me; and like enough may
try again before I die."

"But you were going to tell me about this hole."

"Oh, the hole! yes—that 'ere hole!   You see, when I first
settled, and the Indians was as thick as snakes, so that I used to
sleep with my head in an iron pot for fear they should shoot me
through the logs, I dug that hole and fix'd it just right for 'em, in
case they came prowlin' about in the night.   I laid a teterin'
board over it, so that if you stepped on it, down you went; and
there was a stout string stretch'd acrost it and tied to the lock of
my rifle, and the rifle was pointed through a hole in the door; so
whoever fell into the hole let off the rifle, and stood a good
chance for a sugar-plum.   I sot it so for years and never caught
an Indian, they're so cunning; and after they'd all pretty much
left these parts, I used to set it from habit.   But at last I got
tired of it and put up my rifle at night, though I still sot my
trap; and the very first night after I left off puttin' the rifle
through the hole, who should come along but my own brother
from old Kentuck, that I hadn't seen for twenty year!   He went
into the hole about the slickest, but it only tore his trowsers a little; and wasn't I glad I hadn't sot the rifle?"

## CHAPTER II.

Ragion ? tu m'odii ; ecco il mio sol misfatto.
ALFIERI.

OLD Brand's hatred of the Indians had not always expended
itself in words. When war in its worst shape ravaged the fron-
tiers, there were, besides those regularly commissioned and paid
to destroy, many who took the opportunity of wreaking personal
wrongs, or gratifying that insane hatred of the very name of Indian, which appears to have instigated a portion of the original
settlers. These were a sort of land privateers ;—the more mer-
ciless and inhuman that their deeds were perpetrated from the
worst and most selfish impulses, and without even a pretence of
the sanction of law. We may look in vain among the horrors of
savage warfare for any act more atrocious, than some of those
by which the white man has shown his red brother how the
Christian can hate.

The achievement of which the old trapper boasted loudest was
the burning of an Indian wigwam. He would recount, with circumstantial minuteness, every item of his preparation for the
murderous deed ; the stratagem by which he approached the
place unobserved : and the pleasure that he felt when he saw the
flames curling round the dry bark roof on four sides at once. He
laughed when he told how the father of the family burst through
the pile of burning brush which barricaded the only door, and
how he was shot down before he had time to recognise his cruel
enemy. Then the agonized shrieks of the women and children ;
their fleeing half naked and half roasted into the forest ; and the
mother and babe found dead in the path the next day,—these
were never-failing topics ; and, strange to say, old Brand, though
not born a fiend, could exult in the recollection of such exaggerated wickedness. War, the concentrated essence of cruelty and
injustice, gave the opportunity, and some wrong, real or pretend-

ed, committed by the red man, the excuse; and the outrage was
only remembered as one of the incidental horrors of a border
contest.

As Richard Brand became more infirm, his garrulity seemed
rather to increase, and his grand-daughter, who was his constant
attendant, used to sit for hours drinking in his wild stories, and
imbibing unconsciously, something of the daring and reckless
spirit of the reciter.   She grew up to be a tall, majestic-looking
girl, with the eye of Sappho herself; proud and high-spirited,
impatient of control, and peculiarly jealous of any assumption of
superiority in others; yet capable of attachment of the most ardent and generous kind to those from whom she experienced kindness and consideration.   With these qualities she became an object of a good deal of interest in the neighbourhood, and none the
less that her grandfather was known to have saved property enough
to be accounted rich where all are nearly alike poor.

Julia Brand had just completed her fourteenth year when her
aged relative failed suddenly; as people who have led rough
lives are apt to do; and his mind and body became so much enfeebled that it was thought advisable to remove him to the vicinity of more competent aid in case of illness, as well as to more
comfortable shelter than the old shingled hive could now afford.
More than one offer was made by the neighbours, and the old
man, though seeming at first scarcely to understand or accede to
the plan, yet showed a gleam of his former acuteness by making
choice voluntarily of Allen Coddington's house as his future home.

This Coddington was a man whose early advantages had been
such as to place him far above the ordinary class of settlers in
point of intelligence and ability.   He was an industrious and
thriving farmer, whose education, begun at one of the best New
England academies, had been furthered by a good deal of solid
reading, and made effective by a habit of observation without
which reading can be of but little practical utility.   He stood
decidedly in the first rank among the citizens of his town and
county.   He was among the earlier adventurers in that region,
and, having had the wisdom or the forethought, during the time
of extravagant prices, when producers were few and consumers
many, to bestow his whole attention on raising food for the gold-

hunters, who forgot to plough or to plant, and yet must eat, he had turned the speculating mania to good account, and become comparatively wealthy. His house was ample in size, and well provided with ordinary accommodations, and his farm presented the somewhat rare spectacle (in new country experience,) of a complete supply of every thing requisite for carrying on business to the best advantage.

Whether Allen Coddington was naturally of a self-satisfied and exclusive temper, or whether he had become somewhat over-bearing through success and prosperity, or whether his good fortune, and that alone, had had the effect of rendering him an object of jealousy and ill-will,—he was certainly no favourite in his neighbourhood. He had a certain influence, but it was that which arises from a sense of power, and not from a feeling of confidence and attachment. People found his advice valuable, but they complained that his manner was cold and unsympathizing ; and they remembered the offence long after the benefit was forgotten. Mr. Coddington's family were still less liked than himself, in consequence of their retired habits, which were supposed to argue a desire to keep themselves aloof from the society about them.

To one man in particular the whole house of Coddington was an object of the bitterest hatred and envy. This man was their nearest neighbour ; a person of violent passions, and an ambitious and designing mind, capable of almost any extreme of malignity, when his pride was hurt, or his favourite objects thwarted. Blanchard was not habitually an ill-tempered man. He had often proved himself capable of great kindness towards those whom he liked ; but he belonged to a class emphatically termed good haters—a dreadful anomaly in this erring world, where every man stands so much in need of the forbearance and kindness of his fellow man. Whoever had the misfortune to excite his vindictive feelings was sure of a life-long and uncompromising enmity ; and though prudence might restrain him from overt acts, yet he was not above many mean arts and secret efforts to lower those against whom he had conceived any dislike.

To such a man as Blanchard the peaceful and softening counsels of an amiable and judicious wife would have been invaluable. Many a ruthless and violent character is kept within

bounds by a gentle influence, which is not the less powerful for
being exerted in a manner unperceived by all but the person most
interested ; perhaps unacknowledged even by him.   Blessed, indeed, are such peace-makers, and all who belong to them !   But
Mrs. Blanchard was a spirit of another tone.   Wholly uneducated, both in mind and heart; tormented with a vague and vulgar
ambition to be *first*, without reference to means or ends ; and especially jealous of the pretence to superior delicacy and refinement, which she conceived to be implied in the quiet and secluded
habits of Mrs. Coddington and her children—this woman's soul
was consumed with bitterness ; and her ingenuity was constantly
exercised to discover some means of pulling down what she called
the *pride* of her neighbours ;—a term with which we sometimes
deceive ourselves, when in fact we mean only their superiority.

As was the accusation of witchcraft in olden times—a charge
on which neither evidence, judge nor jury, was necessary to condemn the unfortunate suspected,—so with us of the West is the
suspicion of pride—an undefined and undefinable crime, described alike by no two accusers, yet held unpardonable by all.
Once establish the impression that a man is guilty of this high
offence against society, and you have succeeded in ruining his
reputation as a good neighbour.   Nobody will ask you for proof;
accusation is proof.   This is one of the cases where one has no
right to be suspected.   The cry of " Mad dog !" is not more
surely destructive.

This powerful engine was put in operation by the Blanchard
family, into every member of which the parental hatred of the
Coddingtons had been instilled.   They made incessant complaints
of the indignities which they suffered from the *pride* of people
whose true offence consisted in letting them alone, until the whole
neighbourhood had learned from them to look upon the Coddingtons as covert enemies.

When Richard Brand made choice of the great house as an
asylum for himself and Julia, he unconsciously gave yet another
tinge of bitterness to the hatred of the Blanchards.   They had
been among the most urgent of the inviters, and they felt the
preference given to their detested neighbour as a new insult to
their own pretensions.   We have said that old Brand had shown

a glimmering of his ancient sagacity in the decision.  The establishment to which he was removed was one of extreme regu-
larity, industry and order; the Blanchards were known to be
careless, wild, passionate, and rather thriftless people; whose business was done by violent efforts at intervals, instead of habitual
application and method.  Their children were ill-governed, and
their eldest son bore a character which was by no means to be
coveted, although he maintained an exterior of decency, and
even affected with some success the manners of a squire of
dames.

Martha Coddington was a sweet, gentle girl; lovely in appearance and manners, and in all respects a most desirable companion for Julia, whose education had not been such as was calculated to endow her with all the feminine graces, although she was
far from being deficient in the stronger and more active qualities
which are no less valuable if something less attractive.  Martha
was in very feeble health, and confined almost entirely to sedentary occupations; and she had thus enjoyed opportunities for
mental cultivation which would scarcely have fallen to her rustic
lot if she had been blest with full health and strength.  It was
partly with a view to constant companionship for this beloved
daughter, that Mr. Coddington had been induced to offer a home
to Richard Brand.  The old man himself was becoming almost
a nonentity, and Julia had that indescribable something about her
which attracts the attention and awakens interest without our
being able to define satisfactorily the source of the fascination.
Her manners were singularly simple, child-like and trustful:
while her eye had a power and her step a firmness which betokened her ability to judge for herself, and to read the thoughts
of others.  She was as yet almost totally undeveloped; but it
was impossible not to perceive at a glance that there was abundance of material, either for good or evil, as after circumstances
might sway the balance of her destiny.

Once established in Mr. Coddington's family, Julia enjoyed all
the privileges of a daughter of the house, and shared with Martha, and one or two younger children, the occasional instruction
of the parents.  Her quickness of apprehension was remarkable;
and the activity of her habits and the cheerfulness of her temper

made her a valuable assistant to Mrs. Coddington in the various departments of householdry which would have fallen to Martha's share if she had been stout like the rest. So that the arrangement was one of mutual advantage, and the evening of Richard Brand's life bid fair to be as calm as its morning had been boisterous.

The Blanchards made many attempts at something like intimacy with Julia, but these were quietly discouraged by her protectors, probably from a sincere belief that such association would be unprofitable for her. They were at this time not at all aware of the deep enmity of the Blanchards, although they had not been blind to various indications of ill-will. So, in silence and secrecy grew this baleful hatred! as the deadly nightshade becomes more intensely poisonous when sheltered from the sun-light and the breeze. Imagination is the most potent auxiliary of the passions. Nothing so effectually moderates personal dislike as personal intercourse. Any circumstance which had thrown these neighbouring families into contact, in such a way as to bring into action the good qualities of either, would have done away with much of their mutual aversion. What a world of misery would thus have been spared to both!

## CHAPTER III.

The undistinguish'd seeds of good and ill
    Heav'n in its bosom from our knowledge hides ;
And draws them in contempt of human skill,
    Which oft for friends mistaken foes provides.
  *  *  *  *  *  *
So the false spider, when her nets are spread,
    Deep ambushed in her silent den does lie ;
And feels afar the trembling of the thread
    Whose filmy cord should bind the struggling fly.
          DRYDEN.

NEARLY three years had Julia Brand passed in Mr. Coddington's family ; years, for the most part, of quiet happiness and
continual improvement.  No care had been omitted by her kind
friends to make her all that a woman should be ; and Julia had
imbibed instruction eagerly, and repaid all their efforts by her attachment and her increasing usefulness.  To Martha she was as
a dear younger sister, whose buoyant spirits had always the
power to cheer, and whose kind alacrity could make even the
disadvantages of ill-health appear less formidable.  Yet the un-
tamed quality of her earlier nature broke forth sometimes in
starts of strange fierceness, which struck the gentle invalid with
dismay.  These flashes of passion almost always originated in
some unpalatable advice, or some attempt at judicious control on
the part of Mrs. Coddington, who had learned to feel a mother's
love for the beautiful orphan ; and, although such storms would
end in showers of tears and promises of better self-government,
they were a source of much grief to both Martha and her mother,
who felt the dangers of this impetuosity when they reflected that
no one but the imbecile grandfather possessed a natural right to
direct the course of Julia's actions.

These, however, were but transient clouds.  Peace and love
reigned in this well-ordered household, and the old man, now re-

duced to absolute second infancy, received from the family all
the attention that would have been due from his own children
Every fine morning saw his easy chair wheeled into the orchard,
and there, in the pleasant shade, and with Julia at his side, he
would hum fragments of his ancient ditties, or touch, with aimless
finger, the old violin held up for him by Robert Coddington, a boy
about Julia's age, who shared with her much of the care of her
helpless charge.   The old man's life was certainly prolonged by
the circumstances of ease and comfort which attended its setting;
to what good end, we might perhaps be disposed to inquire, were
it not that he was, in his present condition at least, so like a human grasshopper, that we may suppose he was allowed existence
on the same terms.   His dependent state afforded certainly most
ample opportunity for the exercise of kindly feeling in those
about him; and we must believe this to be no unimportant object,
since one part of the lesson of life is to be learned only by such
means.

Julia, loved and cherished, full of ruddy health, and exalted
by intellectual culture, opened gradually into splendid woman-
hood; her eye deepened in expression by a sense of happiness,
and her movements rendered graceful by continual and willing
activity.   Even in the country, where such beauty and grace as
hers are but little appreciated, she could not pass unnoticed.
Though necessarily much secluded, both by the requisite attendance on her aged relative, and by the habits of the family of
which she formed a part, her charms were a frequent theme with
the young people of the neighbourhood, and it was sometimes
said, half jest, half earnest, that the Coddingtons kept her shut up,
lest she should "take the shine off their sickly daughter."   The
Blanchards in particular, took unwearied pains to have it understood that poor Julia was a mere drudge, and that all their own
efforts to lighten the weary hours of their fair neighbour were re-
pelled by her tyrants, who evidently feared that Julia might be
induced to throw off their yoke if she should have an opportunity
of contrasting her condition with that of other young persons.
There seems to be in the forming stages of society, at least in this
Western country, a burning, restless desire to subject all habits
and manners to one Procrustean rule.   Whoever ventures to dif-

fer essentially from the mass, is sure to become the object of unkind feeling, even without supposing any bitter personal ani-
mosity, such as existed in the case before us. The retired and
exclusive habits of the Coddington family had centered upon them
almost all the ill-will of the neighbourhood.

As a proof of this we may mention, that when a large barn of
Mr. Coddington's, filled to the very roof with the product of an
abundant harvest, chanced to be struck by lightning and utterly
consumed, instead of the general sympathy which such occurrences usually excite in the country, scarce an expression of regret was heard. Mr. Blanchard, who was not averse to " making capital" of his neighbour's misfortunes, declared his solemn
belief that this loss was a judgment upon the Coddingtons, and
one which their pride richly deserved. He even went so far, in
private, before his own family, as to wish it had been the house
instead of only one of the barns. The tone of feeling cultivated
in that house may be judged by this specimen. Evil was the
seed, and bitter the fruit it was destined to produce !

Mr. Coddington felt the loss as any farmer must ; and he
would still more keenly have felt the unkind sentiment of the
neighbourhood if he had become aware of it. But he was on the
point of revisiting his native State with his family ; and in the
bustle of preparation, and the anxiety that attended Martha's
declining health, which formed the main inducement to the journey, the venomous whispers were unheard. He left home supposing himself at peace with all the world, always excepting his
nearest neighbour, whose enmity had evinced itself in too many
ways to pass unregarded.

Julia and her grandfather were left in possession of the house,
with the domestics necessary to carry on the affairs of the farm ;
and she prepared for a close attention to the household cares, and
a regular course of intellectual improvement, which should make
the long interval of comparative solitude not only profitable, but
pleasant. Mrs. Coddington had learned such confidence in Julia,
that she scarcely thought it necessary to caution her as to her
conduct during her absence. Far less did she exact a promise
as to the long-settled point of free intercourse with the Blanchard
family. She gave only the general advice which a mother's

heart suggests on such occasions, and bade farewell to her blooming pupil in full trust that all would go on as usual under Julia's
well-trained eye.

But the Blanchard family, one and all, had settled matters far
otherwise.  The very first time that old Brand's chair was wheeled into the orchard after the departure of the Coddingtons, a
bunch of beautiful flowers lay on the rude seat beneath the tree
where Julia usually took her station.  When she snatched it up
with delight and wonder, she was still more surprised to find under it a small volume of poetry.  Julia loved flowers dearly, but
poetry was her passion ; and she not only read it with delight,
but had herself made some not ungraceful attempts at verse, which
had elicited warm commendations from her kind protectors.  Here
was a new author, and one whose style gave the most fascinating
dress to passionate and rather exaggerated sentiment.  Julia's attention was enchained at once.  When she first opened the volume her only feeling was a curious desire to know whence it
had come ; but when she had read a page she thought no more
of this.  The poetry to which alone she had been accustomed,
was not only of a high-toned and severe morality, but of an abstract or didactic cast ; calculated to quicken her perceptions of
right, rather than to call forth her latent enthusiasm of character.
Cowper and Milton, and Young and Pollok had fed her young
thoughts.  But here was a new world opened to her ; and it was
not a safe world for the ardent and unschooled child of genius,
who found in the glowing picturings of a spirit like her own, a
power which at once took prisoner her understanding, aroused
her sensibilities, and lulled that cautious and even timid discrim-
ination, with which it had been the object of her friends to inspire
her.  She finished the reading at a sitting, and as she returned to
the house with her grandfather, the excitement of her imagination
was such that the whole face of nature seemed changed.  A new
set of emotions had been called into play, and the effect was proportioned to the wild energy of her character.  Poor Julia ! she
had tasted the forbidden fruit.

In the afternoon she repeated the pleasure ; and it was only
when she laid the volume under her pillow before she retired for
the night, that the question as to the appearance of the book re-

curred to her. It surely could not have been any of the Blanchards, she thought; yet who else had access to the orchard, which divided the two domains ? The next day solved the doubt.

Julia was sitting by the side of her charge, holding with one hand the old violin, and clasping in the other the source of many a fair dream, in the shape of the magic volume, when a step broke the golden meshes of her reverie. She looked up, and young Blanchard stood before her. She started and blushed, she knew not why, for she had seen the young man a thousand times with no other emotion than a vague feeling of dislike.

"Have you been pleased with the book my sisters took the liberty of sending you, Miss Brand ?" he said; "they wished me to offer you another, knowing you were fond of reading."

Julia expressed her pleasure eagerly, and received the new volume with a thrill of delight; accompanied, however, with some misgiving as to the propriety of obtaining it just in that way.

Blanchard, encouraged by her manner, proceeded to say that his sisters would have brought the books themselves, if they had supposed a visit would be agreeable. Having accepted the civility in one shape, Julia felt that she could not decline it in another, and the invitation was given, and the visit made.

## CHAPTER IV.

Virtue, and virtue's rest,
How have they perish'd!   Through my onward course
Repentance dogs my footsteps! black Remorse
Is my familiar guest!

\*      \*      \*      \*      \*      \*      \*

Indelibly, within,
All I have lost is written ; and the theme
Which Silence whispers to my thought and dream
Is sorrow still—and sin.

PRAED.

THE accomplishment of the first visit by the Blanchards was only the first step of a regular plan of attack.   Each successive day witnessed successive advances ; and the bewildering influence of poetry, music, and yet sweeter flattery, made rapid inroads upon Julia's prudence.   Still she declined all invitations to visit at Mr. Blanchard's, knowing how disagreeable such a step would be to her absent friends ; and the young man and his sisters found they had reached the limit of their power over her, before they had ventured upon any direct effort to alienate her from her protectors.

Whether they would have relinquished the attempt in despair we cannot tell, for the depths of malice have never yet been sounded ; but a new and potent auxiliary now appeared, who all unconsciously favoured their plans by attracting Julia's attention in a remarkable degree.   This was a young clergyman—a nephew of Mrs. Blanchard's—who had injured his health by study, and had come to the country to recruit.   He was a tall, well-looking young man, with no very particular attractions, except a pale face, dark, melancholy eyes, and a manner which betokened very little interest in anything about him.   He spent his time principally in reading ; but he played the flute very well, and was invited by the young Blanchards to join them in their visits to their pretty neighbour in the orchard.

This young clergyman, who had seen something of society, was not unobservant of Julia's beauty and talent; and although he does not appear to have had the slightest wish to interest her particularly, the silent flattery of his manner,—preferring her upon all occasions,—joined with his graceful person and delicate health, proved more dangerous to Julia than the direct efforts of his coarser relations. In short, he proved irresistible to Julia's newly excited imagination, and after that time the Blanchards found victory easy. Before many days Julia suffered herself to be led a willing visiter to the forbidden doors, conscious all the while that this was almost equivalent to a renunciation of her long-tried and still loved friends.

The main point being thus accomplished, the rest followed as of course. We are not able to trace step by step the process by which the Blanchards sought to root out from Julia's heart the love and reverence with which she regarded Mr. Coddington and his family; but sadly true it is that they succeeded in convincing her that far from having been benefited by their care, she had been secluded from all natural and proper enjoyments, and persuaded to become a family-drudge, under the specious veil of a desire for her improvement. A thousand reminiscences were called up by these designing people in order to find materials for mischief. Long-forgotten occurrences were cited and explained in such a way as to make it appear that the Coddingtons had for their own purposes deprived Julia of the acquaintance and sympathy of the neighbourhood. The seclusion in which she had grown up was represented as the fruit of a sordid desire to get as much household duty out of her as possible, while at the same time her beauty and talents were prevented from appearing to the disadvantage of the sickly Martha. These things cunningly insinuated were like "juice of cursed hebenon" in Julia's ears. In her days of calm and healthful feeling she would have scorned such vile constructions; but under such influences as we have described, and especially wrapt in the bewildering spell of a passion as violent as it was sudden, she was a transformed creature. Her virtue would have stood the test if her judgment had remained clear: but the opium-eater is not more completely the

victim of delusive impressions than such a character as hers when
it is once abandoned to the power of love.

And this love—it carried shame in its very life, for was it not
unsought ?  Had its object by word or even look evinced a preference for Julia ?  Burning blushes would have answered if we
could have asked such questions of Julia herself.  Indeed, this
Mr. Milgrove was a young man of reserved and rather self-en-
closed habits, who, feeling himself quite superior to the people
among whom he found it convenient to remain for the time, had
given himself very little concern as to the impression he was
making.  Thus was unlimited scope given to Julia's unpractised
imagination.  She idolized an idea.  If the object who chanced
to stand for an embodiment of her dreams had made love like a
mere mortal, her naturally keen perception of character would
have been awakened, and she would have become aware of a cold
indifference of temperament in Milgrove, with which her own
could never harmonize, and which would consequently have dis-
gusted her.  But such passion as hers does most truly " make the
meat it feeds on," and in the exercise of this power its growth is
portentous, and all independent of the real value of its material.
It soon filled the heart of the unfortunate girl to the exclusion of
all better sentiments.

Time flew by, until nearly two months had endowed Julia's delirium with the force of habit.  Frequent letters from her absent
friends had brought intervals of self-recollection and self-reproach ;
but the intoxication was too delicious ; and with a sigh over the
conscious disingenuousness, she wrote again and again without
once mentioning her intimacy with the Blanchards or the presence
of their relative.  It is true, she tried to say to herself, that Mrs.
Coddington had no right to control her movements ; but hers was
not a heart to satisfy itself with such fallacies.  She felt deeply
guilty, and she deliberately endured the dreadful load, for the
sake of the dreams which attended it.  Her fear now was the
speedy return of her best friends.  That must, as she well knew,
put a stop at once to all intercourse with those malevolent neighbours, and deprive her of the sight of one to whom she had devoted
her whole soul, unsought and unappreciated.

At length the period arrived when a letter from Mrs. Coddington announced that the family were about to return, travelling very slowly on account of Martha's sinking state, now more alarming than ever before. Julia's emotions on receiving this intelligence were of the most violent kind. She sat with the letter before her—her eyes fixed on the account given by the afflicted mother of the state of her dying child; and as she gazed, her mind may truly be said to have "suffered the nature of an insurrection." All her better self was roused by the thought of Martha's rapid decay, and a flood of tears attested the reality and the tenderness of her affection for this excellent friend; yet, on the other side, the fascinations of the past two months were present in all their power; and as she reflected that these must now be renounced, she groaned aloud, and grasped her throbbing temples with both hands, as if to preserve them during the agony of the struggle. In this condition she was found by one of the daughters of Mr. Blanchard, who had, by various arts, succeeded in gaining her confidence completely.

These young women, who were in every way inferior to Julia, derived all their interest in her eyes from their connection with the object of her mad attachment. She saw them as she saw him —through a medium of utter delusion. The elder, more particularly, was a designing and malicious girl, who hated Martha Coddington with a perfect hatred, and who had always assisted in fomenting the enmity which had arisen between the two families.

Julia's state of mind rendered her incapable of any disguise. Her passionate worship of the young clergyman had been a thing only suspected; but she now threw herself upon Sophia Blanchard's neck, and bewailed herself in the wildest terms, wishing for death to rid her of her misery, and declaring that she would not support an existence which had become odious to her. In the course of these frantic declarations, the whole history of her feelings came out, and Sophia, far from reasoning with her on the destructive effects of such self-abandonment, artfully condoled with her on being obliged to remain with the Coddingtons, and urged her to break with them at once, and remove with her grandfather to a home where she would find welcome and happiness.

But courage for this step was more than Julia could assume. She had suffered herself to receive unfavourable impressions of her

absent protectors, but her habitual reverence for them was such
that she dared not think of braving their ill opinion.   And besides, she well knew that the old man, childish as he was in
many respects, could never be persuaded to the change.   So she
shook her head despairingly, and repeated her conviction that
death alone could relieve wretchedness like hers.

Sophia Blanchard, bold and designing as she was, trembled at
these words.   She knew Julia well enough to believe that such
feelings, acting upon such a spirit, might not improbably result in
some rash act.   Finding Julia resolute in her rejection of the expedient proposed, she set herself about contriving some other
which should serve the double purpose of securing Julia and an-
noying the Coddingtons.

Are there moments when all guardian angels leave us at the
mercy of the evil influences within ?   If it be so, such times are
surely those when we have wilfully given the rein to passion, and
avowed ourselves its slaves, to the scorn of that better principle
which watches for us as long as we allow its benign sway.   " Why
hath Satan entered into thine heart ?"   Alas !  do we not invite
him ?   Poor Julia !  his emissary is even now at thine ear !

Things too wild for fiction must yet find place in a real record
of human actions.   The plan which presented itself to the thoughts
of Sophia Blanchard, was probably suggested by the bitter expressions she had heard under the parental roof ; yet it was too
outrageous to have been broached seriously by a person more advanced in age or better acquainted with the ordinary course of
affairs.   To set fire to Mr. Coddington's house after the family
were asleep ;—then to give the alarm, and remove the old man
and such articles as could be saved—this was the diabolical advice which this ill-taught girl gave boldly to the wretched Julia,
carefully keeping out of view the promptings of her own heredi-
tary spite, and making it appear that the loss would be a matter
of no vital importance to a man of Mr. Coddington's property,
while it would set Julia free to remove at once to Mr. Blanchard's, where Mr. Milgrove had decided to remain for some
time.

# CHAPTER V.

Blessings beforehand—ties of gratefulness—
The sound of glory ringing in our ears—
Without, our shame; within our consciences—
Angels and grace—eternal hopes and fears.
Yet all these fences and their whole array
One cunning BOSOM-SIN blows quite away.

GEORGE HERBERT.

INSTEAD of rejecting this atrocious proposal with horror, as the Julia of purer days would have done, the unhappy girl listened in silence to all Sophia's baleful whispers, and with this tacit permission the whole plan was gradually developed; Sophia's ready ingenuity devising expedients to obviate each objection as it presented itself, till all was made to appear easy of accomplishment, and secure from detection. Still Julia did not speak. She sat with glazed eyes fixed upon her tempter, and not a muscle moved, whether in approval or rejection of the plan. Frightened by her ghastly face, Sophia Blanchard took her hand: it was cold and clammy as that of a corpse. Thinking Julia about to faint, she ran for water, and was about to use it as a restorative, when her victim, rousing herself, put it back with a motion of her hand.

"Enough, Sophia," she said; "no more of this now; leave me to myself! Go—go—no more!" and no entreaties could induce her to say one word as to her acceptance of the proposition upon which her adviser had ventured. Sophia Blanchard was obliged to return home in no very easy state of mind, and all her efforts to obtain admittance again proved fruitless. Julia resolutely refused to see any one of the family.

Three days passed in this sort of suspense—an ominous pause, and one which gave Sophia ample time to reflect on the step she had taken, and to consider its consequences. The old man went not forth to his place in the orchard. He sat whimpering in the

corner, scolding at Julia's laziness, and wishing that Robert Coddington would come back, that he might have somebody to take
care of him.   Julia, stern and silent, moved about the house with
more than her usual activity, regulating matters which had of
late been less carefully attended to than usual, and insisting upon
extra efforts on the part of the domestics, in order that every thing
might be in order for the reception of the family.   On the evening of the third day all was pronounced ready, and the morrow
was talked of as the time for the probable arrival.

At midnight a loud knocking and shouting at Mr. Blanchard's
doors announced that a fire had broken out ; and at the same moment a broad sheet of flame burst from the further end of Mr.
Coddington's house.   The neighbourhood was soon aroused, and
all the efforts that country resources allow, were used to save the
main body of the building.   Meanwhile, old Brand was carried,
in spite of his angry struggles and repeated declarations that he
would not go, to Mr. Blanchard's, and laid on a bed in one of the
lower rooms, Julia herself superintending the removal with solici-
tous care.   This done, she took the lead in bringing out from the
blazing pile, everything of value ; herself secured Mr. Coddington's papers, and suggested, from her knowledge of the affairs of
the family, what might best engage the attention of the assistants.
Most of the effects were thus placed in safety ; but with scanty
supplies of water, and nothing more effectual than buckets, the
attempt to preserve any part of the house was soon discovered to
be hopeless.   The neighbours, having done their best, were
obliged to withdraw to some distance, where they could only
stand and gaze upon the flames, and listen to their appalling
roar.

It was during this pause that the general attention was called
by the most agonizing shrieks, and Julia, who had been all com-
posure during the agitation of the night, was seen coming from
Mr. Blanchard's in a state of absolute distraction.   She had hastened from the fire to look after her helpless charge, but on reach-
ing the bed on which he had been placed, she found it empty and
cold.   A blanket that had been wrapped round him lay in the
path through the orchard, and the conviction had struck Julia at
once, as it did the minds of all present, that the old man, feeble

as he was, had, with the obstinacy of dotage, taken the opportunity when all were engrossed with the fire, to return to his own chamber, now surrounded by flames. Julia darted towards the door of the burning dwelling, but she was forcibly withheld by the men present, who declared the attempt certain destruction. While she still struggled and shrieked in their arms, the whole roof fell in, and a fresh volume of flame went roaring and crackling up to the very stars. The old man was gone!—gone to his account, of which the midnight burning of the helpless formed so dread an item. And Julia—it is scarcely to be wondered at that she envied him his fate. We dare not attempt a picture of her condition.

The grey light of dawn began to chill the glare of the dying flames. The contrast produced a ghastly tint on all around, till the countenances of those who continued to watch the smouldering fire looked as if death, instead of only fatigue and exhaustion, was doing its work upon them. Julia, having resisted all entreaties of the Blanchards to go with them to their house, stood with fixed gaze, and rigid as a statue, contemplating the ruin before her; when the sound of approaching wheels was heard; and the dreary light disclosed the return of the unfortunate family, not with one carriage only, as they left home, but with two; and travelling at so slow a pace that it seemed as if they brought calamity with them in addition to that which awaited them at their desolate home.

"They are coming!" The whisper went round, and then an awe-struck silence pervaded the assembly. Julia's perceptions seemed almost gone, although she was denied the refuge of temporary insensibility. She had already suffered all that nature could bear, and a stupid calm had succeeded her agonizing cries. Yet she drew near the carriage which contained her friends, and cast her eyes eagerly around.

"Where is Martha?" she said, in a voice so altered, so hollow, that the hearers started.

Mrs. Coddington burst into tears, but could not speak. Her husband answered with a forced calmness, "Julia, my love, our dear Martha is at rest! We have brought home only her cold remains."

Julia uttered not a sound, but, tossing her arms wildly in the air, fell back, utterly lifeless, and in this state was carried to the house of one of the neighbours.

\*      \*      \*      \*      \*      \*      \*

The funeral was necessarily hurried, for poor Martha had died two days before ; so that the ruins of the home of her childhood were still smoking when the sad procession passed them on its way to the grave. Julia, recovered from that kind swoon, had made a strong effort to master her feelings, and to take some part in the last duties, but so violent had been the action of the over-tasked nerves, that she was feeble and faint, and utterly incapable of the least exertion. No vestige of the old man's body could be found among the ruins, so that she was spared the vain anguish of so horrible a sight ; yet the reality could have been scarcely more dreadful than the picturings of her own guilt-quickened fancy. She shrunk from joining, according to the custom of the country, in the funeral solemnities of her friend, and passed the dread interval alone in her chamber.

When the bereaved parents returned to the house, Mrs. Coddington went immediately to Julia.

" My daughter !" she said, " my dear—my *only* daughter ! what should I be now without you ! You must take the place of the blessed creature who is gone !" And she threw herself sobbing upon Julia's bosom, clasping her in her arms, and bestowing upon her all the fulness of a mother's heart.

Like a blighted thing did the wretched girl shrink from her embrace, and sinking prostrate on the floor at her feet, pour out at once the whole shameful story of her guilt. Not a shade was omitted, not even the unsought and frantic love which was now loathsome in her own eyes, nor the suspicions of Mr. and Mrs. Coddington which had been instilled into her heart until its very springs were poisoned.

Mrs. Coddington shook like an aspen leaf. She tried to speak —to ask—to exclaim—but words came not from her paralyzed lips. At length—" Julia !" she faltered out,—" Julia—are you mad ? You cannot surely mean, my child—you *cannot* mean all this ! You cannot intend me to believe that you are the—"

She stopped, for Julia, still prostrate, groaned and shuddered, deprecating by a motion of her hand, any recapitulation of the horrors she had disclosed.

"It is true," she said; "I am all that I have told you; I have burned your dwelling, so long my happy home; I have committed murder,—all I ask now is punishment. I have thought of all; I am ready for what is to follow; I wish for the worst; make haste, for I must die soon,—very soon!"

She concluded so wildly, and with such an outburst of agony that Mrs. Coddington again thought her mind had become unsettled by the dreadful occurrences of the last few hours.

But these tears somewhat relieved her, and she was comparatively calm after the paroxysm had subsided. And now, in a collected manner, and in the presence of Mr. Coddington, did she firmly repeat all that she had said, gathering courage as she proceeded, and anxiously entreating to have her statement taken down in legal form.

Mr. Coddington, once convinced that there was a dreadful reality in all this, felt it as any other man would; but he treated it with a calmness and forbearance which not every man could have commanded. He heard Julia's statement through, asked some questions as to certain particulars, and then, taking her hand with his old air of fatherly kindness, he said, "My poor child! you have been dreadfully deluded! Those who have led you astray have much to answer for, and I shall take care that they do not escape the reckoning. You I can forgive. The mental sufferings you must endure are atonement enough; but for those who wilfully poisoned your young mind—"

"Oh no—no!" exclaimed Julia; "no one is to blame but myself. I alone am answerable for my crime! I did all with my own free will—out of my own wicked heart! And oh! how I wish this wretched heart were cold and still, even now! How I envy dear Martha her peaceful grave! Make haste and take down what I have said, for I *cannot* live!"

"Julia!" said Mr. Coddington, interrupting her, with an air of severity very different from his former manner, "do you wish me to believe that all your expressions of remorse and self-abasement are false and hollow? What do you mean? That you would raise your hand against your own life? Rash girl! your thoughts

are impious.  Suicide is not the resource of the true penitent,
but of the proud and self-worshipping hypocrite.  If you are sincere in your desire to atone for the injury you have done me,
show it by entire submission to what I shall see fit to direct.
You know me ; you know you have no reason to dread harsh-
ness at my hand.  Be quiet then; command yourself, and to-
morrow I will talk with you again."

So saying he left the room, seeing Julia too much exhausted
for further conference, but Mrs. Coddington remained long with
her, soothing her perturbed spirit by every thing that a mother's
love could have suggested, and assuring her of Mr. Coddington's
kindness and of his forgiveness.  "You have already suffered
enough, my poor child," said this kind-hearted woman ; "now go
to rest, pray for pardon and for peace, and fit yourself by a quiet
night for the duties of to-morrow."

And such friends Julia had been persuaded to believe harsh
and unsympathizing !

We shall not venture to give a fictitious conclusion to this story
of real life.  It might not be difficult to award *poetical* justice ;
but neither that nor any other was the result of Mr. Coddington's
efforts.  He adhered firmly to his resolution of holding Julia's
advisers answerable for what she had done.  She was not yet
sixteen, and her account of all that had passed during the absence of her friends plainly showed a conspiracy on the part of
the Blanchard family to do him a deep injury.  Slanderous fab-
rications of the vilest character had been employed to prejudice
Julia against her benefactors.  She had been urged to treacherous
and injurious conduct; persuaded that Mr. Coddington was planning to possess himself of her property, on her grandfather's
death ; and frequently reminded that whatever injury should be
done to the Coddingtons, would be considered as no worse than
they merited ; in attestation of which the sentiment of the neighbourhood on the occasion of the burning of the barn, was frequently cited.  On the whole, Mr. Coddington, who was a man
of strong and decided character, was fully of opinion that he had
just cause of complaint against Blanchard, as answerable not
only for his own share of these misdemeanours, but for those
which his family, by his instigation, had carried more fully into

practice.  He refused, therefore, to listen to Julia's entreaties, that she alone might bear the burthen of her crime, and proceeded to seek redress from his malicious neighbour.

His first care was to obtain an interview with Mr. Blanchard, and endeavour to induce him to make reparation and acknowledgment, from a sense of justice.  But this course, however accordant with the sound principles of the injured party, was wholly lost upon the virulent enmity of his opponent.  Blanchard, who did not believe in Julia's deep repentance, treated his neighbour's remonstrances with scorn and derision.  He heaped abuse and insult upon Mr. Coddington, telling him that it was well known that his premises had been insured beyond their value, and more than suspected that the fire had been a matter of his own planning, in order that the insurance money might help to build a more modern house.  He said, as to Julia, that the young men of the neighbourhood had resolved to release her by force, in case she was not given up peaceably, since she was believed to be detained against her will.  In short, this bold, bad man, strong in the knowledge that the prejudices of the country, (so easily awakened on the subject of *caste*,) had been thoroughly turned against the Coddington family, defied him with contempt, and left nothing unsaid that could exasperate his temper.

Mr. Coddington now resolved to appeal to the laws, his last resort against this determined enmity.  That Blanchard was morally accountable he felt no doubt ; to render him legally so, he thought required only that the fact should be plainly set forth to a jury.  The ends of justice seemed to sanction if they did not require such a course ; since it is always desirable to ascertain what protection the laws do really afford to those who give them their support.  He probably thought this necessary also on Julia's account ; for her dread secret was in possession of the declared enemies of the family ; and a judicial investigation, by showing the influence under which she had acted, would place the matter in its true light, and set forth the palliation with the crime.  So the matter was laid before the grand jury.

It might, perhaps, be inquiring too curiously, to ask whether, in coming to this conclusion, Mr. Coddington did not consult his passions rather than his judgment.  It is difficult to know exactly how much love we bear to abstract justice.  That another course would better have promoted both his happiness and his pecuniary interests, is highly probable ; since it is at least as true in a new country, as elsewhere, that the law is a great gulf which is apt to swallow up both parties.  Yet the desire to appeal to public justice was at all events a natural, if not a prudent one.

But a grand jury, though sworn to " diligently inquire and a true presentment make" of such matters as the foregoing, and that " without fear, favour, or affection," are far from being above prejudice, and, perhaps, not always secure from influences likely to obstruct the even flow of justice.  When the matter is not a " foregone conclusion," a judgment prejudged,—it too often happens that the story first told has the advantage.  There is no room for more than one set of ideas on the same theme.  The prominent and tangible fact in this case was, that a young girl confessed having burned a house ; this might bring her to the penitentiary, and the jury would not find a " true bill."  In vain did the deeply penitent Julia make her statement in presence of the court.  She was represented as under compulsion.  She was taken aside again and again, at the repeated instigation of Blanchard, as if, like prince Balak, he still hoped " peradventure *she* will curse me them from thence ;"—but although her story was unaltered, it remained unheeded.  She was now offered half the homes in the neighbourhood, and repeatedly reminded that she was under the protection of the court, and could go where she liked ; but she insisted on remaining with Mr. Coddington, and declared that she desired life only that it might be spent in atoning the injury she had done him.  Foiled, as we have seen, in his attempt to make the shame and the punishment due to so great an offence fall on those whom he considered most guilty, Mr. Coddington's next thought was to vindicate his own character from the boundless calumnies of his envious neighbour.  But a better consideration of the case determined him to let his reputation clear itself ; trusting that the past and the future would alike be his vouchers to all those whose opinion he valued.  So he contented himself with having placed Julia in comparative safety, and resolved to live down the calumnies which had been so industriously propagated against him.  Instead of quitting the neighbourhood, as a man of weaker character might have done, he has rebuilt his house, and adopted Julia as his daughter, fully convinced of the change in her character, as well as of the violent mental excitement under which she yielded to temptation ; and if there be any truth in the doçtrine of compensations, it cannot be doubted that a man of his character must, in time, obtain a complete though silent triumph over the desperate malignity of such people as the Blanchards.

THE END.